He had crossed a line with her.

A very desirable and pleasing line, but one that an honorable man did not cross with an innocent unless there was an understanding between them.

When he attempted to step back she resisted, tightening her grasp on his shirt and leaning against him. She let him go but watched him with wide, intent eyes. Uncertain of what to say, he waited for her, expecting she would be overwhelmed by the power of the passion between them. When she did not speak, he finally found words.

"Do you regret this?" he asked softly as he leaned over and picked her shawl up from the floor.

"Regret?" She shook her head. "I regret only that you stopped."

* * *

The Highlander's Dangerous Temptation
Harlequin® Historical #1162—November 2013

Author Note

Back in 2005, when I wrote *Taming the Highlander,* young Athdar MacCallum did something stupid that started this entire series—he taunted the formidable half Norse/half Scots warrior Rurik, and the debacle ended with Athdar's sister being forced to marry the Beast of the Highlands!

Athdar is now grown-up and laird of his clan. To many, he is cursed with the worst luck in women—having lost two wives, a betrothed, and with another woman thinking about marrying him! He has sworn off the fairer sex—until a young woman grabs his attention and he is drawn to her, unable to resist her.

Since I torment and tease my heroes all the time, it should be no surprise to you that when Athdar finally lowers his defenses, it is the daughter of his nemesis who brings him to his knees!

I hope you'll enjoy *The Highlander's Dangerous Temptation,* this next book in my MacLerie Clan series (which seems to grow monthly!). There are some serious moments, too, as Athdar struggles with the sins of his past and as Isobel tries valiantly to help the man she loves face his greatest failures. But anytime Rurik Erengislsson enters the story, watch out—there is danger and humor ahead!

Happy reading!

The Highlander's Dangerous Temptation

Terri Brisbin

—

HARLEQUIN® HISTORICAL

Recycling programs
for this product may
not exist in your area.

ISBN-13: 978-0-373-29762-7

THE HIGHLANDER'S DANGEROUS TEMPTATION

Copyright © 2013 by Theresa S. Brisbin

This edition published by arrangement with Harlequin Books S.A.

For questions and comments about the quality of this book, please contact us at CustomerService@Harlequin.com.

Printed in U.S.A.

To all of my readers,

You make me stay up nights, struggling to capture the words and images swirling inside my brain and to forge them into a story that's worth reading! You make me want to write the next word, the next chapter, the next book, even when it makes more sense to give it all up and hit Delete. Your notes, mail, emails, Facebook posts encourage me all along the way and especially during those long, intense deadline binges o'writing.

All I can say is THANK YOU.

TERRI BRISBIN

is wife to one, mother of three and dental hygienist to hundreds when not living the life of a glamorous romance author. She was born, raised and is still living in the southern New Jersey suburbs. Terri's love of history led her to write time-travel romances and historical romances set in Scotland and England.

Readers are invited to visit her website for more information at www.terribrisbin.com, or to contact her at P.O. Box 41, Berlin, NJ 08009-0041.

Prologue

'Come with me!' Athdar called out like the commander of his father's warriors would. With his wooden sword brandished high in the air, he pointed deeper into the forest and nodded. 'Our enemies have taken to the woods!'

Athdar led his friends, two his cousins and two the sons of a villager, all almost the same age as him, through the thick growth of trees and bushes. Following the rough path along the river, he sought any sign of movement deep in the shadows.

There! Something moved and he called out orders once more. Deer or some other wild animal—it mattered not to him what the target—scampered ahead of them as the sun's light flickered through the leaves and branches above them. Laughing, they followed the sounds ahead of them as the creature outraced them. After some time and distance, the sound of the river quieted, telling Athdar that their path had changed. Glancing around, he realised that nothing looked familiar to him. Athdar paused for a moment and then raced off, calling for the others to follow him. Without warning, he reached a small clearing bordered by a gully, a remnant of the river's previous path, that blocked their way.

He was tall enough, strong enough, a good runner and jumper, to make it across so he speeded up and crossed the pit with little effort. Skidding to a stop on the other side, he landed in a pile of leaves and quickly stood up.

'Come now!' he called out. 'It is not wide enough to stop us.'

As the chief's son, Athdar was used to being in charge and making the decisions for his ragtag collection of friends and followers. He waved them on now, waiting for them to obey.

'Are you afraid to jump?' he asked, challenging them to the edge. 'Get a running start and you will make it.' He saw the uncertainty on their faces and would not allow that to ruin their adventure.

'Cowards!' he shouted at them. 'Only cowards would disobey their chief.' The words burned his mouth as he said them, but he knew his friends only needed some encouragement to do as he did and cross the gully.

Athdar watched as they nudged each other, nodding and backing up to get a good running start to their jump. Smiling, he crossed his arms over his chest the way his father often did and waited for them to reach his side. One and then another soared into the air above the deep gash in the ground....

Their cries turned to screams as they plummeted down into the dark crevasse below them. Athdar watched in horror as the screams faded into a deathly silence. Only the sound of his breathing broke that stillness as he crept over to the side and peered down.

The bottom lay about twenty feet below him and his friends lay strewn across the small floor of the gully.

Even his seven-year-old mind understood some were dead and the others badly injured. Arms and legs and heads twisted to impossible angles foretold of much sorrow.

He was the cause of this! Searching through his sack, he looked for the rope he always carried and could not find it. More soil loosened as he crept to the edge once more and poured down on his friends. A faint cough told him that someone yet lived. Shaking, he called out names until Robbie groaned back.

'Robbie! I am coming down!' he said, easing his legs over the side and planning to slide the rest of the way down to his friends.

This was his fault. His fault. He must help them.

'Stay,' Robbie moaned out. 'Ye'll be of no help if you get trapped here.'

Athdar paused, grabbing on to the exposed roots of a tree to keep from sliding down into the pit. 'Twas true. Without the means to pull his friends up, he was of no help. The winds rustling through the trees reminded him of the time passing. Soon it would be dark and new dangers would arise.

'I will go for help,' he called out in a loud voice. When no sound answered, he called out again, 'Robbie! I will go for help!'

Gathering up his sack, Athdar glanced around, trying to get his bearings. They'd run through the forest from east to west. Or had they? Now, it all looked the same and he took deep breaths, trying to keep the panic at bay.

He had to find his way back home. He had to get help. He had to…

Athdar ran, ducking through the low branches, seeking the edge of the river.

* * *

It took him hours to find it and then he could not tell which direction was home. Every time he grew too afraid or too tired, he thought about his friends at the bottom of the gully and ran on. Night fell while he searched for home and he collapsed at some point, sleeping a few hours before waking and continuing on.

Daybreak found him no closer to finding home or help and he gave in to the terror and the guilt and cried for his friends.

And that's when his father and uncle came charging through the forest on their horses. In a matter of hours, Athdar had managed to lead them back to the place where his friends lay injured and then he watched as the men in his clan rescued Robbie and the others from the ground below.

It was terrible. His heart hurt as each one was carried out. Only one moved and the silence as the boys were examined tore him apart. Soon, the completely desolate group made their way back to the keep.

Though the parents mostly whispered about the terrible accident, Athdar knew the truth—this was his doing. He had killed his friends just as much as if he'd pushed them from a cliff. For he had pushed them—with words, with insults—using their pride to edge them to the end and fling them into the darkness of the earthen pit. And when he could have saved them, he'd stumbled in the forest, losing his way and wasting precious hours that could have meant saving their lives.

And, even if no one pointed an accusing finger at him, he saw the sidelong glances and questioning stares as three of his friends were buried. He heard the whispered doubts about his part in it and wanted to scream out his guilt. But his father and mother tried to convince him it was not his fault and it had not happened the way he said it had. It was a terrible accident to be put behind him. A horrible event which would fade in time.

And it did. No one ever mentioned it—his father, the laird, forbade it. No one mentioned the children who had died or their parents who had moved away or the injuries to the other one who had survived. No one asked too many questions and Athdar was told relentlessly he must push it all away. In time, all thoughts and memories of it and those friends faded, until, within a few years, it was a muted, empty part of his past.

A part he no longer remembered.

But someone remembered.

Someone mourned their loss and sought solace in the madness brought by the sheer anguish and pain of it.

And that someone decided to seek justice against the one responsible, even if he did not remember.

Someone remembered.

Chapter One

Lairig Dubh, Scotland—AD 1375

'Look! Look! There he is.'

The excited whisper drew Isobel's attention. Her friend Cora rarely took notice of the opposite sex, so this was something different, something special. She turned to see who her friend was watching.

Athdar MacCallum, brother of the laird's wife Jocelyn, strode through the yard, heading for the keep. From the decisive way he walked, looking neither right nor left, he had business with the laird and would not be slowed from his task. Still, he was a fine-looking man to gaze upon.

'He is leaving to return home,' she said. At Cora's questioning frown, she nodded. 'My father mentioned it this morn.'

'Will he be here for the evening meal, do you think?' Cora asked, watching her closely for her reply.

Isobel wanted to show her excitement much as Cora did, but she held back. If she showed her interest in Athdar, word would make it back to her father and then trouble would begin. Just mentioning his name usually caused her father to look extremely bothered. And bothered was not something she, or anyone, wanted her father to be.

The half-Norse, half-Scottish natural son of the Earl of Orkney did not suffer fools easily and at some time in the past, before even her birth, Athdar had done something very foolish and her father would never let it go. It mattered not that Athdar had been young and tended towards brash acts. It mattered not that he had suffered for his misjudgement. And it mattered not that the result had brought Jocelyn MacCallum to Lairig Dubh as the laird's wife. All that mattered to her father was that Athdar's character was lacking then and possibly still. Isobel turned away from the path and faced Cora.

'I know not, Cora. I do not keep watch over his comings and goings.'

Though she would if she could.

As Isobel had watched her various cousins being matched and married these last couple of years and as she'd reached what she considered a marriageable age, the only man who had caught her attention was Athdar. Oh, it had nothing to do with his strong, muscled body or his piercing brown eyes or the way his long, brown hair framed the masculine angles of his face. Dabbing at the perspiration on her forehead with the back of her hand, Isobel realised she'd noticed his physical attributes much too much!

There was also the fact that he intrigued her. Always respectful of her, he spoke to her as though she had a mind and did not shy away from her as all the other men did. Someone who would stand up to her father was not a bad thing. He was a fair and competent man, according to the earl. Compassionate, according to his sister.

And Isobel could sense the pervasive sadness that

lived within him and it called to something deep within her soul—she needed to be the one who gave him solace. Rather than drive or scare her away from him, it appealed to her. She shivered now as she glanced at him again.

Cora noticed her reaction, for her friend squinted and stared at her face. Then the girl smiled and nodded.

'I think you are not so unaffected as you want me to believe, Isobel.'

'Cora, he is kin through my father,' she offered, hoping Cora would allow the issue to settle. Wiping her damp hands on her gown, she tossed her hair over her shoulders and took her friend's hand. 'Come, we have tasks to see to before dinner, whether Athdar attends or not.'

That had been a near thing. Her friend wisely let the subject drop though the man walked half the yard ahead of them as they also headed for the keep. Her mother was attending Lady Jocelyn in the solar and that gave her the reason to follow him inside. Her heart raced in her chest and she tried to keep the anticipation of speaking to him under control…and she might have if someone had not called out his name from behind her. Athdar paused and turned to see who had called out to him. As he did that, his gaze, those intense, brown eyes, fell on her.

Any attempt to continue to behave as though his attention was usual or customary in her life dissolved away when he winked and then smiled at her. She stopped where she stood and tried to remember to breathe. Cora had not been looking so she continued forwards a step or two before realising she'd left Isobel behind. Isobel forced a breath in and out and then glanced back, returning his smile. She was trying to think of something pithy to say to him when Ranald brushed by and stepped between them.

'I am working in the practice yard, Dar,' Ranald called out. 'Come there when ye finish with the laird.'

Isobel watched as Athdar waved to Ranald, nodded his agreement and then turned to enter the keep. Ranald greeted both of them and then went back to the yard. Cora's gaze followed his every step until Isobel cleared her throat to gain her attention. The blush that crept up her friend's cheeks must be similar to the one she could yet feel heating her own. She waved her friend along, not commenting on Ranald's obvious appeal to Cora.

As they entered and walked the corridor to the lady's solar, Isobel decided that she would find a way to watch the two men practice in the yard later. Surely Cora would accompany her on her mission.

Athdar swore under his breath as he walked ahead of the two young women into the dark stone keep to find his brother-by-marriage. He had to meet with Connor and several of his advisors over changes to their plans. As he nodded to those he knew, he cursed himself for his stupidity. Smiling and winking at Isobel? Truly, he was wanting in the head to do such a thing in front of others.

Nay, to do such a thing at all.

Isobel was Rurik's daughter and if Rurik learned of any attention paid by him to her the man would have his head…or nether parts! He'd already faced death at Rurik's hands once before and he never intended to do that again, not even for the lovely Isobel.

Damn his eyes, but she was a beauty! He'd watched as she'd grown from gangly girl to this stunning young woman of confidence and intelligence. Her parents had seen her educated as most of those in the MacLeries' immediate families were. And like many of the other girls and women, they had been encouraged to know and speak their minds. Most unusual, he knew, but here in his brother-by-marriage's keep and village it all seemed the norm.

He sought the chamber that Connor used as a workroom and found him there with several others he knew. As they began their discussion, Athdar found his thoughts distracted by a heart-shaped face surrounded by pale blond curls and the blue-green eyes that were ever filled with merriment when they met his. And the full, pink lips that tempted him to madness. His body went along with these thoughts and reacted in surprising manner. Athdar shifted in his chair, gaining Connor's attention.

'Are you well?' Connor asked, offering him a cup of wine.

'I am,' he replied, taking a mouthful of wine to give him a moment to focus his thoughts on the business at hand and not on the lovely and forbidden Isobel. 'About the preparations for winter?'

Try as he might, even as Connor went back to explaining their plans, and his clan's part in them, Athdar thought about Isobel.

And the fruitlessness of any interest he might have in her.

Glancing around the chamber and realising that most of those there were happily married, he felt the heartache pierce through him as it always did.

Happy, he might be, but married he would never be again.

The disasters of his previous marriages and the most recent betrothal had made his decision for him—he would not subject any woman to the dangers of marrying him.

Especially not the lovely Isobel.

The tragedies of his past would haunt his every day and night, but he would not risk someone as precious and vibrant as her to the chance that he was truly cursed.

Some would laugh and call him foolish. People died. Women died, especially in childbirth or such manner. But then they would recall that he'd lost two wives to death, a betrothed to an accident and two possible wives to the fear of all that would befall them if their fathers agreed to matches with him.

So, in spite of any desire he had to find a wife and have a family as these men had, Athdar understood that the fates stood against him. Standing and walking to the window, he listened and replied to Connor from there.

As though his thoughts had conjured her up, Rurik's daughter passed into his view as she walked through the yard in the direction of the practice yards. She and her friend had their heads close together, conspiring no doubt on some feminine matter, as they laughed and glanced at the men practising their fighting skills. He emptied the cup and placed it on the nearby tray.

'I will accept your invitation to stay for a few days, Connor.' He strode towards the door, ignoring any questioning glances. 'I must check with my man about some of the supplies we need.'

'Your sister is in her solar, Dar,' Connor said.

'I will seek her out later.' Lifting the latch on the door, he pulled it open. 'I will return shortly.'

His feet led him outside before he could consider how strange his behaviour was. Something, someone drew him as though a rope connected him with…her. When he realised his dangerous actions—dangerous to his own well-being and hers—he slowed down and sought Ranald instead.

A good fight might beat this madness out of him. It might make him remember his reasons for being here. And his reasons for avoiding marriage completely.

His plan almost worked, too, until he heard Isobel gasp out his name as he landed face first in the dirt from a well-aimed punch. How was he ever going to ignore her when every fibre of his body and soul wanted to claim her?

'Rurik thinks to marry her elsewhere.'

Connor stepped closer, watching the scene in the yard from above—in his favourite place and standing behind his beloved Jocelyn. He leaned nearer, placing his arms on each side of where she stood, and inhaled the scent of whatever she used to wash her hair. His body grew hard just thinking about her…taking a bath…naked. Shaking his head, he laughed at the ever-present temptation she presented to him, regardless of their decades-long marriage and age.

'Has he finally realised she is of age to marry?' Jocelyn asked, turning into his arms. 'He has resisted for a long time.'

'Two offers have come in recently. We discussed them at length which forced him to accept that it is time.'

'And you support these matches?' she asked. A hint of something—suspicion? sarcasm?—entered her voice as she asked.

Connor laughed. 'Is the game on then, wife?' Kissing her, he watched as her eyes lit with mischief. 'So it is, then.'

He released her and looked over the side of the battlements down to the yard. Her brother had left their meeting abruptly and now he fought with one of the younger warriors, Ranald, before a shouting and cheering crowd. Even from this distance, Connor could read the distraction in Dar's fighting style. And, if he was right, he knew the person causing it.

'He notices her.' He felt Jocelyn tense and waited for her to object to his guess. 'Rurik will not be happy.'

'Athdar has sworn not to marry again,' Jocelyn whispered as they watched her brother losing control of the match below. 'He keeps so much pain within himself.'

Connor remained silent then, knowing that it could be telling their own story again—the pain, the refusal to marry, the inability to hope that love could be within their grasp until it was nearly too late. Only the woman before him had saved his soul and his heart from eternal darkness.

'Rurik has hopes she will settle her heart elsewhere, and that's without Dar's name being mentioned.'

'I did not think Rurik one to hold a grudge for so very long,' Jocelyn said, facing him once more and searching his face. 'It was so long ago and Athdar was so young. And it was only an insult, not an attack.'

'You have not involved yourself with Dar's affairs before. Why take up this challenge now?' he asked. He was trying to figure out if this would indeed become their next matchmaking challenge.

'It was not my place, Connor. I had accepted that,' she said, as sadness filled her voice.

'Had?' That was not good.

'I see the longing in his gaze at gatherings. He wants what we have. He wants a wife, bairns. Love. He wants it and yet he fears taking another chance.'

'So mayhap you should leave him to making that decision?' It could not hurt to nudge his beloved in the right direction. 'He is a chief now, with responsibilities. I do not think he would take it well to know you plot about him.' Hoping that was enough to push her away from making this attraction between Dar and Isobel more than that, he added, 'I have to see to things. I will see you at table?'

She smiled, acquiesced even, but he knew in his soul that she would not turn her efforts from a possible match between her brother and Rurik's daughter. And there would be hell to pay on all sides if that happened. He did not have the time to make her see the folly and danger in her choice, but he would see to it later. This night. In their chambers.

'Until then,' she whispered, reaching up on her toes to touch their mouths together.

He watched the seductive sway of her hips as she walked away and realised she'd not denied that she would pursue a match. Outplayed once more by desire for his wife, Connor cursed under his breath and walked away in the other direction. He needed to have a conversation with Rurik.

Or mayhap not.

For, once fired up, the commander of all his troops was formidable even for him. Mayhap this time he would hold back and see how this all played out?

With thoughts of what would await him in his bedchamber tempting him, Connor walked off to find someone to fight. It was a good way to clear his mind and sharpen his wits. And if his wife and the other mothers had decided on a match, he and the other fathers would need their wits about them.

From the smug expression that lay across her lovely face as she turned from him, he knew that even his wits might not win this battle.

Chapter Two

Since he was a visiting nobleman and considered more family than ally, Athdar was not surprised by the lack of formality during the evening meal. He'd shared many meals here in Connor's hall and most of them were like this one—family, friends, villagers and anyone in need of a meal. Conversations ebbed and flowed throughout the meal, laughter echoed high into the rafters and those dining moved between the small gathered groups to talk with others.

As always, his eye was drawn to Connor, his brother-by-marriage for this last score or so of years. His mentor in many things, his nemesis in others, Connor never minded his presence or his opinions, but, watching as the man's gaze softened each time he glanced at one of his children or at his wife, Dar's gut tightened with a mix of envy, jealousy and admiration. That the fearless, ruthless Earl of Douran could yet have a soft place in his heart made Dar want everything Connor had… yet again.

Drinking deeply from his cup of ale, he nodded to several who passed by and offered greetings to him. Glancing around the hall, he found Rurik sitting at a table with his wife and their children. The son, a year or so younger than Isobel, would be as formidable as their father in a few years. His height and build spoke of his Norse forebears and heritage. Then Isobel laughed and Dar felt it ripple across his skin. As she raised her eyes, their gazes met.

He knew he should look away. She was too young for him. She was too innocent of life and the horrors he'd seen. She was her father's daughter. For once, he simply enjoyed the innocence and freshness he saw in her eyes and did not question his need for such things… from her. At least he did until someone stepped between them, ending whatever connection had begun.

'Athdar,' his sister said as she sat on the bench next to him. 'When will you return home?'

He laughed at her remark. If he did not know her as he did, he would have thought his welcome was over.

'I expect to be on the road in the morn, dear Jocelyn,' he replied. 'My business with your husband is complete now.'

She reached over and plucked a morsel from his plate. 'I have been thinking…' she said, before tossing the bit of roast fowl into her mouth and savouring it.

Jocelyn thinking usually meant trouble for him—it had as a boy and it usually did now that he was grown and laird in his father's place. 'That is never good, Joss,' he said. 'Connor should discourage such things.'

She smacked his shoulder and shook her head at him. 'You are a lackwit at times. 'Tis no wonder…' Her words faded off as she realised that any jest about married life would fall like rocks thrown in the air. But the pity that replaced the mirth in her eyes hurt more than the memories. 'Dar…' She reached out to touch his hand, but he pulled back before she could.

'What have you been thinking about, then?' he asked, hoping she would allow the change of topic without comment.

'Will this be your last visit before the year's end? I know you and Connor made arrangements for supplies and other things, but I knew not if that meant your journeys here are done until spring?' she asked.

'Connor invited me to visit again and I will, unless the weather turns.'

Jocelyn glanced away from him. 'Unless the weather turns…' She remained silent for a few moments and then shook her head. 'Good. I am always glad to see you.'

He was certain she wished to say something more, but Connor called out to her first. She stood, as did he, and nodded to him. After taking a couple of steps towards her husband, she turned back to face him. 'Did he speak of…helping you to find…arrangements…?'

Athdar knew of what she spoke. Though he'd couched his words in diplomatic terms, his sister's husband, his overlord, had offered to broker a marriage contract. He'd done so many times in the past for other allies and kin, so it was not so strange. But he had no need for such aid.

'Aye, he did, Joss,' Dar replied. 'I declined his offer.' Best to have things clear between them. An unexplained frustration and anger grew within him then.

'You need a—'

'Stay out of this.' His voice must have been louder than he thought, for most in the hall stopped talking and looked over at them.

Including Connor.

Including—damn him for noticing!—Isobel.

And her father.

Rurik had long been Jocelyn's champion, loyal to her in every way, so an insult to her would not go unnoticed or unanswered by him. The commander of all the MacLerie warriors began to walk towards him, but was waved off by Connor who reached them first.

'Jocelyn?' he asked as he held his hand to his wife.

'I am meddling as you have warned me not to, husband,' she said, smiling into the laird's concerned face. 'My brother has been my target and an unwilling one at that.'

And as usual during their lives, she tried to take the brunt of displeasure for him. She ever did so when they were children and would still do so now in spite of their ages and positions. It had changed their lives irreparably before.

'Your pardon, Jocelyn, for my sharp tone,' Athdar offered the apology so that all could hear. Brother or not, laird in his own right or not, here he was a guest and she was their lady. Jocelyn's reaction removed the tension from the situation as she threw herself into his arms and hugged the breath out of his chest. He allowed himself a moment of weakness and then eased himself from her grip.

'I take my leave now, sister,' he said. Nodding to Connor, he waited for the laird to give him leave. 'I leave at first light and would not disturb you so early.'

Connor offered his hand and Rurik, convinced now that his services were not needed, walked back to his own wife. The others drifted back into their own conversations and Dar finished his ale. Walking back to his room, he realised that, once more, he was alone.

And no matter what he'd said to his sister, it was a condition he did not like and he did not want. But the danger of taking steps to make it different overrode his own personal needs or desires. For after the death of two wives and one betrothed, he would not put any woman in danger by being associated with him.

That dark night passed slowly and he rose at dawn to ride out as he'd planned.

Isobel had watched as he'd finished his meal and spoken to Lady Jocelyn. Something very strange and strained happened between them and she winced as he uttered the harsh words that made the lady turn the colour of Isobel's newest chemise. Then her father and the laird both went to her side and the hall grew silent.

Somehow, she could not imagine the lady needing protection or aid against Athdar. Her father had championed Lady Jocelyn for as long as Isobel could remember, and if the laird questioned it he never put a stop to it. Isobel's mother did not seem bothered by this protectorship, for she and Lady Jocelyn were the closest of friends. When the laird was absent, her father stood behind the lady. When the lady travelled, her father made the arrangements. It had always been that way.

So why had the hostility between her father and Athdar started? As she had watched the scene resolve, she tried to remember any clues about the beginning of the bad feelings. Then her father had returned and Athdar left the hall and she knew she would not see him again on this visit. As her father bade them go with him back to their cottage in the village, she knew that, unless she did something, Athdar would always wear the expression of grief in his eyes. And that she simply could not accept.

As she had lain in her bed, seeking sleep while finding a restless night, Isobel realised that the only way to make that happen would be to get her mother on her side. Lady Jocelyn's support would be a good thing because her father would listen to the lady. Plans and ideas had come and gone as the hours did and soon the weak light of a cloudy dawn had begun to seep into her bedchamber.

Dressing quickly and quietly, she made her way through the dark cottage, trying not to wake anyone. If her luck held, she could be back, in her bed, before the rest of her family rose. Already some of the villagers were about their daily tasks and she nodded as she passed them. Uncertain of why she wanted to speak to him now, she accepted it and continued walking towards the main gate.

She wrapped her shawl tightly around her shoulders to fight off the early morning chill and lifted her head to watch as those gates opened. A small group rode through and in her direction, so she stepped back off the path to let them pass. The lead rider waved the others on and drew his horse to a halt before her.

''Tis a bit early to be out this morn, lass,' Athdar said in a quiet tone. 'Does your father know you prowl about the village alone?' His voice was deeper after sleep than it usually was, sending shivers through her for some reason. She tried to ignore the reprimand.

'I have an errand to see to with Lady Jocelyn, if you must know,' she said. Turning towards the keep, she walked around him, now hesitant to say too much to him.

Why and how could he do this to her?

The poise and self-confidence that her parents often praised in her deserted her, leaving her feeling like a halfwit in his presence. Instead of carrying on a reasonable conversation—as she could with most any of her kin or those who visited the MacLerie laird—she turned into a babbling fool who could not utter a bit of sense.

Even now when she wanted to speak to him about his journey or his duties as laird, to ask sensible questions or offer a sensible suggestion, she could only blush and stammer.

'I would not keep you from your duties to my sister.'

He turned his horse once more so that he was headed down the path through the village and out to the main road. Before he spurred it on, he nodded and smiled to her and she wanted to melt into the ground beneath her feet.

'Go on now, lass. I will wait until you go inside,' he said.

Athdar was making certain she was safe before leaving.

'Safe journey, Laird MacCallum.'

'My name is Athdar, lass.'

She had never called him that to his face—he was older than she was and held a higher position, as well. But…

'Safe journey, Athdar,' she repeated with a nod.

The edges of his mouth curled and a rough smile changed his entire countenance from foreboding and serious to wickedly handsome. Her breath caught at how very handsome it did make him. Grasping for some of the boldness that would have caused her father's brow to rise, she called out once more, 'And my name is Isobel.'

His laughter rang out in the quiet of the early morn and a ripple of satisfaction pulsed through her at the sound. 'Good day, Isobel!' he called out as he turned his mount and rode off down the path to join the rest of his men.

Isobel walked quickly in the gate, greeting those on

guard duty as she did and fighting the urge to turn and watch Athdar with each step. Winning that battle but not having a specific errand in mind, she decided to seek out the lady and begin her campaign to fight for Athdar.

Chapter Three

MacCallum Keep—Two months later

Athdar rode back through the gates and called out to his men as he approached the stables. He'd spent two days riding his lands, overseeing the end of the harvest and the laying in of the crops for the coming winter. Though he'd lived through many changes of seasons, this one felt different somehow and he wondered if the winter storms would come through the mountain passes sooner than usual.

'Laird.'

Athdar turned to find the steward walking in his direction. 'Broc,' he said, waiting for the man to reach him. 'The preparations look well in hand…as you said they were.'

'There is still the butchering to be seen to, but that will be done in the next weeks.'

'Will this be a quiet winter, then?'

Padruig MacCallum had a habit of sneaking up on people, having perfected a silent, light step. It helped many times in dangerous situations, but he could drive Athdar to madness with the habit, too.

'The MacLerie has strengthened his control and his influence over the entire south-west of Scotland since the king does not act. Connor predicted no outbreak of hostilities…yet.'

From the expressions on the faces of the two men who served him most closely, he could not tell if they were joyful or saddened by this news. He liked a good fight the same as any man. Yet, now that this clan and its welfare was his responsibility, and now that supplies, crops and food were ready, he could admit a quiet winter had its appeal. Well, he could admit it to himself.

'What other news do you have for me, Padruig? How is training coming along? Has your son mastered swordplay yet?'

A good way to change the direction of his friend's talk was to bring up his son. Padruig doted on the boy, now almost a man, and his skills and talents. As he watched the man's usually dour face brighten, he knew the conversation would turn and braced himself for the pain he brought on himself once more.

And it did.

It took Broc only minutes to utter about things to do and leave and return to his duties, as Athdar wished to do. With each passing moment and with every word Padruig spoke, another dagger plunged into his own heart. But Padruig was his friend, in addition to being the commander of the MacCallum warriors, and it was not long before he realised what he'd said and the price of it to Athdar's heart and soul.

'Did Broc tell you?' he asked while kicking the dirt at his feet.

'About the cattle?'

'Nay, about your sister. Lady MacLerie,' Padruig said.

'Broc!' he shouted as he walked towards the keep. Padruig grabbed his arm to stop him.

'Jocelyn is on her way here. An outrider brought the message.'

'Why is she coming here now?' he said, tugging free and continuing to head for the keep...and some answers. He paused. 'Send two men out to meet them.'

'Dar.' Padruig let out an exasperated breath.

If Jocelyn was travelling, and Connor knew about it, she would be well provisioned and well guarded. Connor would never allow it any other way. So, his sister's safety was not an issue. 'Never mind.'

Still, he needed to know more so he walked into the squat, stone keep and searched for his steward— the one who'd conveniently forgotten to tell him of the visit. When he found him, Broc stood in the corner in one of the storage rooms under the kitchens.

'My sister?' he called out, trying to gain the man's attention.

An unexpected visit could be because of a problem or not. His sister and her husband did journey here several times a year, sometimes to see him and sometimes as they travelled onwards to other places, so there was no way to know. Except for Broc, who had not answered him.

'Broc!' His shout echoed through the small chamber and caused the servants in the kitchen and corridor to stop and stare. Finally, his steward straightened and turned to face him.

And that was also when a comely young woman stepped out from behind Broc's shadow and made her way out of the chamber and past Athdar. Damn, but Broc moved quickly with the lasses. From the smile on her mouth and the blush in her cheeks, he knew Broc had another conquest.

'Laird,' she said quietly with a nod as she passed him.

'Ailean.'

Broc waited as she sauntered down the corridor before coming to meet him at the door of the chamber.

'Another minute and you would have had her naked,' Athdar said. 'My God, man, you move quickly. You left the yard only minutes ago.'

His steward had always been so—a man with more women than other men could handle. It had been like that through their younger years and showed no sign of diminishing now that they'd reached manhood and more. Broc shrugged and smiled, accepting his words as a compliment…which they were.

'My sister is coming?'

Broc pulled the door closed and walked with him back to the kitchens. 'Aye. Her messenger said they are about a day's ride from here and should be here by midday on the morrow.'

'Is aught wrong? Did she say the reason for the visit?'

'Nay, no word about why. Just that she travels with a small group and will stay about a week. I was just on my way to ready the large chamber for her and her women.'

His keep was nothing like Connor's with its many storeys and bedchambers and towers. There was one large chamber on the lower floor, off the main hall, that was used for guests along with four chambers on a second floor. And one small tower for the guards. The great hall and kitchens took up most of the lower floor, with a stable and chapel set apart from the rest. But it was clean and comfortable and it was his.

A chill raced along his spine and he wondered if

it was the weather or the visit that worried him more. 'Twas unlike his sister to visit without an invitation or arrangements being made in advance. With her many duties as Lady MacLerie and the Countess of Douran, she simply did not rush off across Scotland to visit him. He hoped the ill-at-ease feelings he had were not portents of something bad.

He nodded as Broc went off to see to arrangements and then he went to the small chamber he used to keep his records and rolls. As they were not significant enough to warrant the use of a priest as clerk, Athdar kept his own records and was proud of that. Reviewing them now, he was confident his kith and kin would weather the coming winter well.

The chill of foreboding built within him, even as he saw to his duties throughout the day.

By the next day, he'd convinced himself that he was getting up in years and would soon be complaining of the aches and pains of the elders in his clan. He laughed at himself as the call came from the gates announcing his sister's arrival.

But when he saw who accompanied Jocelyn into his yard, he knew the feelings had been a warning of things to come, for following his sister on her horse was the woman who confounded him the most—Isobel Ruriksdottir.

Excitement hummed inside her as the gate and the stone keep beyond it came into view. Isobel could not believe her plan was succeeding so well. Oh, there were no guarantees that her mother would support her in this or that Lady Jocelyn agreed that she was the perfect choice for a new wife for her brother. There were so many things that could yet go wrong.

As they rode on through the gate, Isobel sat up a little straighter on her mount and glanced around the yard, hoping he was here waiting. Lady Jocelyn had sent him scant warning of their arrival and nothing of her reasons for visiting her brother.

The lady did have a reason—a flimsy one, true— but it would make sense. The herbs that Athdar's healer needed to replenish her own stores had not been included in the last supplies sent here. Those herbs and plant cuttings lay wrapped carefully in moist cloths in her own bag, just as Margriet had prepared and instructed. These would be needed before winter fell, so there was a need…other than hers.

Their party drew to a stop and Isobel waited as she heard Athdar call out greetings to his sister. From her position behind and to the side of her mother's horse, she could not see him or be seen, so she listened as he greeted the lady and helped her down. Several young men approached to help with the horses and one lifted her down to the ground. With his help, she also untied the bag from her saddle and took it with her. Her mother held out her hand and Isobel took it, walking with her to greet the laird appropriately.

'Margriet!' he called out as he saw her mother. 'Isobel,' he said as he met her gaze. 'Welcome to my home.'

Although her mother had visited before, this was her first time in his home. She followed as they walked into the keep, looking at everyone and everything. Jocelyn had grown up here until her marriage to Connor Mac-Lerie—something caused by Athdar's youthful antics, if she understood it correctly. She'd only heard bits of the story, but the results had turned out more happily than anyone at the time had dared hope.

The keep was stone—not as large as the MacLeries', having only two storeys and one guard-tower. Athdar had made changes since becoming laird and since marrying that made the keep more comfortable, according to Jocelyn. More importantly, the MacCallums had become close allies with the powerful MacLerie clan.

Soon they reached the other end of the large hall and Athdar led them to a table set with platters of food and pitchers of ale.

'Broc thought you might need something since you have been on the road,' he said. The lady and her mother both acknowledged the man who must be Athdar's steward.

Broc seemed of an age with Athdar, but where Athdar always wore a serious expression that furrowed his brow, Broc wore one that spoke of mirth…and something more that she could not decipher. He wore his long black hair pulled back and his eyes were the colour of the stone that lay in the walls around them. His smile caught her eye and she could feel the heat of a blush moving into her own cheeks. Athdar brought him closer just then so he could greet her and her mother.

'Margriet, welcome,' he said, bowing to her mother. 'It has been several years since you last graced us with a visit.'

His deep voice affected even her mother and a blush that matched Isobel's filled her cheeks. Then she giggled! She'd watched untold numbers of women react this way to her father, but had never expected to see her mother fall under this kind of spell.

'Isobel, welcome,' Broc said, taking her hand and smiling. 'We met a few years ago at Lairig Dubh, but you were only a wee lass then. Now…' Athdar cleared his throat loudly and Broc continued, 'I hope you enjoy your stay here.'

She thought herself immune to such clear and blatant flirting, but she was not. And since neither her mother nor Jocelyn was resisting it, she smiled back, too.

'My thanks for such a warm welcome,' she said. 'I am certain I will enjoy my visit here.' Broc guided her to a seat.

'Can I have your bag placed in your chamber?' he asked while waving to the waiting servants to begin.

'That is for Laria,' Lady Jocelyn said before she could. The healer for Athdar's village would be in need of what they'd brought.

'Should I have it taken to her or would you rather have her come here?' Athdar asked.

'Mayhap Isobel could take them after we finish here?'

'Certainly, lady,' she replied. It would give her a chance to look about the village. And stretch her legs after long days of riding.

Taking the seat that Broc indicated, she watched as Athdar spoke to his sister in hushed tones. An expression of relief crossed his face—he must have been expecting bad news with this sudden visit. Then the tension between brother and sister eased and his face took on a boyish look and it took Isobel's breath away.

She allowed herself but a moment of appreciation before turning to speak to her mother about the plants they'd brought. Marian, Duncan's wife, had a talent with herbs and plants and oversaw the keep's gardens. Isobel herself had worked with Marian at times, learning from her store of knowledge for use when she married and supervised her husband's household. The plants they brought would add to the ones needed to treat fevers and pain, important for the winter and in time to have them dried and ready for use.

Athdar and Jocelyn joined their conversation and brought him news of the comings and goings at Lairig Dubh. Soon they had finished eating and the steward directed them to the chamber where their bags had been taken. Isobel excused herself from her mother and the lady and approached Athdar.

'Can you tell me how to find Laria's cottage?' she asked, smoothing her hair back from her face.

'Come, I will take you there,' he said, guiding her down the steps.

'You must have more important things to do,' she said. Though it worked into her plans well, she did not want to take him from his duties as laird.... At least not yet.

'One of a laird's duties is to show hospitality to a guest, so you take me away from nothing more important.' From the tone of his voice and the serious look in his eyes, he did not seem to be joking. So, neither did she.

'I am honoured, Athdar.'

Isobel nodded at him and took his arm when he held it out to her. He matched his longer stride to hers as they crossed the hall and left the keep through the kitchens. He introduced her to relatives as they passed by, pointed out places along the path and kept up a steady flow of conversation along the way.

The keep was not as large as that in Lairig Dubh and neither was the village, but everyone they met looked hearty and well. No one seemed to fear approaching the laird and speaking to him, whether they were old or young, man or woman. The completed harvest and the coming winter were the two most common subjects raised, but some of the younger boys challenged Athdar to battles and he accepted them in good cheer.

Though he released her arms several times as they stopped to talk with others, he offered his once more as they began walking again. When she tripped over the exposed root of a tree, he held her steady and did not let her fall. The path meandered through a thick stand of forest before opening into a clearing. A small cottage lay within a still-lush garden, surrounded by a low wall. Curls of smoke drifted up from the chimney and wicked away into the air, leaving a hint of peat to scent the coolness. Athdar opened the low gate and let her pass him. Before they reached the door, it opened and a woman stepped out.

'Laird,' she said, nodding to Athdar. 'Good day,' she said, as she glanced at Isobel.

'Good day, Laria,' Athdar said, letting her arm slip down now. 'This is Isobel Ruriksdottir, from Lairig Dubh. She has something for you from my sister.'

'You are Margriet's daughter, then?' Isobel nodded as the woman continued to examine her face. 'You do have her look.' Laria stepped back and motioned for them to enter.

'I must return to matters in the keep. I will send someone for you?' Athdar remained on the narrow walk, waiting for her answer.

'I can find my way back,' she said as she followed Laria inside. 'Again, I am grateful for you bringing me here.'

The short, wonderful walk they had together over, Isobel watched as he strode away from the cottage and her. No matter that he had spared her this time, he was an important and busy man here among his clan with much to do besides seeing to one guest. Still, it had been a boon granted to her and it pleased her.

'You brought the plants?' Laria asked.

Isobel realised the woman had moved across the cottage's main room to a large worktable already crowded with jars and bowls and plants and leaves. She walked over and placed the bag she carried in a clear spot.

'Marian sent along the ones you asked for and a few others she thought you might have need of,' she said as she opened the bag, lifted out the wrapped bundle and handed it to Laria.

Isobel watched in silence as the older woman handled the cuttings and plants with almost reverence, unwrapping and gently easing the stems and roots and leaves apart. Some she placed directly in bowls of water, others she pressed into bowls filled with soil. Isobel did not know enough about the various herbs to know which ones were which or which needed what. Laria worked on, without giving any attention or notice to Isobel, so she wandered around the cottage, examining some of the covered jars, sniffing some of the more aromatic plants. But when she reached out to touch one, Laria called out to her.

'Do not!' she said sharply.

Her words and tone surprised Isobel and she jerked her hand back away from the dark, dense plant that had gained her attention. 'I am sorry,' she offered as she returned to the table where Laria yet tended to the newly arrived plants.

'Some of these are more de…delicate than others and must not be touched,' Laria explained and she held out the empty bag to Isobel. For a moment, Isobel thought the woman was going to say something else, something other than 'delicate'.

'Your pardon. I will be more careful, Laria.'

Isobel felt a shift in the tension between them in that moment. Something had changed and she was at a loss to explain it. Mayhap the plants had been damaged before by a careless touch? Laria's next words confirmed her feelings.

'If you have nothing else for me, I must get to work with these,' she said, motioning to the plants she'd unwrapped and separated. Though her face was emotionless, her eyes showed something more, for a dark, suspicious glare met Isobel's gaze for a brief moment.

Mayhap she was overtired? Or was it simply the woman's disposition? Isobel brushed the few strands of loosened hair away from her face and nodded.

'We are visiting for a sennight. If you have need of anything else from Lairig Dubh, just inform me or Lady MacLerie and we can arrange to have it brought to you before the winter sets in,' she said.

Isobel walked to the door, but stopped before leaving. She could not explain, even to herself, why she asked the question.

'Athdar has spoken many times about your skills and talents in healing with them, Laria. If I promised to be careful and obey your instructions, would you teach me some of what you know? While I am here?'

'Why?' the woman asked, with no inflection to reveal if she was even thinking about her request.

'My knowledge of plants and herbs is sorely lacking. With my parents considering offers of marriage, I realise that I may be overseeing such matters in my husband's home much sooner that I thought. I would gain some knowledge before I marry.' It was true, even though another, less identifiable reason lurked deeper in her mind.

Laria stared at her as though evaluating her words in a silence that drew out past the simple few seconds Isobel thought she needed to refuse her. Then, surprising her, Laria agreed, though it was clear with some reluctance.

'I can spare you some time each morn, if you want to come,' she said.

'Aye, I would like that. My thanks, Laria,' Isobel said.

'And you touch nothing without my saying so.'

'Certainly.' Isobel lifted the latch on the door. 'I will come on the morrow then.'

At once pleased and puzzled, Isobel gained her bearings and headed back through the forest towards the keep in the distance. Passing some, she offered greetings as she walked back. All were friendly, many having seen her pass this way earlier with Athdar and some whom she had met when they'd visited Lairig Dubh with their laird on previous occasions. She did not remember all the names, but a number of faces were familiar to her.

She arrived at the gates and was waved through by the guards watching from their posts. Everything along the way was pleasant and welcoming and she saw her mother sitting with Lady Jocelyn and other women at the end of the hall.

So, if all was well, why did she feel the distinct chill coursing through her bones? Why did it feel as though someone had just walked on her grave?

Chapter Four

Jocelyn sat with Margriet and several of her own cousins in the hall, all of them working to repair a large tapestry. It had always been one of her favourites, a scene that included figures of all the animals that inhabited the forests and lakes in the surrounding area. As a child, she would look at this on the wall and make up stories about all the animals, giving them names and occupations. She'd noticed the damaged and fraying corners on her last visit and took advantage of this one to work on it.

This was one disadvantage of Athdar being without a wife—there were simply some things that a woman needed to see to in the keep and village. One of their cousins had stepped in, and oversaw the keep and the duties of chatelaine, working along with Broc. And Laria served as healer and watched over the village concerns.

But Athdar needed a wife. His clan, their clan, needed their laird to marry.

More than that, her brother deserved a lasting happiness. Her heart ached for all he'd lost and all he lived without and the fact that he wanted it, but would not allow himself to hope for it, tore her soul in pieces. That was the reason she had decided it was time to meddle here. Winning or losing the matchmaking challenge between her friends and their husbands meant nothing to her in the face of Athdar's continued pain and unhappiness.

Everyone deserved the chance for a family. If her husband, the Beast of the Highlands, had found redemption, her brother should, too.

'Do you think this is wise, then?' Margriet asked her quietly as they passed threads around the circle of women embroidering. The other women spoke amongst themselves, carrying on conversations about their tasks and their families.

'Should you even be asking me that question? You know our agreement,' Jocelyn said, smiling at her friend.

'You broke all the rules when you brought me along on this mission of yours,' Margriet replied, resting her hands on her lap and pausing in their work. 'You cannot expect me to sit back and observe when my daughter is part of your plot.'

'Margriet, there is no plot. We know Isobel is attracted to Athdar and he to her. I wanted to see if there is any true spark before encouraging this match to proceed.'

'But he has sworn not to marry again. How do you think to overcome that?' Margriet asked.

'I think the better question would be how do we get your husband to accept a marriage between them? Neither one has got over their incident.' Margriet blanched at Jocelyn's words, her pale skin going even whiter at the mention of her husband.

Rurik and Athdar's first meeting and the altercation

that followed Athdar's stupid behaviour and insults had led to Jocelyn's forced marriage. For some male reason, the eventual happy outcome between her and Connor had not smoothed the road between two of the important men in her life and her connected family. Each of them gave the other the respect they deserved due to their roles and positions, but it was a begrudging deference and nothing more.

'He is protective of her,' Margriet said. 'He did not take Connor's suggestions for possible matches any better. Rurik yet sees her as a child. If he has time to consider the good things about a marriage between them…' Her words drifted off into silence as they each contemplated Rurik's reaction.

Jocelyn snorted first, laughing aloud, and then Margriet joined her, gaining the full attention of the rest of the women there. Greeting their puzzled looks with a shrug, Jocelyn waited until everyone had returned to their own conversations before speaking again.

'Mayhap 'tis better to beg forgiveness than to ask permission?' Jocelyn asked in a whispering voice, not really wanting an answer.

If Tavis MacLerie had asked permission to marry Marian and Duncan's daughter Ciara, it would have been refused. If Ciara's betrothed had asked permission to break their arranged marriage to marry another, it would have been refused. Sometimes it was better to take matters into your own hands than doing the proper, formal thing.

'That may be premature, Jocelyn. We do not even ken if this is anything more than a mere attraction between them. If my daughter is to marry, I want her to be happy in that marriage.'

'True. Which is the reason I invited her, and you,

on this visit. To see how they are together. In a place where he is in charge and not affected by Connor's, or Rurik's, presence. To see the real man that Athdar is.'

They fell back into companionable silence and worked on the tapestry for some time before seeing Isobel enter the hall. Jocelyn had been pleased when her brother offered to escort Isobel himself to the healer's cottage and from the blush in her cheeks and smile on her face, it had been a good idea.

'Lady Jocelyn,' Isobel said, with a bow of her head as she approached. 'Mother.'

Margriet held out a needle and threads to Isobel, who took them and sat on a chair next to her. Isobel's skills with a needle were excellent, but her other talents were more impressive and would be a boon for any man lucky enough to wed her. She had a level head, was intelligent and kind. She had grown into one of the best chess players amongst those in the family who played, beating her father and Marian with ease now. That demonstrated her logical mind and ability to see how things worked and progressed.

'Did Laria have anything to say?' she asked.

'Nay, not much. I told her if there was anything else she needed, to speak to you.' Isobel lifted the material closer to her and then glanced up at Jocelyn. 'She is not a friendly person, is she?'

'Nay, she is not,' Jocelyn answered. 'But she is skilful and has always worked for the good of the clan.'

She watched as Isobel absorbed the meaning of her words. Laria's temperament had never been the same after losing her two children, but what woman would be unchanged by such tragedy? Still, she worked tirelessly to provide herbs and medicaments to anyone in need.

Jocelyn's father and Athdar after him always provided Laria with a living so that she able to continue her work.

'Her gardens must be impressive when in full bloom,' Isobel said. 'I asked if she will teach me about her work while I am here.'

'Did you?' Margriet asked, putting down her needlework. 'Why? You have never shown an interest in such things.'

'I know that you and Father are considering possible marriages and that I will need to oversee such things for my…husband.' She paused for a moment. 'This seemed an advantageous thing since we are here and I have no other duties to see to.'

Jocelyn smiled to herself and glanced over at Margriet. Isobel did understand that it was time. Now, all she…they…had to work out was if marriage to Athdar was the right path for both Isobel and him.

A small thing to accomplish when she put her mind to it.

Athdar had accepted two things as inevitable when he received word of Jocelyn's pending arrival with Isobel and her mother as travel companions. The first was something that always happened during Jocelyn's visits—the keep would be better after she tended to things. The second was that he would be spending time, and a good amount of it, with the fair Isobel. Ever a man to know his limitations and his strengths, he understood the true purpose of his sister's journey here and it had little or nothing to do with some damned plants for Laria.

As he swallowed another mouthful of ale and contemplated his reaction to Jocelyn's, and Isobel's, visit and his plans for this incursion into his life, he accepted another inevitability—Jocelyn had not given up on pursuing another marriage for him.

She said something then, about the cook's recipe for the fowl before them, and he nodded and muttered something acceptable. But his mind turned the situation over and over. He knew she did most things to protect or help him. It had ever been that way between them—as children and even into adulthood, she had been the buffer between him and whatever came his way.

Her marriage to Connor, though now a happy one, had been her attempt to get him out of a bad situation he'd caused—one of many in his childhood and as a boy and even young man. Now, he wondered if the sins of his past were catching up to him, taunting him even, with the nearness of Isobel.

Isobel smiled just then and said something softly to her mother and Athdar watched her mouth curve and her eyes brighten. So young, so beautiful.

And so tempting.

He leaned back and listened to the discussion about some household matter and then realised he was not the only one watching and listening to her. She held the attention of Broc, Padruig and many other men at the table and nearby, whether they be married or bachelor. When Broc caught his eye and winked, Athdar knew she had another conquest if she wanted one or not. The way that she engaged in conversation, offering her opinion when asked and questioning to clarify, demonstrated her innate intelligence.

When had she grown from child into…this?

While he was living in hell.

The hell that began with his first marriage to the woman he'd loved for years. The hell that included watching her die, after she struggled to give birth to their child, and then losing the child, his son, within days. The hell that continued through another wife and another death and a betrothed and her death.

While Rurik had kept his daughter safe and sheltered, he'd failed three women.

No wonder he'd missed the changes in her as she reached womanhood.

He drank again trying to wash the bitter taste of those memories away and continued to watch the women discussing Jocelyn's latest plan to improve the hall. He did not mind her ministrations, no matter that they reminded him that he had no wife to be in charge of his home, as his mother had done for his father. She saw that things were cleaned and repaired and freshened and they were usually tasks that he would never think of himself. Broc oversaw the important tasks a steward did—supplies, foodstuffs, livestock and such—but that left many less critical things undone. The empty platters were being removed when he drank the last of his ale.

'Isobel, do you play chess?' He knew her parents did as did his own sister and husband. Chances were Isobel did. Something within him pushed him to offer a challenge when she nodded. He wanted to speak to her, with her. 'Play with me?'

'Athdar, it has been a long day,' Jocelyn answered before Isobel could. 'On the morrow?'

Isobel responded as the well-behaved guest and lady would. 'I must agree with Lady Jocelyn, Ath—my lord,' she said quietly, as she slipped up and used his name in front of others. His body reacted to the hint of his name on her lips. Bloody hell to that!

'We are kin here, Isobel,' Jocelyn replied. 'I am certain my brother has no objections to you calling him by his given name. We are families connected now.' Jocelyn arched an eyebrow at him. As though he would refuse when he'd already given her leave to do so.

'None, Jocelyn,' he said. 'You all must pardon my boorish ways. I should have remembered about your travels these last few days and not imposed.' He stood and held out his hand to his sister. 'I will see you in the morn.'

Athdar hugged Jocelyn and bowed to Margriet and Isobel and he waited for them to leave the table before sitting back down. As they walked towards the back of the hall and the chamber they would use, Isobel paused and looked around as though searching for something. He glanced to where she'd been sitting and saw her handkerchief on the table. Athdar grabbed it and walked towards her, holding it out.

'You left this,' he said.

'If you will wait, I would like to play chess,' she whispered.

He tried to hide his surprise, both at her acceptance of his invitation and her boldness in planning to return, clearly without her mother or his sister. If he did the right thing, it would be to order her to remain in her chambers until morn. If he did the right thing, it would mean lying awake another night. If he did the right thing... Damn! He always did the right thing.

'I will be here.'

She turned and made her way back to where her mother waited and Athdar watched them leave, all the while smiling over this small transgression. Oh, Isobel was completely safe with him—he would never overstep with Rurik's daughter and would never dawdle with an unmarried woman in a way that would call her honour,

or his, into account. They were family, Jocelyn had said.
So he would treat her as such.

And he would wait.

For her.

Chapter Five

Isobel lay on her cot in the darkness, listening to the sounds of her mother and the lady as they fell into sleep's grasp and wondering at the boldness of her actions. Once their breathing grew deep and even, she waited a few more minutes and then climbed slowly and silently from under her bedcovers, pausing after each movement, committed to returning to the hall. It took her several more minutes to get off the cot, get dressed in her simplest gown and make it across the chamber to the door.

She did not know what madness claimed her in the moment when she told Athdar she would return, but it seemed simpler than contradicting Jocelyn and making it seem more important than it was. At the same time, she did want to see him and play against him…now, and not wait for another day. Their walk to Laria's cottage had been pleasant and she'd managed to lose the nervousness that always plagued her when he was near.

Isobel lifted the latch with care and eased the door open. The hall lay quiet and in darkness. The hearth at the other end was the only thing giving off light to guide her path. She gathered her hair and tied it with a strip of leather and then inhaled a deep breath. Letting it out slowly, she took the first steps across the stone floor. As she grew closer, she saw a small table and two chairs arranged in front of the fire. Athdar stood, leaning his arm against the mantel of the hearth, staring up at the tapestry above it.

'Did you help to repair that?' he asked quietly. He had not acknowledged her arrival, so his words surprised her. Pleased that he had waited, she moved closer.

'Aye. I worked with my mother, your sister and the others to fix it. It was unravelling there near this edge,' she said, walking up next to him and pointing to the lower, closest corner of the large woven and embroidered piece. 'Lady Jocelyn fixed the fraying bear and deer there.'

'They were her favourites.' He reached up and touched the edge of the tapestry before turning to face her. 'She would tell tales about each of the animals after our mother finished them.' He held out his hand and guided her to sit, still smiling at what must be pleasant memories.

Once they were seated, he held out a cup to her, one he had on a tray next to the board. She accepted it and sipped the watered ale.

The light of the low flames flashed to life for a moment and illuminated his face to her. For once, he lost the pain that she could see in his gaze and took on the look of the younger man she remembered from her childhood. She could imagine for a moment the adolescent who vexed his sister and his parents. The man before he…

Lost so much.

She lifted her cup and leaned forwards to look at the

board. If she continued to think about the many tragedies he'd faced, she would cry.

'So, are you better than your father at this?' he asked, as he settled in his chair.

'He will never admit it, but, aye, I am,' she confessed quietly. 'Though I cannot win over Duncan's wife on a regular basis.' Duncan's wife Marian was a formidable opponent in this game. Even her father had given up trying to beat her.

'But you have tried?' he asked, as he moved the black pieces to his side. She scooped up the red ones and began to put them in their places.

'She taught me the game.'

His swallow was audible and she laughed at his reaction. 'Mayhap I should seek my bed after all?'

'Nay. I will not surrender this early. Let us test our abilities before calling for a retreat.' His eyes sparkled then and she found herself lost in them for a moment longer than it took for him to notice.

'Very well, if that is what you want,' she teased.

They fell into a comfortable silence as she made the first move and then studied the one he made. She neither rushed nor delayed, but took her time and learned his method and strategies. He was skilled, though he played discreetly. Several times he surprised her with a riskier choice, but each risk taken was rewarded with success. In the end, Isobel struggled to make her loss appear real and not to lose in earnest.

'You are a dangerous opponent, Isobel Ruriksdottir.'

'But you won, Athdar,' she said. Lifting the cup to her lips, she drank before she said anything more.

'You let me win. You should have claimed several of my pieces when I put them in jeopardy.'

She had learned long ago that men did not particularly care for women who could best them so she had no intention of admitting he was right. But, when she met his gaze, she decided differently.

'Are you insulted?' she asked, watching his response.

'Aye. Insulted that you think I need to be coddled like a bairn.' The sparkling was back in his eyes, so she doubted he was truly insulted.

'We could play again…'

'An honest game?'

'If that is what you want?'

They launched into the game without another word, the play going back and forth between them and the outcome was never a certainty for either of them. Finally, Isobel made her last move and won. She placed all the pieces she'd collected in the wooden box next to the board before raising her eyes and looking at Athdar.

Would he truly accept defeat well? Or would he be angry in spite of his words?

'Well played, Isobel,' he said. 'I thought I might be the victor until you made those last three moves. More than skilful, lass. You have a real talent for this.'

His compliment and his appreciation of her skills brought a blush to her cheeks. The warmth of it spread through her.

Athdar stood, gathered the rest of the pieces in the box and closed it. He lifted the board and tucked it under his arm. She waited for him to put it up in its place on the mantel.

Isobel had no idea of how much time had passed while they played. She looked at the hearth and realised it had burned down quite low. A few lamps around the hall still threw some light down its length and shadows into its dark corners. No one had entered since they'd been there—most likely all were in their beds asleep as they should be.

'Athdar, I...'

'Isobel...'

She laughed softly and waited for him to speak first. Just as he opened his mouth to begin, a cough echoed through the emptiness. They both turned to find her mother standing outside their chamber's door.

'I should go,' she whispered.

'Aye. Go on then,' he said. 'If you need me to speak to her, I will.'

'Goodnight, Athdar,' she said, taking the first step away from him.

'Goodnight to you.'

She'd taken a few steps towards her chamber when his voice came as a whisper from behind her.

'Isobel.'

She shivered at what her name sounded like when whispered so.

Isobel quickened her steps when in fact she had no wish to face her mother's ire too soon. She wanted to savour the pleasure of being with Athdar, alone, as a man and woman. She let his words of praise repeat in her thoughts until she was but a few paces from her mother.

'Who won?'

The words were not the ones she had expected to hear when she'd clearly misled her mother and Jocelyn. At the least, she expected a warning about such behaviour. Instead her mother surprised her by asking about the game.

'I did,' Isobel whispered as she followed her mother back inside the chamber. Lady Jocelyn sat up in the bed, watching her enter.

'How did he take the loss?' she asked, smoothing

the bedcovers over her lap and pushing her long sleep braid over her shoulder. Isobel's mother sat on the edge of the bed and listened.

'He complimented me on my playing.'

The two older women exchanged some glance she could not read. Then they looked back to her.

''Tis now the middle of the night, child,' her mother said softly. 'Seek your bed.'

When she had expected a reprimand for ignoring the lady's words and for sneaking out of her chamber in the dark of night to meet with Athdar alone, all she received instead was an enigmatic expression. Isobel sensed that both women supported her exploring the possibility of a relationship with Lady Jocelyn's brother. Though separated in age by almost a score of years and though her parents must have some other marriage plans in mind, her mother did nothing to warn her off. And the lady had specifically invited her along on this visit. Kn ving they would both speak their minds when they wished to, Isobel undressed and slid back under the bedcovers on her cot.

Try as she might, sleep would not come to her. She tossed and turned, reliving each moment spent with Athdar, replaying the games in her thoughts. And watching the way his mouth curved when he laughed…and the way his eyebrows gathered tight when she'd made an unexpected move. But mostly she thought about the way they'd simply been together and how comfortable it felt to be in his company.

If they'd played through half the night, then she had spent the other half going back over every minute of it. Sooner than she thought possible, the faint light of the rising sun pierced the darkness of the chamber with thin beams around the edges of the window shutters. Isobel turned for the final time and listened as the sounds of the keep's inhabitants waking and beginning their day also crept into the room.

She waited for her mother and Lady Jocelyn to stir before sitting up on the cot and loosening the tangles in her hair, which had come undone from its braid during the restless hours. Stretching her arms over her head, she settled at the side of the cot and watched as a serving woman brought in a bucket of steaming water to them, then it took little time to wash and dress and prepare for the day.

Planning on breaking her fast and then seeking out Laria for her first lesson, Isobel was surprised to find Laria in the hall.

'Good morrow,' she said to the older woman as she walked towards the table in the front of the room. 'I did not expect you to come for me.'

'I need to finish harvesting some plants to the south of here, so it seemed the practical thing to do,' Laria replied before turning to Lady Jocelyn and Isobel's mother. 'Lady. Margriet,' she said with a nod. 'The air has turned colder. Bring a sturdy cloak.'

Lady Jocelyn smiled at her, letting her know that this brusque approach was the custom for the healer. Isobel rushed back to their chamber to get her heavy cloak and leather gloves. Knowing she would be working alongside Laria this morn, she'd already pulled on her short boots which would protect her feet from the damp grass and mud. Within minutes she was ready and back in the hall, listening to Jocelyn talking with Laria. Her mother held out a small parcel to her as Laria turned to leave.

'You did not eat. Some bread and cheese.'

In many other noble houses, great store was placed in the conducting of meals with formality, but as long as she could remember the laird and lady ate among their kith and kin. If tasks were to be done, a simple meal like this one was enough. So, it might seem unusual to many others of the same rank as Lady Jocelyn to dispense with a meal with little comment, yet it was not for them. If Laria thought it strange, she did not say. A nod to the others was the only signal that they were leaving and would be about their day's work.

She spent the chilly, cloudy morning following Laria across fields and into forests as she collected the last fresh leaves and cuttings from many different plants. The healer spoke about each one as she cut, wrapped and placed it into the large basket she gave Isobel to carry. There seemed to be none of the reticence that Isobel had first felt from the older woman. Indeed, she now seemed pleased to have an assistant as she carried out this important task in preparing for the coming winter.

They spoke little other than Laria's instructions about how each plant would be preserved and prepared, all the time walking across MacCallum lands. Though the air warmed a bit as the sun rose higher in the sky, it lost only the coldest bit of chill and never grew to the point that she could remove her cloak completely.

After several hours, they neared the keep and Laria dismissed her until the next morn.

Isobel had never thought herself pampered or lazy. That is until Laria dragged her to and fro for these last hours, leaving her exhausted. She drew nearer to the gates of the keep, watching villagers on the way back to their cottages, and found a place where the sun's rays warmed a section of the low wall of a narrow bridge. She sat, gathering the cloak around her and leaning her face back to feel the sun's warmth on her cheeks for a few moments before going inside.

Some quiet seconds passed and Isobel thought she might doze, tired as she was, so she leaned back against the trunk of a tree that grew next to the wall. Sitting still for the first time since getting out of her bed this morn just past dawn felt good. She knew people passed her by, but the sounds faded away as sleep overtook her.

'Isobel?'

She heard someone saying her name. Sleep held her firmly and she just could not open her eyes.

'Lass?'

Then she felt a large hand on her shoulder, squeezing it as her name was spoken again in that deep, appealing voice.

'Isobel? Are you well, lass?'

He watched as her eyes fluttered open and, as she recognised him, Athdar began to reach out to steady her, placing his other hand on her shoulder and waiting for her to wake completely before letting go. There was going to be hell to pay from her mother already from last night's infraction of manners, but if Margriet saw her daughter asleep on the bridge because he'd kept her up half the night, body parts might be maimed or removed. His body parts.

'Athdar,' she whispered as she straightened up and stretched her neck and shoulders a few times. Then she smiled at him and stood. 'The sun felt so good when I sat down, I must have drifted off to sleep.' A wonderful blush crept up into her cheeks, showing her embarrassment about being caught.

'It was a cruel thing I did to you, Isobel. Kept you

up most of the night. Then I allowed Laria to find you just as you left your chamber. And now, puir wee lass, you've had to find sleep sitting on the bridge. I am a terrible host.'

Isobel stood and he moved back so she could. He wanted to touch the dark shadows that marred the creamy colour of her cheeks and make them go away. As he lifted his hand towards her, he heard people nearby. People walking across the bridge. People who could see everything he did and hear everything he said.

He took another step back and then another and then waited for her to step away from the place on the wall where she'd been sitting. After she shook out her cloak, he held his arm out to her.

'Come, let me see you back to the hall.'

Isobel glanced around them and nodded to the men he'd left sitting on their horses waiting for him.

He'd forgotten them when he noticed her asleep on the wall.

'You have duties, Laird MacCallum, and I must not keep you from them,' she said, loudly enough for them to hear. 'But I thank you for your kindness.'

Athdar wanted to thank her for saving his dignity in this. He'd, again, lost his mind at the sight of her and forgotten the tasks he was in the middle of doing.

'We go to check on the repairs to the mill.'

From the sly glances from Padruig and the others, he would suffer for this. So, after she bid him farewell, he nodded and watched as she turned and walked towards the gates. He'd only just climbed up on his horse when the whispered taunts began. He listened in silence, for responding to them would make it worse and draw attention he did not want. Then as they reached the road that led to the mill, his destination, he realised what he must say.

'I was showing her the hospitality of my home,' he said to them. 'But what excuse do you have for not paying attention to a young, attractive woman who is of marriageable age?'

He rode off then, while kenning two things. He knew that the young bachelors among his men, especially Fergus and Niall, and even the recently widowed Connal would look a bit differently at Isobel at supper. And he knew that he had made a grievous error in dealing with his own attraction to the lass. If he did not strengthen his resolve never to marry again, a lass like Isobel could make him change his mind.

Chapter Six

Warmth surrounded her and Isobel did not wish to move. She pulled and tucked the bedcovers high around her neck and dipped her face down to stay warm in the cooler air of the chamber. Dawn must have come and gone some time ago from the brightness of the room. Still, considering that yesterday had been busier than she'd thought possible when she accepted the lady's invitation to visit her, a sense of guilt filled her as she realised how late it must be.

She'd expected to be a guest, possibly working on embroidery—which she had—or making the acquaintance of some of the lady's other kith and kin—which she had. Instead she'd worked more and harder than she did at home, mending clothes and linens, cutting and cooking vegetables for preserving, cleaning two storerooms and visiting most, if not all, of the villagers.

And she'd spent most of each morning working with Laria and learning about the healing arts and herbs. She now kenned the difference between an intinction, a tincture, an infusion and a tea, a poultice, a posset and a rub, and how to grind the dried leaves of many plants to make a passable paste to treat all sorts of ailments and complaint.

The most disappointing part of all this work was that she had not been able to challenge Athdar to another match—because each night she'd barely made it through supper awake. And try as she might, she could not rouse herself once she'd got into bed to see if he'd waited for her in the hall.

Now, on her fourth morning, she decided she was going to have a lazy day and remain abed until the sun. No more climbing through bushes and marshes. No more crawling along the streambed searching for certain grasses and flowers.

No more.

Mayhap she would read, selecting a book from the MacCallums' collection, which Jocelyn had described to her, and finding a sunny place in the hall to enjoy it. Then, after a day of leisure, she would be rested enough to stay awake and try to sneak back and play chess with Athdar.

Or…

The knock surprised her. The second, louder knock forced her from her cocoon. The third, more relentless knock told her clearly that lazy day was at an end.

'Come in,' she called out, still lying abed.

The maid called Glenna entered and closed the door behind her. She waited until Isobel had climbed from the cot and faced her before speaking.

'Lady Jocelyn said to tell you she is waiting at table for you, mistress,' Glenna said.

'At table? Has she not broken her fast?' she asked as she dug into her travelling trunk and found a clean shift, gown and stockings. No matter the place or time or reason, she did not want Lady Jocelyn waiting for her.

'Aye, lady. She called for a small meal for you since you…' The words drifted off when the girl could not come up with a polite way of saying 'since you have been lying in your bed like a lazy twit', no doubt.

'Tell her I will be there,' she said, tugging the shift she'd worn to sleep in off and pulling the clean one on.

She was struggling with her gown when she felt Glenna's hands make fast work of the laces. Isobel sat down and pulled the stockings on, tying them to keep them in place, as Glenna began untangling her hair. Within a few minutes, she was dressed and ready to find Lady Jocelyn. Glenna handed her a shawl before they left the room.

'The weather has turned colder, lady. You may need that,' Glenna said, walking just behind her to the front of the hall.

Isobel looked up to find that it was not only the lady waiting for her at table. Her mother smiled at her as she approached…as did the five young men and one older man who sat there. All of them stood as she grew nearer. If expressions could tell tales, her mother's would be an endless one filled with laughter. Isobel paused and offered a slight curtsy to Lady Jocelyn.

'My lady,' she said as she sat in the empty chair, 'forgive my tardiness.'

'Isobel, Athdar asked that we introduce his kin to you,' her mother said. 'He thought you might like to meet Tomas, Dougal, Angus, Connor and James.'

Each man nodded when introduced to her. Once they were all named, and at her mother's behest, they sat on the stools that now surrounded the table. Isobel understood her duty in this and engaged each man in conversation, eating the stew that appeared before her in between questions. Though she doubted any of these men could lay claim to a title, she suspected that they were among the wealthier landowners or craftsmen of the village.

The meal progressed and her mother and the lady joined in to keep it moving if she slowed. Soon, a reasonable time had passed and Isobel thanked them for visiting with her. The men each nodded, but no one moved until all the others did, apparently not willing to give any of them an advantage the others did not get. They walked away as a group and Isobel was so tempted to laugh at their boyish antics.

'Your father would never approve of any of them, I fear,' Lady Jocelyn said.

'I wonder why your brother suggested they meet Isobel?' her mother said.

That was exactly her own question. She waited for the lady's answer, but none came. If she had not glanced up at just the right moment, she would have missed the look shared between the other two women. Now, she was more puzzled by their reaction than even to Athdar's decision.

'I told Laria I would come later today if I was able,' she said, standing. 'If neither of you needs me for anything, I will go there now.'

'Do not exhaust yourself, Isobel,' Lady Jocelyn warned. 'I think this turn in the weather is a bad sign and we may have to leave sooner than we'd planned.'

'Very well,' she replied. In her mind, she made plans to work with Laria for a short time and return well before it grew dark. As the winter drew nearer, that happened sooner each day.

'And take your heavier riding cloak. The day grows colder,' her mother advised.

Isobel sent Glenna to bring her cloak and left through

the kitchens, checking with the cook and the steward to see if they needed anything from Laria before making her way through the yard and gates and village to the woman's cottage.

'So, you came,' Laria said, greeting her in the same brusque manner as was her custom. 'I am nearly done my chores for today.'

'Is there anything else I can help you with?' Isobel asked. She'd learned the first day not to try to assume that Laria meant anything more than she said. And it seemed that no one was addressed any differently by her—whether man or woman, visitor or villager, laird or servant.

Lady Jocelyn's words ran through her thoughts about Laria's past and her manners now, but she hesitated to ask anything of a personal nature. Isobel was a guest and had no place to ask such things. She would ask Lady Jocelyn or her mother instead.

The cottage filled with the smell of some concoction cooking in the hearth. The aromatic puffs of steam that rose from the bubbling pot scented the entire room with something very appealing and soothing. Isobel paced around the work table, looking at the various piles and bowls.

'The winds have changed. Winter will be upon us sooner than we thought.' Laria pointed to two sacks on the end of the table. 'I must get these to the miller.'

'Is there someone to take you there?' she asked, uncertain of what arrangements were made for this.

'Nay, not now. The mill is not a far walk.'

The mill. Athdar was overseeing some work on the mill. He'd arrived back at the keep late each day because of it.

'Should we go now?' The words were out before she could stop them.

'Aye. Let me move the pot,' Laria said. She wrapped her apron around her hand and pushed the pot over into the corner and away from the flames. 'That will keep.'

Though she'd not walked to the mill, Isobel knew the direction of it and estimated it would take about an hour or so to reach it.

'Is this to be milled?' she asked once they were on the road that led along the stream to where it grew wider and where the mill sat. 'Athdar has been overseeing repairs to it these last few days.'

Isobel felt that same shift between them that she'd noticed the first time they'd met—and at the mention of Athdar. Mayhap Laria was offended by her casual way of speaking about the laird? Glancing over at the woman, she thought it might be something more than that. But as quickly as the chilliness came, it left Laria's voice and face, making Isobel question whether it had happened or not.

The rest of their journey was accomplished in silence, only occasionally interrupted when Laria pointed out something of interest. A scurrying animal moving in the bushes. A different plant or tree she'd not seen before. A villager passing by on their way to their chores. Although the day was colder than the previous one, Isobel hardly noticed it as they walked away from the village.

And as they walked, the anticipation grew within her at the expectation that she would see Athdar. They had not really spoken since they met on the bridge the day after her arrival. Now she would have a chance to watch him in his duties as laird. Familiar with him more as kin or family of kin, she'd had little experience with him in his position over his clan.

They heard the sounds before they reached the curve in the road. As the mill came in sight, Isobel saw a group of men struggling to move a new millstone into place. The side wall of the millhouse was gone, taken down to allow them access. She looked for Athdar, but she did not recognise the man directing the work.

Walking closer, she watched as the men hauling the stone worked together. Isobel recognised the man guiding it to its place on the frame—Athdar, in the thick of things, doing the hardest part of the labour. Not wishing to disturb or distract them, she touched Laria's arm and held her back.

It took only a few more minutes before the stone dropped into place. A cheer went up from those watching at the successful—and critical, she knew—placement of it. Soon, others began reattaching ropes and the connections that would allow the stone to be turned by the waters coursing beneath the mill. That was when Athdar glanced up and met her gaze. Waving to her, he left the millhouse and strode towards her. Laria walked towards the man who had been directing the work—he must be the miller or stonemason—while Isobel waited for Athdar.

She tried not to notice that he wore no tunic. She tried not to stare at his sculpted chest and stomach. More, she tried not to imagine what the rest of his body looked like as he grew closer. Suddenly the day was not cold at all. Now, she wanted to peel off the heavy cloak and dab her face.

Athdar did not seem to notice the cold, either, his body giving off steam as he reached her. Isobel fought the urge to follow a trickle of moisture down his chest as it made its way beneath the trews he wore. Thankfully, he seemed not to notice her own discomfort.

'Your mother said you were indisposed this morn. 'Tis good to see you up and about.'

She held up the sack she'd carried from the cottage. 'Laria needed my help,' she said. It was the weakest excuse she'd ever given, but Athdar didn't seem to recognise it.

'Broc! Take this to Lyall,' he called out to his steward as he took the sack from her. 'Ask Laria about it.'

Broc, the sinfully handsome man, stopped before her and bowed. 'Isobel. How do you fare?' His green eyes sparkled and his gaze focused on her mouth. 'I feared you were taking ill when Lady Jocelyn said you would remain abed this morn.'

Athdar elbowed Broc before she could say anything about her condition, or lack of one, to either of them. He stumbled away, with a nod to her. The man was an unrepentant flirt and she'd watched as other women fell under his spell. For some reason, though she would admit she liked him and had blushed at their first meeting, his antics did not affect her the same way now. Not after spending more time with Athdar.

'In all seriousness, Isobel…' Athdar began. He took his shirt and a cloth from the young boy who brought them to him. 'How do you fare this day? In speaking to your mother, I realised that you have been doing much during your visit.'

'I am well, Athdar. Truly,' she said. 'I was simply feeling lazy this morn and my mother and your sister indulged me in it.'

'You are a guest here, Isobel. I would not see you abused and overwrought because you fear saying no to someone's request. Even my sister can be a bit of a tyrant at times.'

He used the cloth to dry his chest and back and then pulled the shirt over his head. She did not turn her gaze away as a demure maiden should—she could not help but notice the way his muscles rippled and flexed as he tugged on the shirt. Her cheeks heated then and she touched them as he finished putting his belt in place, accepting the length of plaid from the boy who tended him. He sent the boy back to the others and then held out his hand to her. She gave him hers and he wrapped his fingers around her hand, tugging her along with him.

'Come meet Lyall and his sons.' He held her hand tightly until they reached the others who continued to finish work on the mill's walls. 'He and his father before him have worked the mill for my clan. Lyall, meet Isobel Ruriksdottir.'

'Lady,' Lyall said, bowing to her. A gaggle of boys surrounded the man and he touched some of their heads with clear affection. 'These are my sons.' He laughed as one or two of them pushed forwards to be introduced. 'No matter their names, they belong to me.'

But one stood out. Not a boy, but a girl dressed as one.

'Ah, my wee lass who tries to keep up with her brothers. Ye noticed her, did ye? That is Elizabeth, named after her maither, God rest her soul.' Lyall leaned in and whispered to Isobel, 'She has the look of her maither, too.'

Isobel's eyes began to burn with tears at the thought of these children without a mother, but Lyall's love for them shone brightly in his gaze when he looked at them and in the way he watched them.

'You are a lucky man to have such a family, Lyall,' she said.

She'd grown up with a younger brother and sister and her parents, but she'd been surrounded with love and hoped to have such a family of her own, God willing, one day. Isobel glanced up at Athdar just then and he would not meet her gaze, staring at something a distance away among the trees. She recognised the pain in his eyes and her heart hurt for him.

In that moment, she promised herself to do something to help him, even if she was not the woman for him. Even if this ended as nothing more than a simple visit and she returned home with her mother with no betrothal in the plans, she would find a way to release him from the pain that marked and marred him now.

'Well, I'd best be getting myself back to the mill. 'Tis a pleasure to meet ye, my lady.' Lyall bowed and took the children with him back towards the building being repaired. Isobel laughed at their antics, which continued all the way back.

Isobel watched as Laria finished giving Lyall instructions on how finely she needed her flour—well, her dried plants and beans—ground. Athdar stood a few paces away from her, still not giving her his attention, drowning in his sorrow so strongly she could feel it.

'Athdar?' she said quietly. 'We will take our leave now.'

He shook himself free of the melancholy feelings that always struck when he thought about his dreams of having bairns of his own and faced Isobel. The expression in her lovely blue eyes told him she knew what he was thinking about. She saw the pain that never left his heart and soul.

'Let me take you back to the keep,' he said, motioning for his horse. 'The winds are picking up and it is getting colder.'

'Laria…' She had not said no.

'One of the boys will take her in Lyall's cart.'

She looked to Laria for consent for only a moment and then nodded to him. The older woman's brow gathered before she nodded. He did not think she would naysay him—she had never while he'd been laird—but he suspected she was thinking about doing just that. Not waiting for permission to be given by someone not entitled to do so, he took the reins and climbed on to his horse. Then he turned and held out his hand to Isobel.

If he thought she might hesitate, she proved him wrong for she took his hand, placed her foot on his and let him help her up to sit behind him astride the horse. He gave her a few moments to right her skirts and cloak before calling out to Broc and urging the horse to move. Athdar felt her hands slide around his waist to hold on and he placed one of his on top of hers.

Damn, but it felt so right to have and hold her close!

Once they followed the road around the curve away from the mill, he slowed the horse's pace and found a comfortable gait. Her arms remained around him. It must be the chill in the air, he thought, or she would loosen her hold.

After a few minutes' travel, she leaned her body away from his and he waited for her to move her hands. When she did not, he decided it felt good to him.

The strange thing was, he did not lack for feminine company. Not at all. There was a widow in the village who enjoyed his attentions. Another in Lairig Dubh as well. So, why this particular woman, why Isobel felt so right to him was a mystery and one he was not certain he wanted to solve.

A young woman of her standing and wealth was not suitable as a bed partner. She and her family, and Connor as her laird and his overlord, would have every expectation that any interest in her would be followed by an offer of marriage.

And that was the reason he would and could never pursue her. He could not and would not offer marriage to any woman and risk losing them to the strange twist of fate that dogged his life. Though others might laugh at the thought of a curse, that was exactly what it felt like to him—a curse placed by an angry god or spirit. A curse that killed anyone he loved or cared about. A curse that tore apart any bit of happiness he found.

Isobel did not deserve to have such a thing touch and possibly take her life.

Chapter Seven

The ride back to the keep had been a quiet one. Riding behind someone was not truly conducive to conversing, so she'd remained silent. He decided he liked the way she held on to him and he did nothing to change it. Isobel sat sheltered behind his body and when she leaned against him, he realised she must need the heat of his body to stay warm in the now much colder winds that blew along the road as the sun readied itself to set. Riding along in the many shadows caused by the forest that blocked the sun's light, he did not mind providing her some shielding.

From the way she began to shift as they got nearer to the keep, he knew she thought he'd stop and let her down there. He did not. Instead he rode right through the gates, waving to the guards, until they reached the steps. Taking her hand, he helped her to slide down and stand, not waiting for anyone else to come forwards to help her.

'My thanks for that,' she said.

The winds had loosened her hair, so she brushed it back over her shoulder as she adjusted her cloak. For a brief moment, he imagined running his hands through its length of white-golden curls, spreading them over his pillow as he pleasured her.

'I did not want you so exhausted that you cannot accept my challenge this night,' he answered as his body took all the meanings possible from his words and accepted all of the sexual innuendos in them. Before he could embarrass himself and her, he climbed down to walk the horse to the stables.

'I think I can stay awake for a game after dinner,' she said. Then she traced her bottom lip with the tip of her tongue and drove him mad. He coughed several times and bade her farewell. He needed to regain his control before going near her.

Athdar walked off, tugging his horse behind him and cursing himself for ever allowing her to affect him like this. She could make him feel what he longed to feel once more. She could make him dream for things he'd always wanted. She could make him…

It was only as he passed the cemetery on the way to the stables that sanity once more settled over him. Those gravestones, large and small, reminded him of his failures and brought back his control. He could recite each name even though some of the stones had grown smooth over the years. He'd never forgotten until a certain pale-haired woman entered his keep.

At least there would be peace for him once she left. If he was a little sadder to see her go, it was the price he had to pay for his failures.

He handed the horse off to one of the boys working in the stables and walked back to the keep. Supper would be ready soon and then the last game he would play with the fair Isobel. Broc had already mentioned Jocelyn's plans to leave on the morrow to get ahead of what felt like an early winter change in the weather.

The mountain pass would be deadly if a storm hit while they traversed it, so it seemed sensible and cautious for them to travel now before it grew dangerous. Mayhap he should ride with them to the edge of his lands and see them safe to the pass?

Jocelyn would have an opinion on that, so he would wait to speak to her first. His sister was as stubborn as her husband, though she never recognised that she'd picked up and refined the trait from him. Once her mind was on something, she would not be turned from it.

He thought about that and wondered what else Jocelyn had her mind fixed to. If she was set on some plan that involved him and Isobel, he would have to make certain she knew it was not possible. Athdar climbed the steps into the keep and up to his chambers to wash the day's grime from him before presenting himself at table. Not too much later, he made his way down to table and to the challenge he'd made to Isobel.

Jocelyn peered out the window of their chamber. The winds seemed to pick up with each passing hour and it was not a good sign. Her bones, in spite of her attempts to ignore how old they were getting, ached much as they did before any bad storm. Winter would come early this year. From the various signs and symptoms, winter was coming fast.

'Aye. I think we need to be on our way at first light.' Jocelyn turned to see the reactions of the other two women in the chamber. One looked accepting and understanding, the other disappointed and almost mutinous. 'We cannot take the chance of being trapped here or, worse, trapped in the mountains once we leave.'

'I will pack after supper,' Margriet said, standing and

coming closer. 'Connor and Rurik would not be pleased to have to come to our rescue in those mountains.'

Jocelyn smiled. Both of their husbands would walk through the fires of hell if their wives needed them, and both she and Margriet knew it, as did most anyone who knew either of the men. They might be ruthless, brutal even, warriors, but Jocelyn and Margriet were their husbands' weaknesses and nothing—not weather, war or God—would keep them apart if they needed them.

Isobel remained silent through this. She missed nothing but did not speak. A good trait, for she listened well before saying anything. Another reason why Jocelyn believed she would be a good match for her brother. She had a calm head and a good heart. But now they would leave and any chance of the two of them spending meaningful time together to learn if they did truly suit was gone.

'Well, let's get down to the hall and have our supper. We can pack and the men can make preparations after that and be ready to leave at first light.'

Margriet held out her hand to her daughter and Jocelyn walked behind them out of the chamber. Once they were near the centre of the hall she stopped and gazed around the place where she'd grown up. Most of the family she'd known were gone—her mother passed first just after Jocelyn's marriage to Connor and then her father about a decade ago. Her older cousins had married and moved away. Joy and sorrow had lived in this hall, but now only sorrow remained. Isobel noticed she'd stopped and came back to her.

'Is ought wrong, lady?' she asked quietly.

'Nay, just some memories of long-ago days here,' she answered. 'My cousins and I had the perfect hiding place when I wanted to avoid Athdar's teasing. Up there,' she said, pointing to the small, almost invisible alcove that sat up on the walkway of the top storey. Isobel nodded as she saw it. 'Some days, some lazy days, I would hide up that so I wouldn't have to do my chores.'

'Surely not, lady!' Isobel laughed.

'Oh, I could be a tyrant in my childhood. Athdar was my target as frequently as he vexed me.'

Margriet turned to them. 'Come, they are waiting for us.'

Jocelyn smiled at Isobel and wondered if she would need to beg forgiveness over this attempt of hers to match these two. The girl had been bold in coming directly to her about her interest in Athdar and, watching Isobel, Jocelyn knew she had tender feelings for him. If the girl was bold enough to take that chance and if she was wise enough to get the message Jocelyn was giving her, she could be the one to draw the poison from Athdar's festering wound. Forgiveness would be the least of her troubles.

Athdar and the other men at the table stood when they approached and waited for the three women to be seated. She hoped that she was not wrong about Isobel. So much depended on Jocelyn not being wrong.

Chapter Eight

Jocelyn was up to something, of that he had no doubt. He recognised all the signs of it from a long history of doing battle with her. Athdar could feel it. A shiver ran down his spine as a warning to remember that his sister could be devious and stubborn when it was to her purpose. And watching her walk to the table along with Isobel, he knew she was up to something. The good thing was that she was leaving on the morrow. And that was the bad thing, as well, for Isobel would leave, too.

He let out a breath and watched as the servants began to serve bowls of thick, aromatic meat stew. Platters of roasted fowl and steaming loaves of bread followed. Soon the table was filled and everyone began passing the food and eating. Athdar tried to, but the tight feeling in his gut put off his appetite for food. The meal did pass by easily, talk of travelling and preparations filled any gaps in conversation and when it was over, everyone had tasks to complete before seeking their rest. He recognised the feeling as they finished eating.

Disappointment. He did not want Isobel to leave.

'Will there still be time for a game, Isobel?' he asked, not wanting to let the chance pass because he did not speak. Isobel glanced at her mother for an instant before answering him.

'Aye. I will make time, Athdar,' she said quietly. It felt as though she spoke only to him, but from the startled expressions, he knew others had heard not only the words, but also the tone. 'If you are so willing and eager to face defeat again,' she added.

He laughed. 'Not willing or eager, Isobel. But I cannot allow that kind of challenge to stand without my honour being questioned. So, you shall have your game.' He stood as the women did and watched them walk to their chambers.

She would return.

'What the bloody hell was that about, Dar?' Padruig asked, as he sat down next to him and put a full goblet of ale before him.

'A game. We played the first night my sister arrived, but have not played since. I should have lost the first game and did lose the second one.'

'You were not speaking about chess to the young woman just then.' Padruig was too keen and saw too much. 'You remember who you will face if there is anything untoward between the two of you?'

'Aye.' Athdar took and swallowed a couple of mouthfuls before saying more.

Both he and Padruig had been at Lairig Dubh when young Rob Mathieson arrived to demand the hand of Connor's eldest daughter. Rurik had met him first, as the MacLerie champion, and Rob had barely survived it. Despite his age, Rurik was still the fiercest fighter Athdar had ever seen and one he did not wish to face on a field. And since he planned to do nothing that would dishonour Rurik's daughter, he was not worried about it.

'So, do you want to tell me what the hell you are trying to do?'

'I like her, Padruig. I like her.' It felt good to admit it. He faced his friend then and waited for Padruig's reply.

'Anyone with eyes can see that. And she likes you. But what will come of it since you've sworn not to marry again?'

He would not admit it, even to his closest friend over a mug of ale, but she'd begun to make him want to forswear his oath.

'We will play a game or two of chess. She will leave on the morrow and return to Lairig Dubh.'

Padruig mumbled something as he took another swig from his mug. He did not need to hear the words to know the curse within them. Padruig relied on a few, favoured, well-chosen words when he was angry, ones his friends could repeat along with him.

The servants approached to clear the table and Broc ceased flirting with both women and went off to see to preparations, leaving only him and Padruig at table. Rubbing his hands over his face, he suddenly felt as old as every year he had lived. Padruig had a family, a wife of more than a score of years along with three children—one, a son nearly full-grown.

Athdar had nothing.

'Have you thought of trying—?' Padruig began.

'I have thought of nothing else.' He slammed his fists down on the table. 'After Mairi, I did. After Seonag, I did. But Tavia's death made it clear I could not put another woman in danger. And you know what happened then.'

He did not want to talk about or even dwell on these matters—they were better left in the dark of an unhappy past. Padruig must have realised he'd overstepped for he sat and drank the rest of his ale without uttering another word.

'She comes,' Padruig whispered.

Athdar looked up and saw Isobel approaching. She walked quickly and decisively towards him. Padruig stood to leave, but he put his hand on Athdar's shoulder and squeezed.

'You do not stand a chance, my friend.'

Athdar wanted to ask what he meant before Isobel got close enough to hear. Padruig laughed then, smacked his back and moved away.

'Lady,' he said as he passed Isobel, 'he mounts a strong defence, but dinna be fooled by it.' Padruig warned her loud enough for Athdar to hear.

If Isobel was disturbed by it, she showed no sign of being so. Athdar dragged two chairs close together, near the warmth of the hearth. Isobel grabbed the small table and pulled it between them.

'You finished packing quickly,' he said as he reached for the wooden box and game board. 'I did not expect you for nigh on another hour or more.'

'My mother said I was making a mess of things, so she told me to leave!'

He waited for her to sit and then did so. 'I suspect you have used that tactic in the past with great success.' Her cheeks took on a pale pink hue as she blushed, confirming his suspicions without answering. 'Which colour would you like?'

'I like the black pieces,' she said. Lifting one up, she wrapped her fingers around it and rubbed the edges of it. Athdar swore he felt her touch on the hard parts of his anatomy and tried not to show it. 'The dark appeals to me.'

Though he would die before doing anything dishonourable, he was thinking of many, many things he would like to do with her as he watched her caress the carved wooden figure. He shook himself free of desire's control and took up the red pieces, arranging them in lines on the board. With the way she'd played the first night, he needed his wits about him if he stood a chance of winning or even drawing a tie.

He allowed her the first move and it was not long before she began taunting him with risky moves, placing her pieces in harm's, or his, way. Athdar resisted the urge to fall for her feints. She would make a remarkable strategist in any battle or war, he thought, as she claimed yet another of his. It took losing nearly half of his 'army' before he saw her pattern. He laughed aloud when he did, finally seeing the simple way she tested and took or tested and retreated from a confrontation.

Then it was too late for him, so caught up in appreciating the intelligence of her play that he missed her final series of moves that took his queen, then his king. This time she laughed, too, along with him. A few of the servants still working in the hall turned at the sound of it.

'Another?' he asked, motioning at the main table for cups and a pitcher. Ailean saw it and brought them. Isobel glanced around the hall and then back at him.

'The polite thing for me to do is to beg off from another game, but I would like to continue,' she answered.

'Then, let's,' he said, with a motion of his hand to let her take the first move.

He'd learned much about her style of play and he was prepared for her this time. This game moved at a leisurely pace, each of them studying the board a bit longer than in the previous games. They'd taken several moves each, and he'd already lost a piece when she spoke.

'So, what do you call your keep?'

'The keep?' he said, looking up at her. 'I have no name for it.' He thought about it for a moment and then realised what she meant. 'It is not big and grand enough to have a name.'

'Oh, it is big enough. And you could make it grand, if you wanted it so,' she said.

'Have you ever visited your grandfather's?' If she had, 'twas no wonder she thought of grander places—Rurik's father was the Earl of Orkney and one of the wealthiest men in Norway.

'I have met him, aye.' She leaned in closer and lowered her voice so only he could hear it. 'Father does not wish me to become accustomed to the way his father lives. But I have visited my grandmother in Caithness and stayed several months with her.'

Her father's father had extraordinary wealth and power in the northern islands while her father's mother was a nun, supervising a convent in the north-east of Scotland—two extremes in life—and yet Isobel seemed no more impressed by one than the other.

'Your father is a practical man,' he said.

Her eyes flashed and her cheeks turned bright red then. She laughed, leaning back against the chair and holding her stomach. She was so vibrant he thought the hall grew brighter from it. Only then did he notice that her hair was not bound up in a braid, but hanging loose and swirling around her as she moved.

'In all my years…'

He frowned at her. *All* her years?

'For as long as I can ever remember, you and my father have had nothing good to say about each other. Ever,' she said, wiping her hand across her eyes. 'I do not understand the basis for your animosity, though I have heard various rumoured bits of it…. That is the only good thing you have ever said about him.'

Her laughter yet echoed through his hall and he wanted to hear it go on and on. For so long, this had been a place of sadness, and would be again, but for now, he enjoyed her mirth.

'I am certain I have said good things about him.' Athdar searched his memory for that good thing now and could not bring it to mind. 'I have admired his fighting skills.'

She stopped laughing, but her mouth curved in the most appealing smile then. 'So tell me how it happened. I would like to hear the truth of it.'

Athdar hesitated. To put one's humiliation on display was not done easily. Yet…

'I was but ten-and-five and full of myself.'

'As most young men are at that age,' she added. She was much closer to that age than he was.

'I travelled through Lairig Dubh on my father's business and had the opportunity to watch your father in a fight with Connor. Apparently, it was a custom of theirs to engage in swordplay when they met up and I was witness to both their skill and strength. Scared the bravado right out of me.'

He shifted in his chair, wondering how to tell her the rest of it. She was, after all, a young woman with certain sensibilities.

'I was a guest there and managed to get myself rather drunk one night at dinner. I insulted your father and found myself the victim, though at my own instigation, of his fury and his strength. I ended up with broken arms, nose and many, many bruises.'

It was worse than that, truly. The worst was not the two broken arms or the other physical injuries. The worst was when he understood the situation he'd drawn the unsuspecting and unwilling Jocelyn into because of his youthful stupidity. Her dreams of marrying the man she loved were torn apart by his foolish, drunken challenge that put him in the custody of the Beast of the Highlands.

Rurik had visited him in the depths of Broch Dubh and told him exactly what he would cost Jocelyn. All because he could not control himself. All because he did not think of the consequences of his actions. Not unlike an earlier time when…

A memory flared and faded in that moment. Something dark and terrifying flitted across his memories and sank back into the murky depths from which it had risen. Nausea followed, then his head felt as though struck from behind.

'Athdar?'

His vision narrowed and then widened. He could hear only a buzzing in his ears. Then all of it began to fade away.

'Athdar?' Isobel said, caressing his face. When had she touched him? When had she risen from her chair and approached him? 'Are you ill?' She crouched down closer before him and stroked his forehead and cheek with the back of her hand. 'No fever.'

'I am well,' he said, though he was trying to convince himself of it more than her. 'What happened?' He swallowed, but his mouth and throat were parched. She noticed and held out a cup to him.

'You were telling me of your confrontation with my father and then something happened. You looked as if in pain and then ill. Now?' she asked, taking the cup from him and kneeling next to him.

Strange. He had been thinking about the true humiliation of learning the unintended consequences that Jocelyn suffered when some other memories or feelings surged forwards. Now they were gone and he felt fine.

''Tis a painful thing—exposing a man's youthful stupidity to a beautiful woman who is the daughter of the man who exposed it in the first place. You now know my sordid past with your father, Isobel.'

Her hand still caressed his face and, with her kneeling at his side, it would be easy, oh so easy, to lean down and kiss the lips that tempted him so much. When she lifted her head and her mouth opened slightly, he did what he wanted to do.

Her lips were soft and warm against his and he could feel her heated breath against his mouth before he touched it with his. Athdar did not touch her, but she did not let go of his face, stroking it as he deepened the kiss by sliding his tongue along her lips until she opened to him.... For him.

God, but she was sweet.

He knew not when it happened, but his hand slid up and he tangled his fingers in her hair. Then he cupped her head, and held her against his mouth. His tongue felt the heat deep in her mouth and he tilted his head tasting her and kissing her. For a moment, he drew back, but she looked at him with such wonderment in her eyes, that he kissed her again and again and again.

'Isobel?' Margriet called out.

She pulled away and pushed up to her feet faster than she realised she could. Her mouth, her lips and tongue, tingled from the way he'd touched her, kissed her. Isobel lifted her hand to touch her mouth, but her mother's voice came again through the corner of the now-darkened hall.

''Tis late and you need your rest for the journey.'

Had her mother been watching? Had she seen…?

'Go, lass,' Athdar said as he stood up and took a step away. 'I will see you in the morn before you leave.' His hand grazed hers as she turned from him and she fought the urge to hold him. 'Sleep well,' he whispered as she passed him.

Her body hummed with some kind of heat and every part of her felt alive and achy at the same time. But her mouth… Her mouth hungered for more. More of him. More of his mouth against hers. More…

She knew he watched her until she reached her mother for she could feel his gaze on her skin. This was unexpected. This was unplanned. This was…wonderful.

This was over.

The wave of sadness hit her as she walked through the door to the chamber for her last night in Athdar's keep.

She could not meet Lady Jocelyn's eyes or her mother's as she undressed and prepared for bed. Her trunk was packed and a fresh gown lay there for use in the morn. Her heavy stockings and boots waited next to the trunk, as well as her travel cloak with an extra plaid to keep her legs warm along the road.

Soon, the chamber grew silent except for the occasional soft snores and squeaking of the bed-ropes. Isobel lay awake thinking about everything that had happened between them. It had been a good start and he certainly found her pleasing or he would not have kissed her so. Would he?

Men, she knew, did many things that made no sense. The explanation of what had happened between Athdar and her father was but one example of that. Men would kiss any woman who would let them. She'd seen it, been warned against it and had wanted it. She wanted him.

Unfortunately, any chance she had of making him see she was right for him ended now. In the morning, they would ride out before the storms closed the mountains to them. And by the time the spring came and the roads opened once more, her father would have arranged a marriage for her elsewhere.

Her father would not settle her on someone she objected to. He would make certain her prospective husband was a good man who would provide for her and oversee her person and her dowry. Since her father was an important man within the Earl of Douran's household, and the natural son of the Earl of Orkney, her husband would be a nobleman who had some position within the Scottish kingdom or connections to another.

But, she did not want to marry for those connections or to move away from all and everyone she knew. Oh, that was what she'd been raised to do and trained and educated to do, but she did not want that.

If only there was more time.

Minutes, then hours passed and she tried to quiet the turmoil in her mind and the tumultuous feelings in her now-awakened body. Just when she began drifting off to sleep, words began echoing in her thoughts. Lady Jocelyn's voice whispered them.

Mayhap 'tis better to beg forgiveness than to ask permission?

Forgiveness for what? she asked to the voice within her.

My cousins and I had the perfect hiding place when I wanted to avoid Athdar's teasing. Up there. Some days, some lazy days, I would hide up that so I wouldn't have to do my chores.

Up there. A hidden alcove. The perfect hiding place.

Isobel sat up, suddenly knowing what she needed to do.

The girl could be a problem.

He watches her and dotes on her. Attends on her words and follows her steps.

Worse, he laughs with her.

He does not deserve to laugh.

Ever.

He deserves nothing but pain.

She should leave...

Now...

Before it is too late for her, as well.

Chapter Nine

Athdar sought his bed, but never found the sleep he wanted. Instead, he could taste her on his tongue, a sweet flavour of innocence and desire that remained after their mouths parted. He could smell the scent of the soap she used as he had tangled his fingers in her hair and held her head. He could hear the soft sigh against his mouth as he'd kissed her.

Over and over.

His body hardened at her touch and at her kiss.

It was still hard and his blood rushed through his veins, heating him and pushing his desire for her to his limits.

From a kiss. It was only a kiss. Their first kiss.

But, if one kiss from her could do this, it was good that she was leaving at dawn's light.

When he did drift into sleep, something from the depths of his memory moved again, bringing dread and terror and pain with it until he woke, silently screaming into the quiet of his chambers. Covered in sweat and unable to breathe.

He'd rather remain awake and think of her kiss.

He was no youth in the bud of first passion and yet

he felt as if he were. He'd had women in his bed, and in his heart, for more than a score of years and Isobel made it feel new again.

He wanted her, he would not deny it, and it was in spite of every vow he'd made and every bit of opposition he would encounter.

Mayhap it was a good thing—for his peace of mind and survival—that she left in the morn?

Aye, a very good thing.

Finally the light of the rising sun brightened the darkness of his room and he rose. As laird and as a brother, he would see Jocelyn and her party off. Due to concerns about the weather and their overall safety, he ordered that six men would accompany them—three would ride ahead and three would travel as far as the pass and then return here to let him know they had made it through.

He dressed quickly and made his way down to say his farewells. Jocelyn and Margriet stood ready near the back of the hall, but Isobel was nowhere in sight. Worried over Margriet's reaction to what she'd undoubtedly witnessed, he was instead greeted with a warm smile from both women.

'Are you ready to leave?' he asked. It was an indirect way of asking about her without drawing attention to his desire to know.

'We waited to see you. The horses and cart are packed to leave.'

'You are dressed warmly?' He hugged his sister and kissed her cheek. 'To be this cold this soon is not a good sign.'

'Aye. Heavier cloaks and stockings. Boots—' she held up her foot to show him '—and we have some extra woollen blankets for our legs.' Jocelyn stepped back, allowing Margriet to say farewell.

'If you hit bad weather, come back. I do not want to risk your safety in an unpredictable storm,' he said. Finally, he gave in to the temptation. 'Is Isobel not ready?'

'She has already gone ahead with the outriders. She was up early and decided not to wait for us. We will meet them at the pass,' Margriet said.

'If the weather holds, we should make it through before nightfall,' Jocelyn said.

'Give her my regards,' he said. 'Let me walk with you,' he added, trying to understand the disappointment and not let it show. Surely this was the easier way, instead of facing her this morn after last evening's kiss? What could he say when he did not know what it meant?

They walked outside to where the rest of the group was assembled and he helped Jocelyn mount. Checking the straps on her saddle and reins, he touched her leg and then her hand.

'Be well, Jocelyn.'

'Be…well, Dar.'

He nodded to Margriet and waved to the man leading the group. Following them to the gates, he watched as they rode into the forest along the road west. When he could no longer see them or hear them, he returned to the keep to break his fast.

The keep was once more his own.

He went into the kitchen to eat as was his usual custom when no guests were there. The servants knew it and a bowl of oat porridge was waiting for him.

Now his life would settle back to what it usually was and winter would come.

* * *

The day passed slowly for him; all his duties were the same. Meals were accomplished without much talking. He met with Padruig, trained in the yard with his men, made arrangements with Broc to send people to the mill to help Lyall finish up the season's grinding before the water began to freeze upstream. Though the stone could be turned by men, travel between the keep and village and the mill would become difficult and nigh impossible once the storms of winter struck.

Since some of the more distant villagers would be stranded when the snows of winter came, they needed to be moved. And other tasks needed accomplishing.

Somehow, though, it all felt empty this day.

He had drifted through the rest of it and joined those who lived in the keep at supper, though he was not interested in the food. The exhaustion of having not slept the night before caught up with him as the food was being cleared away and he'd decided to seek his bed when a flicker of light caught his eye.

Glancing to the back of the hall and then up to where the walkway along the top floor met the wall, he saw it again. There was no one staying in the chambers there so there should be no lamps, lanterns or candles up there. Yet clearly someone was.

Athdar walked to the stairway and climbed to the second floor where his chambers were. Then he followed the corridor to the second stairway that led up to the battlements and roof. He'd almost reached the alcove where Jocelyn liked to hide as a child when he saw it. There, in the recess on the wall, was a small candle, its flame flickering as the air moved around it.

Had someone, one of the servants, left it here?

As he moved closer he heard a noise. Stopping and listening, he recognised the unmistakable sound of snoring coming from the alcove.

Who needed to hide here and sleep? All of those serving in the hall had a place below stairs. He had no guests. No one was unaccounted for. So who…? A runaway? A spy? Who…?

'Bloody hell!' he muttered under his breath and he peeked around the edge of the alcove and found…

Isobel asleep, wrapped in her cloak and blankets and tucked into the small corner space. Her head tilted back, she licked her lips several times as she snored softly. Then she shifted and leaned her head down against the wall to her side.

How?

When?

Why?

Questions flooded his mind as he watched her there. Well, unless and until he woke her, he would not find out, so he reached down and touched her shoulder. He shook her gently, whispering her name as he did.

'Isobel.' Then, louder, 'Isobel.'

She stirred then, her eyes fluttering and then opening slightly. Her back arched and she turned her head back and forth as though working out a cramp in her neck. It would be no surprise if she was quite uncomfortable after being in this cramped place for however long she'd hidden there.

'Here, let me help you,' he said, holding out his hand to her.

At first—still asleep, he thought—she frowned at him. Then she rubbed her eyes and whispered his name. 'Athdar.'

She accepted his hand and he guided her to her feet and out of the alcove. Near to the steps that led to the roof it was always cold. Even with the heavy travel cloak and blankets, she must be chilled to the bones. Without delaying, he scooped her up in his arms and carried her down to the main floor and took her to the hearth.

'Ailean! Some hot cider! Broc, send someone to get her things in Jocelyn's hidey hole. Bring the chair closer.'

He continued to call out orders until he had her wrapped in several more blankets, close to the now-blasting fire and with hot cider to sip. Athdar read the shock and surprise in everyone's gazes—hell, he was surprised to find her here—but did not slow until he could see some colour in her fair cheeks and the shivers disappearing.

Then, with a nod of his head and a meaningful glare, the servants and others left…quickly, though he would be surprised not to find them listening at any and every crack. He pulled a chair up next to her and waited.

Minutes passed. The logs in the fire crackled, sending off sparks and bits of burning wood into the air above it. He could be a patient man when need be, but he was not now. Especially not when so much—her reputation, his life—was at stake.

'When did you return?' he asked.

She squinted and pursed her lips. Then she grazed the edges of her teeth over her lower lip, all the while looking as though she could not find the words to say. But it was the guilty glance that gave him the answer.

'You never left?' He stood up and looked down on her. 'Bloody hell! Does your mother know?'

'By now, aye.' Her gaze darted to his and then away.

'And Jocelyn?' Again, her guilt shone on her face.

Added to his own misgivings and suspicions about Jocelyn's behaviour about and through this visit, there could be only one answer. 'Jocelyn put you up to this?'

'Nay,' she said, standing and letting the blankets fall around her feet. 'I did this. Jocelyn only...'

'She told you about that?' He nodded up to the alcove.

'Aye,' she said. 'She and my mother thought I'd ridden ahead. I stayed behind.'

He walked closer and studied her face, trying to discern the truth as he asked his next question. 'Why, Isobel? Why did you do this and stay behind?'

She thought about how best to answer him. Honesty was crucial, yet how much did she dare reveal to him when she had no idea of his own feelings? Saying too much would make her appear a foolish, infatuated girl. Not enough and he would never realise how serious she was that he should consider a future with her.

So she decided on the real reason, unadorned and true.

'I did not wish to leave.'

He seemed to begin to argue with her several times before stopping and just watching her. Then he dragged his hands through his hair and shook his head.

'Jocelyn knows you are here and safe? You are certain?'

'Aye.'

'Isobel, you cannot remain here without your mother or my sister. On the morrow, when my men return, we will make arrangements to return you to Lairig Dubh.'

She would not argue—it was futile at this point. But if all the signs were correct, there was a storm moving towards the pass and only those already through would make it the rest of the way. That was why Lady Jocelyn left when she did.

'Very well,' she said, backing away a bit.

He smiled then and picked the blankets up off the floor. 'Did you hide food with you, as well?'

At that exact moment, her stomach made its emptiness known with a loud, grumbling growl and she smiled.

'Not as much as I would have liked.'

'Come then,' he said, motioning in the direction of the kitchen. 'It is not so far past supper that we cannot find you something to eat.'

She followed him into the warmth of the kitchen where a fire was tended at every hour of the day. Servants and watchers scattered as Athdar walked with her to a table set off to one side of the large room. The cook's wife approached them.

'Jean, Lady Isobel missed supper. Can you find something for her?' Athdar asked.

'I do not need much,' she said, knowing how inconvenient it was to expect to be fed now that the kitchen's work was done for the day.

'No matter, lady,' Jean said, with a smile nearly as large as the woman was herself. 'We always keep a pot warm since many of the laird's men come back late after their duties. Finding enough for ye—' the woman paused and examined her shape for a moment as though she found her wanting '—'twill be no bother at all.'

'My thanks,' she called out as Jean walked to one of the cooking hearths, pulled a large pot to her and began ladling some of it into a bowl.

Soon, the large bowl, a crust of bread, a piece of cheese and some ale sat before her and her stomach answered with its own reminder of how hungry she truly was. He said nothing as she ate, standing a few paces away, arms crossed and leaning against the wall, watching everything she did. Her hunger assured that his observation of her did nothing to stop her or slow her down as she ate and drank all but a few crumbs of the food.

'My thanks, Jean,' she said once more as she finished, wiping her mouth and hands on the piece of cloth left for her use. 'It was quite good.'

Jean strode over and collected the bowls and plates, smiling at her. 'Did ye eat yer fill?' The woman squinted, looking at the bowl and then at her.

'Aye.' Isobel made a great show of sighing deeply and patting her mouth once more. 'I could not eat another bite.' She thought Athdar laughed then, but when she glanced over at him, he was staring off in another direction.

'Verra weel, lady.' Jean carried everything away, leaving the two of them alone now.

Silence settled over the room and she waited for his next reaction or question. Before he did anything, Broc walked in and greeted her before speaking to Athdar.

'I have made one of the chambers above ready for the lady,' he said to Athdar. 'And her belongings are there, awaiting her arrival.' Then the man had the audacity to wink at her. Did he know he was too attractive for his own good? If he was not careful, a wise woman would see through his games and claim him for real.

'Which chamber?' Athdar asked, speaking for the first time since they arrived in the kitchen.

'The far one,' Broc answered with a laugh, as though sharing a private joke with his laird. 'Shall I escort her there?'

Certainly Athdar would escort her himself? If she'd

thought so, she would have been mistaken, for he nodded then at Broc.

'Aye. If you will?'

'Come, lady,' Broc said, holding out his arm to give her something to hold on to. 'Glenna is waiting there to attend you.'

He talked in a constant stream of words about nothing of consequence as they walked, tracing again the path she'd taken from Jocelyn's alcove, but stopping in front of the third chamber. The door was open and Glenna worked at the hearth, starting a fire to warm the chamber.

'Sleep well, lady.'

With those words, he left her and closed the door.

'It will be warm in here verra soon, lady.' Glenna took off her cloak, the one she had not even realised she yet wore, and hung it on a peg by the door. 'Let me help ye get under the bedcovers.'

Isobel's custom was to undress without the help of a maidservant, but she allowed this luxury because the fatigue of another sleepless night, along with a nervous day of hiding and expecting to be discovered before it was too late to send her away, assailed her at that moment. Now exhaustion flooded through her and the urge to do as Glenna suggested was irresistible. She stood while the girl loosened her braid and brushed the tangles free. Then she held up the covers and Isobel climbed in.

Within minutes, sleep rushed up to claim her. Though she should have been restless and spent the night tossing and turning and worrying about being forced to leave, Isobel had the feeling that she was in the place she was always meant to be.

Chapter Ten

Though all the signs of an early winter were there, the next morning dawned clear and bright with little indication of impending doom or bad weather. Athdar was not fooled.

As long as Isobel was under his roof, doom impended.

When she did not come down to break her fast, he knew she must be exhausted and did not pursue it. He had duties and as long as he remembered those, it was better for him and his peace of mind. Always with an eye to the gates and waiting for the return of those assigned to escort his sister to the pass, Athdar accomplished many things. And the one thing he did not do was to ask after Isobel.

Broc joined him in the yard, commenting on the miller's progress and asking about other tasks and villagers yet unready. Athdar ignored the smirking expression that dared him to ask about Isobel and went about his tasks, deciding that he needed to take Broc over to where his men practiced their sword skills and let them beat some of the arrogance out of him.

One of his oldest friends, the son of his father's steward, they'd grown up together as boys and it was always assumed that Broc would serve Athdar when the time came for him to be laird just as Broc's father had served Tavish MacCallum for decades. For a time, for a long time, Broc had lived with kin in a distant village, returning here only when his father took ill and then died.

No longer the serious boy Athdar remembered from their youth, or the one he thought he remembered, Broc carried out his duties well. But somewhere along the way, he'd also become the inveterate womaniser and though he never forced himself on anyone, he also never committed to one woman and settled down. In a youth, it was to be expected, but now, these many years later…?

Athdar ended up taking up a sword and they spent about an hour in practice. He did not look cowed when they finished, but a few new bruises showed and he was out of breath, so Athdar felt some satisfaction. Steward or not, sword and fighting skills were critical, so he did not feel any guilt for putting the man through some intense training.

And yet, Broc yet wore the irritating smirk.

'Fine!' he yelled as they left the yard, the keep their destination. 'How fares Isobel?'

Broc laughed. 'I thought you would never ask. She rose just before I came out to speak to you. She seems well.'

'Shouldn't the riders be back soon?' he asked, glancing up to see the position of the sun in the sky. 'Without the women to slow them down, they should be back.'

'Aye. And especially with a day as clear as this one.'

Athdar stopped before the door. 'Is she in the hall?'

'Nay. I forgot to tell you. She said she was going to

visit with Laria until the riders returned. Said you could find her there.'

Was he stating it that way simply to annoy him? As though Isobel was giving orders now? Athdar rubbed the back of his hand across his forehead, staving off the need to kill his steward. Knowing Isobel was busy and out of his way…out of his sight and not able to constantly tempt him… Athdar went to the kitchen and took his midday meal there.

Called in many different directions, the rest of the day and daylight sped away and supper approached. With no sign of the riders, he considered sending more men out and would if the men did not return by late this night. Those he'd sent knew the roads and had the light of the full moon to allow them to travel at night.

They should have returned by now.

They had not.

By the time everyone gathered in the hall for supper, Athdar was worried. Had they encountered trouble along the way? He trusted those he'd sent as well as the MacLeries who travelled with his sister, so he would wait for word before believing anything else.

One thing Broc had done correctly was to assign Glenna to serve Isobel and see to her needs until she returned to Lairig Dubh and so when he saw the maid returning from the upper chambers, he called to her.

'Has the lady returned from Laria's?' he asked when she approached him.

'Aye. She asked for a tray to be brought to her for supper,' Glenna said.

'Is she well?' he asked. *Why else would she eat in her chambers?* he wondered.

'I think she seeks to avoid your temper, laird,' the girl said as a hint of laughter trickled out with her words.

'She thinks I am angry with her?' he asked. Not waiting for an answer, he was walking towards the stairway before he realised he'd taken a step.

It took him no time at all to reach the top floor and find himself standing before the door of the chamber he'd sworn not to enter. Had he unconsciously indicated to Broc to place her in Mairi's old chamber? Athdar hesitated for several minutes there, fighting off the old demons and memories without uttering a word. If Isobel stayed, he would move her…

If she stayed?

Hell, not even putting her in Mairi's room lessened the hope or the knowledge that not only did she not want to leave, but he did not wish her to. Before that thought could finish, he knocked on the door.

'Come.' He lifted the latch and opened the door, forcing his feet to move into the room he'd not entered in years.

'Athdar,' she whispered once she saw that it was him. 'Have the men arrived?' She wore a plain gown with a woollen shawl around her shoulders. Her hair lay in loose waves of curls and floated around her hips with each step she took towards him.

Part of him, the heart that had never healed after Mairi's death in this room, was horrified that he noticed her appearance. Another part of him, the randy part that found her immensely appealing, pushed him to watch the way her eyes brightened when she spoke to him and the way his heart pounded when he listened to her voice.

'Nay,' he said, clearing his throat and trying to concentrate on his reasons for coming to see her. 'I fear they may have had to escort Jocelyn all the way through the pass.'

'Are they safe?' she asked, clenching her hands and twisting them. A worried frown marred the usual bright expression. 'I should have been with them.'

'Aye, you should have,' he said, a bit sharper than he wanted to. 'But, you are here and safe and my men and the MacLeries will have one less woman to worry over.' She nodded. 'If not this night, we will know by the morn.'

She shook her head but did not look reassured. 'Will you send more men?' Isobel met and held his gaze. 'On the morrow?'

'I sent a man out ahead of them, two days ago. He will reach Lairig Dubh and let Connor know of their early departure.' He should not have, but he reached out and touched her hands. 'They will be safe.'

A trembling smile lifted the corners of those tempting lips and she nodded as she laid one of her hands over his. 'Thank you for your words. Especially when you have every right to be angry with me.' She acknowledged his original reason for coming here just as he remembered it for himself.

'I am not angry with you, Isobel. I do not understand why you engaged in such subterfuge or why my sister helped you.' He paused when she started to object. 'Or why my sister *inspired* you to such behaviour,' he finished, convinced completely that Jocelyn and Isobel had conspired—either openly or in secret—for her to remain behind.

Something inside pushed at him to be honest with her. Something strong forced the words out of his mouth before he could stop them.

'I am not unhappy that you wished to remain here.'

Isobel looked up at him, unable to believe the admission he'd just made to her. 'You are not?' He shook his head and his stern expression softened just the scantest of bits. 'But you are angry?'

He let out a breath and released her hand. Walking back to the door, which she noticed he seemed to glance back to every few seconds, he shrugged.

'I should be. You purposefully misled your mother, my sister and me. Although I think my sister knew or prodded you in this matter.' The stern look was back in his brown eyes, making them darken to almost black. But the attractive dimple in his cheek twitched and she knew now he fought back a smile. 'Still, I am glad you are safe.'

'And glad I am here?' she asked, not wanting to miss the chance to see his reaction. He stood now in the frame of the door and shook his head once more. In regret?

'Since no one offers me such a challenging game of chess, I suppose I am.' She could tell he would give her nothing more than that, but it pleased her. 'I came up here to invite you down to the hall for dinner. If you remain up here, they will all think you are more prisoner than guest.' Athdar extended his arm to her. 'Worse, they will know I subjected you to my terrible temper.'

'I do not remember your temper flaring at me in the past. But I thank you for that warning—I will have a care for overstepping your hospitality,' she said and she meant it.

Isobel had heard tales of his temper from kith and kin who visited here and she'd witnessed a few strange outbursts from him during his visits to Lairig Dubh, but never directed at her.

But any man, be they laird or servant, could reach

their limit and strike out. Though she knew her father had never lifted a hand to any woman, she'd also seen many a man who did. Embarrassing a man in front of others risked his displeasure and her being discovered here without the laird's knowledge could be embarrassing.

'Does this reluctance to anger me mean you will not defeat me in chess again?' he asked, his eyes narrowing as he waited for her reply as though trying to discern the truth of her words.

She walked to his side and placed her hand on his arm. 'If losing to me again will anger you, then I could promise to let you win.' She knew him to be jesting, as she was. 'Truly, I feared you were angry and did not want to force my company on you in front of your people.'

They walked down the corridor to the stairs and then down to the main floor. Before they entered the back of the hall where others had already gathered to eat, he drew her to a stop.

'Isobel, we must have a care for your honour, now that you are here without my sister or your mother. So, before we go in, you should know…' He stopped and faced her, his face once more serious. 'We cannot meet for chess in the hall after supper. Well, not alone, we cannot.'

Athdar was having a care for her reputation, though knowing her father as they both did, she did wonder if fear of him was the cause. Almost as though he'd read her thoughts, he laughed then and began walking once more.

'Besides, if word gets back to your father that I did anything the least bit questionable regarding you, drawing and quartering would be less painful than what he would do to me.'

They approached the table and Athdar led her to an empty seat next to his, and waited for her to sit. Those waiting greeted her and the meal was served. Strange, it seemed more companionable now without Jocelyn than when she was here. She wondered if Athdar felt pressured by her presence. She was, after all, his older sister, and had attained a position of higher power and wealth with her marriage to the MacLerie.

Broc seemed more subdued at this meal than before, as did Athdar's commander, Padruig. Their quietness made her realise that they were distracted, not inattentive. Looking around the table, she noticed a similar expression on the faces of several others there.

Worried. They worried. Leaning over to Athdar, she spoke in a low voice so that only he could hear.

'The men still out there—your people worry over them?' she whispered.

'Aye. Padruig's son accompanied Jocelyn back. They wait for word.'

She felt terrible, as though responsible for this delay, and telling herself she was not did nothing to assuage her feelings. Isobel realised that the woman next to Padruig must be his wife. Then she felt Athdar's hand on hers under the table.

'You are not the cause of their delay. If anything, you being here, talking with them, is easing their worry. Speak to Nessa there about your weaving.'

He knew she liked to weave? Jocelyn must have shared that with him, for it was not something most men took notice of.

'Nessa, did you know that Lady Isobel has a talent for weaving?' Athdar asked.

'My wife is one of the best weavers here,' Padruig said, pride clear in his every word. 'And our eldest is showing some of her skills, as well.'

'Where is your loom?' she asked, having not seen one here in the keep. 'Has the wool been carded and spun yet? Or dyed?'

Once they started talking, it continued for some time. Soon Isobel found the two of them alone at the table while the men had moved to one end of the long table and were now involved in some heated discussions— about what she could not tell.

After some time, the table was cleared, the floors swept and the hall readied for the night—and still the men did not return. Nessa stood and bid her farewell. Walking over to her husband, she took him by the arm and pulled him aside, whispering to him with a glance or two over at Isobel. Then Padruig said something to Athdar who also looked over at her.

She wanted to examine her gown for holes with the way the whole group began to look in her direction!

'Glenna,' Athdar called out. The young serving maid came at his call. 'Take Lady Isobel back to her chamber.'

As she began to follow the maid away, dismissed with a simple command, he spoke again. 'I will send word when the men arrive.' It pleased her that he understood she worried over their safe return.

'My thanks, laird,' she said.

As she returned to the chamber above, she realised two things. In spite of its inauspicious beginnings, the day had some good results—the best one being Athdar's admission that he was glad she'd not left. And she believed that he was beginning to see her as something other than too young or too this or too that, or just as

Rurik's daughter. Between their kiss and the way he touched her hand under the table and his attempts to ease her worries, she suspected he was thinking about her in the way she wanted him to do so—as a woman.

She'd been so exhausted the night before that she had fallen deeply asleep within moments of settling into the bed, but this night it took more time. Time enough to realise that Glenna shared her chamber, sleeping on a pallet near the door. And that only convinced her more that she was correct about Athdar's attitude towards her.

Isobel felt as though she'd slept for only minutes when the knock came on the door, telling her that the men escorting Jocelyn and her mother had returned. She dressed quickly and hurried down to the hall to learn if the fates were going to be kind—to the men and to her plan.

Padruig grabbed his son and dragged him into what could only be a chest-crushing embrace. Athdar gave him a chance to privately greet Tavish, named after Athdar's father, before asking the men to give their report. It did not take long for others to arrive at the hall—the men's families as well as some of the servants. Athdar gathered everyone at the large table and let them eat and drink before asking them all the questions he had for them.

Just as he was about to begin, Isobel arrived.

She was sin personified walking across his floor, just woken and looking fresh from bed. Her hair was loose and tussled and it begged him to wrap it around his fist. From the way his body reacted at the sight of her, he knew he'd made the right decision in having Glenna share the chamber with her. When he glanced

over at Padruig, the man winked at him as though reading the temptation Isobel presented to him on his face.

He rose and offered her his chair. She sat and he noticed she smiled when she saw Padruig's son next to his
father. She must be as worried for news of her mother as
he was, but she waited for him to ask the questions.

'Are they safe?'

'Aye, laird,' Dougal answered. 'They made it through
before the worst of the storm hit us. Gavin travelled all
the way when he headed back.' Her body relaxed at the
news and he let out the breath he did not know he was
holding. Jocelyn was safe.

'What took so long?'

'Well, Niall had to give over his horse for the lady's
group. The cart was slowing them down, so they took
what they needed and used Niall's to carry the extra
supplies.' Athdar realised that Niall was not with them.

'Where is he now?'

Tavish and Dougal chuckled. 'Still walking, laird.'

Athdar did not have to say a word. Padruig was on
his feet, calling out orders to two of the men listening.
The light of the moon was enough to see their way and
retrieve Niall.

'So the storms came, then?' he asked.

'Aye. One moment it was clear and sunny, the next it
moved in like a wall of snow. Lucky we were far enough
in that they could get through the rest.'

'My thanks,' Athdar said to them. He held out his
hand to Isobel for he wanted her to hear news about her
mother without the others listening.

'Dougal?' They walked far enough from the table so
the others could not hear. 'Did my sister or the lady's
mother give you messages for her?'

'Only to tell you that they are safe and someone will come for you as soon as the pass opens once more.'

'My thanks for your assistance to them, Dougal,' Isobel said in a tone that made the man instantly her admirer.

Dougal left them and Athdar looked at Isobel, trying not to let his fear and pleasure over this *setback* show. He would have to take steps to ensure her honour was protected and that he protected her honour, as well. That, he suspected, would be the bigger problem.

'It seems you will have me as a guest for some time longer, Athdar. I hope I will not be too large a burden to you.'

Words escaped him in that moment. This would be the biggest challenge he faced in a long time. To have her so close and want her so much and not to touch her. And not to let her batter down his resistance and his resolve about accepting another woman into his torn and shattered life.

Looking into those eyes the colour of the northern sea and knowing she was truly an innocent and must remain that way, he vowed to respect her honour…

For if he did not, he dishonoured himself, as well.

And he would end up in little pieces spread all over the Highlands of Scotland by her furious, half Scots, half Norse, very dangerous father.

Chapter Eleven

Although, from the sound of it, it was a severe early winter storm that had closed the pass, the weather at the village and in the lands around them was beautiful and sunny. Harvest was done and now everyone did their part from the oldest to the youngest, from fit to shut-in.

And for Isobel, guest or no guest, it would have been inconceivable to remain inactive and not help, so she did. She spent a few hours each day with Laria, helping her dry, crush and mix her various herbal concoctions. She spent other hours visiting with Nessa and the other weavers spread throughout the village, helping as she could and wishing she had her loom here so she could work alongside them.

But the best time of each day was the evening.

Supper brought her together with Athdar who seemed to enjoy her company and her conversations about many topics, from warfare and the political alliances in Scotland to how to preserve more meat for the winter. Sometimes she would catch him watching her or see him smiling over something she'd said to Broc or Padruig.

He was very much like Connor in that he did not

mind having his opinions challenged, though when he made a decision, that was the end of the matter. She witnessed that when it came to arrangements for the village and when it came to some decisions about the training of some of his men.

They did play chess, but always in the middle of things, with others around and though she often found him staring at her lips, that kiss was never repeated. She certainly would have been willing to, she told herself, if he'd only try to. He did not…. Nothing about his behaviour towards her could be considered anything but polite and respectful and honourable.

And she wanted to scream!

Isobel had thought of ways to spend some time alone with Athdar and yet could come up with nothing that would not be obvious. With each day's report of the snows in the mountains and her visit extending came the hope that something would happen between them. She just did not realise that weaving would be the way it would begin.

Isobel was leaving Nessa's cottage when she spied Athdar riding through the village. The cold winds whipped around her, catching up her cloak and her hair and tugging her along the path faster than she would have walked. Laughing as she went, she soon found herself standing before Athdar. He smiled at her and her heart warmed.

'Come now, Isobel,' he said, leaning over and reaching out his hand. 'If you are making your way back to the keep, let me take you there.' She accepted his hand and pulled herself behind him on the horse.

'Are you certain I am not keeping you from duties?' she asked, as she settled on the horse, tugging the length of her gown and cloak down to cover her legs. A cold burst of wind made her laugh once more as she fought it.

'Isobel!' he whispered over his shoulder as the horse danced beneath them. 'Here now,' he said, reaching around and dragging her across his lap. It took him no time at all to place her over his legs, wrap the bulk of the cloak around her, and surround her with his arms. 'Ready?'

He asked, but did not wait for a reply, kicking the sides of the horse until the giant black lunged forwards carrying them both along the road to the keep. She sat, unmoving, both out of fear of upsetting the horse's movements and out of the desire to not leave his arms. After they'd gone a short distance, she relaxed against his chest, enjoying the feel of his strong muscles and the warmth his body gave hers. He tensed for a moment as she did it, but then allowed it, even cushioned her more as they continued up the path. Several villagers called out or waved and she noticed more than one of them giving a knowing nod.

If the weather held out…

If she demonstrated her usefulness…

If she made him want her…

If only…

'You do not need to work in the village, Isobel. You are my guest.'

'Aye, a guest, but I cannot abide being lazy. And truly, I would rather stay busy than sit idly by when there is so much to be done.'

He seemed to think about her words. When she lifted her head up, she could imagine him tilting his down and kissing her. She did lift hers and inhaled the warm, masculine scent of him, so close to her, wishing he would…

'It is getting too cold for you to traipse around the village like this,' he said. His concern warmed her, too.

'Would you…?'

She stopped before asking him to do something for her. If word came that the pass was cleared of the early snow, and chances are that it would before winter set in for real, she would be gone. So, she did not want to ask him to change something for her. Still…

'Go on, Isobel. What is it you want?'

His deep voice grew a bit huskier then, sending shivers unrelated to the wind down her spine, and she thought about what she really wanted from him. Then she shook herself free of this madness he caused in her.

'Would you permit me to have one of the looms moved into the keep so I can continue to work on it there?'

He remained quiet as they passed through the gate and rode up to the keep. When he stopped there, a boy ran up to take his horse. Athdar handed her down and she was sad for the loss of his heat. The winds buffeted her on the steps until he jumped off the horse and wrapped his arm around her, guiding her up to the door and through it.

He was not going to allow it. She could tell by his delay that he would not. She waited until they were inside so she did not have to shout against the winds. Isobel needed to make her case for this change to the way he did things here.

'Nessa said there is a loom, unused, in the storage room below. I could set it up…here,' she said, pointing to the first corner of the hall as they entered it. 'The sunlight will make it bright enough during the afternoon for me to work here.'

'And this will please you?' he asked.

It was not what she had expected him to say. He'd shown her the hospitality of his clan and his home so he did not have to do anything for her.

'And it will keep you from freezing because you walk from one side of the village to the other, visiting each of the women who weave for our clan?'

He knew what she did each day? She thought that as long as she kept herself out of his way, he cared not. But he was keeping track of her during the day?

'Aye, I know what you do with your days, Isobel,' he said, almost reading the questions in her thoughts. 'I hear reports from my men because you visit their wives and mothers. I hear reports from Padruig because Nessa is happier than she has been in a long time to have such an accomplished weaver among us. And I hear from Broc about how much you are helping Laria as she prepares for the winter and to move into the keep.'

Part of her was embarrassed that he knew so much, but more of her was thrilled he'd taken note of what she did. She nodded at him and smiled. 'It would please me greatly, Athdar.'

For a moment it was only the two of them there. The noises and chatter of the hall faded away and Isobel swore she could hear the breaths he took. Her heart pounded as he stepped closer and took her hand in his. She gazed at him as he leaned his head down and touched his lips to hers. Isobel stood up on her toes so that she did not lose contact with his mouth. This kiss, so different from the first one, had barely got started when he abruptly ended it.

He stood very still and she finally heard what he clearly had—the voices coming closer and closer. His wide shoulders and height hid her from their view and he was giving her the opportunity to move away before this scandalous behaviour was seen by anyone. She did as he indicated and took a pace back away from him just in time, for Broc appeared at his side.

'You may be our guest for the whole of the winter, Isobel,' he said. 'Or we will have to send you through the lowlands and out to the sea to get home.'

'I think I would not mind being here all winter,' she said to Broc, though the whole time she stared back into Athdar's eyes. He broke contact with her gaze first.

'Broc, the lady asked if she can have the old loom from the storage room brought up here,' Athdar said to his steward.

'You are making her work for her meals, then?' Broc jested.

'It would please her to do so,' Athdar said, glancing briefly at her. 'And I know how much you like to please our guests.' He smacked Broc's shoulder and nodded to her. 'See to it?'

She watched him leave, speaking to several others as he made his way through the hall to the small chamber he used as a place for his records and rolls. Once he'd gone, she turned to Broc. *May as well get this handled*, she thought.

'So, would you like to come with me to find out if the loom is in any condition to bring out?' Broc asked.

'I would like that.' Isobel took off her cloak and carried it over her arm as she followed Broc.

It took only a short time to find the disassembled loom, which Broc told her belonged at one time to Lady Lilidh MacDougal, Athdar and Jocelyn's mother, before being stored away at Jocelyn's departure and her mother's death. With the help of some of the kitchen workers, they had the loom's pieces carried to the corner of the hall.

* * *

She spent the rest of the afternoon working to assemble the frame and to begin to hang the weights. To her surprise, the men found another, smaller loom and brought it out from the storage chamber to the hall. Broc was convinced it belonged to Lady Jocelyn as a child, her practice loom where she learned her skills. Jean told of Jocelyn's first attempts to use it and entertained them as the men worked now to set up both of the looms, side by side.

Soon, their usual tasks called them away and Isobel knew it would take several more hours to get the looms set up and working. Since Nessa would see them when she arrived to take supper in the keep, Isobel was certain she could gain her assistance on the morrow.

Supper came and went. The pleasant companions at table made the meal go quickly and Isobel found herself fighting to stay awake after the busyness of the day. She and Glenna returned to her chamber and she fell into bed, expecting to be asleep quickly.

First, it was the maid's snoring that kept her awake.

Then the howling winds and rain that began some time later slammed against the stone walls and wooden shutters.

Finally, Isobel realised that she was not ready for sleep; her thoughts kept going in different directions and would not quiet. Giving up the fight, she climbed from the bed and, having a care not to wake Glenna, she wrapped her heavy woollen shawl around her shoulders and left the chamber. She found a lantern hanging on the wall, so Isobel took it with her, guiding her way through the darkness.

Some people did sleep in the hall, though now they

placed their pallets near the hearth for the warmth they could claim. Walking down the stairs to the back corner, she put the lantern down on the floor and studied the wooden beams and pieces. The stone weights lay in a pile, ready to be strung and placed over the main beam to hold the warp threads in place as the shuttle worked the weft, over and under, tightening the growing fabric after every pass.

She sat in the near dark, attaching the ends of large balls of spun threads that would be used. Occasional snores or coughs echoed through the hall and she remained as quiet as she could be, using her body to keep most of the lantern's light blocked. How much time passed, she knew not. She continued to sort and organise the parts and pieces until she felt sleep's call. Placing everything where it could be used on the morrow, she rose, picked up the lantern and walked quietly back to her chambers.

She was driving him to madness.

With each passing day that she remained in his keep, in his village, in his world, she stole a bit more of his resolve until he wondered how he could continue the farce of resisting her.

Isobel had breathed life back into his home and his people…and into him. She had done what years and wisdom and fortune had not—she had made him want to try again. His sworn oath was crumbling more each day and with each smile and cheerfully done task, with each gracious favour and suggestion, she made him want her.

And he did want her.

Although he had much more experience in the physical pleasures than she, he'd thought about those two simple kisses they'd shared more than he'd thought about any previous ones. Even those of his first love faded now and the ones in more recent memory paled when he compared them.

Those kisses would be his downfall…and hers if they were not careful. He sensed her curiosity and budding passion and knew she wanted to know more. He prayed nightly that the snow would recede and save him from the desire for her that grew with every encounter.

He could not sleep and decided to go down to the small chamber off the hall and review some documents he'd found from his father's time. When he walked into the corridor, he heard sounds from below. Leaning over the stone wall, he saw her, in the corner, moving some of the pieces of the loom and sorting through the pile of weight stones.

He wondered how it felt to be those stones, resting in her hand, encircled by her fingers. He reacted as he expected, growing hard at the thought of her touch. As he watched in silence, she organised the threads and began tying on some of the stones. After a while, she slowed and stopped. Picking up the lantern from the floor, she began walking towards the stairs…and him.

Not wanting to frighten her or startle her and cause a scream, he backed up against the doorway and waited for her to approach. When she reached the top of the stairs, he lifted the latch of his door, jiggling it enough to warn her of his presence, but not to scare her. Instead of fear, her face brightened when she realised it was he.

'Athdar,' she whispered, smiling. 'I thought you might be Glenna following me.' She held the lantern up higher, revealing that he wore a shirt and trews only. And revealing her undergown and shawl. 'I hope I did not wake you?'

'You did not. I am having some trouble sleeping this night, Isobel.' He looked past her towards her chamber. 'And where is Glenna? Is she not supposed to attend to you?'

'The girl works unceasingly all day, Athdar. And then she sleeps like the dead.'

She did not understand that she'd just given him both an excuse and a reason in revealing Glenna's pattern. The girl would hear little or nothing that went on outside the chamber, nor in it, he suspected, once she retired for the night.

Done waiting, done resisting, done…just done, he took the lantern from her and put it on the floor.

'Isobel,' he whispered, sliding his fingers into her hair and drawing her close. 'I want to kiss you, lass.'

He could feel her breath against his face, they were so close, but he waited for her to object to his attentions. When she did not, he lowered his mouth to hers the way he'd wanted to for days…for weeks…for ever, it seemed.

She sighed against his lips at the first touch and leaned into him, opening to him. He smiled at that, almost laughed really, and then placed kisses on her cheeks, her forehead, her chin and the edge of her jaw before joining their mouths and tasting the wonderful essence of her with his tongue. He plunged deeply within and then mimicked the movement another part of him wanted to take, sliding in and out. Tilting his head so that he could access every part of her mouth, he kissed her until she was breathless as he'd wanted to do.

When she drew back from him to take a breath, he kissed down the line of her jaw and on to her neck. She lifted up towards him, seeming to urge him on, but he did not trespass further. Touching, tasting her skin, licking and nipping his way back to her lips, he discovered that she had grasped his shirt and her shawl had fallen away from her shoulders.

She did not move away. She did not stop him. She pulled his shirt, bringing him closer to her. Dar dropped his hands from her head and stroked down her arms before sliding his hands around to her back and embracing her. Pulling her up against him hard, he had no doubt she could feel his rigid flesh between their bodies.

But did it frighten her? Nay, not his Isobel. She let out a slight gasp and then met his gaze. 'Kiss me again, Athdar.'

And he did. He wrapped himself around her, lifting her up to meet his mouth and taking hers. The feel of her tongue against his nearly undid the control he was struggling to keep strong. He stopped and let her explore his mouth, ignoring the blinding need to lay her down and fill her with himself. Every touch of her tongue, every time she clutched at his shirt and slid her fingers unknowingly across his nipples, his body screamed for him to break free and take her.

Then a sound from below broke into the heated haze surrounding them and he lifted his mouth from hers and listened. Other than the sound of their breathing, both of them panting from the pleasure, none other came to them. But it gave him a chance to realise that he had crossed a line with her.

A very desirable and pleasing line, but one that an honourable man did not break with an innocent unless there was an understanding between them. When he attempted to step back, she resisted, tightening her grasp on his shirt and leaning against him. She let him go, but watched him with wide, intent eyes. Uncertain of what to say, he waited on her to speak, expecting she was overwhelmed by the power of the passion between them. When she did not, he finally found words.

'Do you regret this?' he asked softly as he leaned over and picked her shawl up from the floor.

'Regret?' She shook her head. 'I regret only that you stopped.'

Did she have no idea of the enchanting temptation that she was to him? Of the danger someone like her, *her*, presented to him? Clearly not.

'Someone had to or…'

'So you regret…this?' she asked. 'That you acted this way, then?' Sadness seeped into her voice. Something he never wanted to hear there.

'My behaviour has been less than honourable towards you, Isobel. You should go now.' He whispered that warning, praying she would understand how close to disaster they now stood.

'I should go? To my chamber? Back to Lairig Dubh?'

She put a pace's distance between them and crossed her arms over her chest, pulling the shawl tight over her breasts. Breasts that had recently been pushed up against his chest. Nipples that had tightened against him even if she was unaware of it. Considering the path of his thoughts, there was only one answer.

'Both.'

Her gaze narrowed and, for a moment, he recognised the same glare her father was so famous for being sent in his direction.

'You would send me away?' she asked.

'This was wrong,' he said, nodding at the area around them. 'No man should touch you that way, kiss you that way, unless you are betrothed.' He knew she waited on that offer, but it was not coming. It could not come from him.

Instead of going to her chambers, she stepped closer, studying his face. Then a mutinous expression filled her face and her lower lip curled. No matter what she would say, Athdar understood he was in trouble…. Big trouble.

'You would send me away out of fear?'

Had it been so clear in his expression, then, that she could read it?

'Aye. Fear,' he answered, crossing his arms, as well, but more in an attempt to keep himself from grabbing her once more. 'Fear of you. Fear for you. Fear that I will take your virtue but am unable to offer you more than that passion. Fear that I will—'

He stopped himself then. He could not admit wholly the control his past yet held over him, not to her. His true fear was that he would break her heart and be unable to protect her. That whatever deadly fate had stalked the other women in his life would pursue her. Now, looking at her face and in her eyes, he knew that if anything happened to her, it would be the death of him.

'You must go,' he whispered. 'Back to your chamber. We will talk about the rest in the morning.' He pointed down the dark corridor towards the room.

'Tell me why? Tell me why this promising beginning cannot continue towards something else? Is it because of Mairi's death? Or Seonag's?' She reached up and touched his cheek, forcing him to meet her eyes. 'I do not believe you are cursed, Athdar.'

'Neither did they. Neither did Tavia. But they are dead now, are they not?' He could not stop the frustration and resignation from bursting through now. She'd unleashed it, first with her innocent passion and now with her insightful questions. 'Any woman who ties herself to me dies. I will not risk you.'

'Well, I do not regret what happened between us,

Athdar. And I will not act otherwise.' She lifted her chin and watched him, and though he should say words that would scare her away, he just did not want her to believe he regretted what happened between them this night or over these past weeks.

He placed his finger under her chin and lifted it even higher. Then he leaned over and touched his mouth to hers, just to feel the heat and the passion that simmered inside of her once more before he sent her away. Her mouth, with its mutinous firmness, softened under his touch and her lips moulded to his. Then he lifted his head and stepped away, allowing his hand to drop.

'Regret that? Never? But you…you I will always regret.' Not taking the chance of her misunderstanding, he made it clear between them. 'Nothing more can or will happen between us, Isobel. Nothing. So return to your chamber and, on the morrow, we will find a way for you to return home.'

Other than a slight narrowing of her gaze, she did not react. She stared at him for several moments before turning away from him. She gathered up her shawl and picked up the lantern from the floor before walking back to the end of the corridor and her chambers. Nothing, not a word or gesture, spoke of her acceptance of his decision or her abidance of his orders. Instead, she tilted her head as though studying him before lifting the latch to her door and going inside.

Athdar returned to his chamber. He should have felt content that she understood the situation between them and that nothing more could come of this desire and attraction they each had for the other. He undressed and climbed into his bed, but as he lay down and tried to find sleep, the truth struck him.

Isobel had not taken his words, his declaration, as

the fact of how things would be between them. Nay, she had not. Instead he understood now the parting glance she had given him for he'd seen it in his sister's gaze and in Mairi's and Seonag's at times.

The expression was one of accepting a challenge made.

God help him, he was in more danger now than ever before.

He does not remember.
He does not remember the cost that he will pay.
He desires her and cannot stay away from her.
Her father is not the only danger he faces if he continues to pursue her.
A reminder is needed.
He must remember the terrible cost he must pay.
For ever.

Chapter Twelve

The next few days were strange ones for Isobel.

After her encounter with Athdar and the passion that had flared between them, she could not go back to being ignorant of his feelings. And she did not wish to.

The morning after had been awkward at first, but she moved through the day, helping move Laria into the keep and setting up the workroom she would use. Laria's cottage was much too far from the keep during winter's storms, so her practice over the last decade or so had been to situate herself in the keep from which she could reach or be taken to places in the village more easily.

It took most of the next day to finish setting up the looms with help from Nessa and others. Some of the older kin who visited told tales of Jocelyn working side by side with her mother when she was just a young girl. In spite of any unease, Athdar did help out, getting everything set up and then watching as she began weaving. Unused to this loom, it took her a while to get things adjusted, the correct tensions on the threads, the positioning of the weights and the choice of a pattern, but by late in the afternoon she sat working in a familiar rhythm and soon produced a length of fabric.

There was a moment that felt unreal to her.

While still working on the first few inches of fabric, Athdar walked up behind her and watched. She nearly lost her pace when he placed his hand on her shoulder and leaned in close to speak.

'Does this please you, Isobel?' he asked, not moving his hand from the comfortable place on her shoulder.

'Aye, Athdar,' she answered without taking her eyes off the loom and the moving threads. She dared not look to see if anyone else noticed their familiarity. 'It pleases me.' Before he could lift his hand away, she posed a question to him.

'Does it please you to see your mother's and sister's looms at work once more?'

He squeezed her shoulder then, sending a tingle all the way down along her spine. 'It does please me, lass.'

Having witnessed the fierce fight he was having with himself over the way things stood between them, she decided to let it pass. They had discussed travelling back to Lairig Dubh, but his men returned with reports that the pass was, well, impassable. So, her visit here would continue, while he wished for a bout of warmer weather to clear the pass and she prayed for the winter's early arrival to spread.

If she had more time…

So, three days had passed and she bided her time, enjoying the time with Athdar and his kin, using her skills for weaving to spend her time being useful. And using the time with Laria to increase her knowledge of plants, herbs and medicaments. Isobel felt useful and needed and as though she fit in quite well. And, if the time came—which she knew it would—that the roads opened and she was able to return home, mayhap he would ask her to stay instead.

Then, on the fourth day, everything changed in ways that she could never have expected or known.

'Something strange is going on,' she said to no one.

Sitting alone at the loom, working the dark green and brown threads into the fabric, she noticed a number of people she did not recognise entering the keep. A woman about Athdar's age was the centre of it and her grief was palpable to her. Though she wanted to go to her, Broc was there and then Jean came from the kitchens.

Watching the scene unfold from her place in the back of the hall, Isobel wondered about what had happened. When Broc sent servants and men off in different directions, she put down the shuttle and rose. Nothing could console or calm the woman's agitation and finally Broc sent for Laria.

This was wrong. Something was terribly wrong— even she, a stranger here, knew it. Broc must have sent for Athdar, so she knew he would take care of this when he arrived. She sat back down, keeping watch, neither happy nor good at waiting.

She was on her feet again and found herself taking slow, measured steps forwards just as Athdar did arrive.

The shouting shocked her.

'This is your fault!' the woman cried out at the sight of Athdar. 'Everyone now suffers because of you!' The colour drained from Athdar's face and she moved a few more paces closer.

'Ailis? What has happened? Where is Rob?' he asked as he tried to take the woman's hand, but was shaken off by her. Broc leaned over and told him something that made him grow ashen.

'Aye, Dar,' the woman said. 'My Robbie is dead, just like the others. Just as ye should be!' Her voice broke into wailing and she crumpled at Athdar's feet. 'But nay, 'tis never ye who suffers the cost, is it? No' the laird's son…. No' the laird.'

Athdar staggered a pace back at her accusation and Isobel went to his side. Whispers spread quickly through the hall and she saw many others coming in to see to the matter. When she would have offered to help, Athdar spied her and shouted, 'Go to your chambers! There is nothing for you to see here.' Though some of those watching threw sympathetic glances in her direction, no one intervened. No one would.

Though hurt by his callous words and manner, she understood that he was profoundly affected by the death of this woman's Robbie, causing him to react to her. Rather than arguing or giving him cause to do something he would regret later, she backed away, allowing others closer. Others of his kith and kin. Not outsiders like her.

Isobel walked to the bedchamber and watched from the doorway as more and more people came to the hall to speak to Ailis. Athdar remained there, but did not try to approach her again. Indeed, from where she watched, he did little but stand and stare. Though some of his men approached, and both Broc and Padruig spoke to him, he did little more than shrug or wave people off. Then he called for whisky and began drinking deeply of it.

Soon, servants began putting platters of food and pitchers of ale on the table. Some of those in the hall partook of it, but most simply spent time trying to console Ailis over her loss.

Was Robbie her son? Her husband? Her brother? What was Athdar's connection to him and his death? Why would Ailis blame Athdar? So many questions swirled around in her thoughts, but there was no one to answer them.

When she could, she watched, but sometimes, the grief was too intense to witness. She offered up some prayers for the man's soul and for his family when she could no longer watch. Standing by helpless was not something she was accustomed to doing.

Jean had Glenna bring a tray up to her, but the girl did not remain long enough to answer her questions. The gathering in the hall had turned quiet now and Laria had given something to Ailis before she was taken back to her cottage. A group of women, some old, some young, accompanied her from the keep.

Still, she had no answers. She would have to wait and find out more on the morrow. Resigned, she worked on some mending and then decided to go to bed early since there was nothing more she could accomplish. Some time later, she was awakened by the sound of someone lifting the door latch. Expecting Glenna, she pushed herself up on the bed and waited for the girl to enter. Mayhap now she could gain some information or insight into what was going on and why Ailis thought Athdar was to blame.

But, outlined by the light of lanterns along the corridor, the person who stood at the door to her bedchamber was not Glenna at all.

'Are ye awake, lass?' His words slurred and she could smell the pungent aroma of *uisge beatha* as he walked inside and closed the door. He'd been drinking whisky and now stunk of it. She slid from the bed, not knowing what to expect from him.

'Athdar? What is wrong?'

His heavy breathing echoed across the chamber, but he had not moved since closing the door. He would never hurt her, so she had no fear of him. But drunken, he could hurt himself or her unintentionally. She walked slowly towards him, stopping at the table near the hearth to light a candle.

He looked as if he'd seen death and it was coming for him.

So haunted were his features that she gasped as she got a look at him. Isobel put the candle down so she did not drop it and walked to him.

'Here now,' she whispered softly. 'Let me help you back to your chamber. Some sleep will help you.'

'I came here... I forgot... Mairi...' He slurred the words and sloughed off at the end into nothing.

So this had been Mairi's chamber, then? He might have mumbled something more, but he was wobbling and making noises as he shuffled on his feet, so she was not certain. She did not remember him ever mentioning Mairi, his first wife, until a few nights ago, though others here had spoken of her openly. 'Why did you come here, Dar?'

'Robbie is dead,' he said. 'Robbie.'

She walked to his side, planning to at least get him to sit on the bed before he fell to the floor. 'Who is Robbie?'

He allowed her to guide him to the bed and he sat, but he did not answer right away. Instead, he lifted the jug he'd been carrying up and drank deeply from it. Then he put it on the floor at his feet, covered his face with his hands and sat motionless.

Had he caused Robbie's death?

A laird and chieftain sent men into dangerous, even

deadly, situations and sometimes men died. Her own father had spoken of losing friends in battles and even when he had had to fight to rescue her mother from outlaws who had taken her. Death was the only certainty in their lives. And a laird held the ultimate authority—and responsibility—over his people's lives and deaths. Still, why did this one devastate him?

'Ailis was right. It should have been me who died. Not the others. Not Robbie now. Me.' His voice sounded both empty and so overly full that it hurt to listen to it.

He reached for the jug and she was tempted to take it out of his hand. Instead she let him drink more, thinking that it would make him fall asleep sooner. 'Tell me of Robbie.'

Athdar sat quiet for a few minutes and then spoke.

'We were friends. Robbie and Duff and Kennan and Jamie and me.' He smiled then, but it broke her heart with its sadness. 'We ran and fought and…' His words slipped off and it was then she noticed the tears. His tears. 'It should have been me.'

Isobel was puzzled and suspected that whisky and grief added to his confused thoughts, as well. He lifted his head then and seemed to realise his surroundings and her. He began to stand and she moved closer to help him. Then he staggered back and tripped, falling on the bed. When his feet flailed out, he kicked the pottery jug and broke it. It roused him and he reached for the pieces, apparently aware of her bare feet.

'Stay!' he said, scooping the pieces of broken clay aside. 'Have a care.'

She walked around the puddle and the jug and patted the pillow at the top of the bed.

'Here now, lie down,' she said, taking him by the shoulder and guiding him down. 'Sleep, Athdar.'

She thought he was going to lie back until the last moment when he reached out and grabbed for her. Only able to grasp a bit of her gown, he pulled her along with him. She moved with him so that her gown did not tear. Finding herself on the bed, next to him, she could only laugh softly as she tried to free herself from his hold.

'Stay with me, Mairi, love. They are all dead now. I should be.' He wrapped his arm around her and held her close. His next words broke her heart. 'I should not have lived when you died.'

He said nothing more which was a good thing, for she felt her own tears flowing at the hints and signs of the deep wounds he had suffered because of these deaths. She lay at his side, tucked half-under him and let him drift off to sleep. Her intention was to wait for him to be deeply asleep so he would not feel her move and then slide out from under him.

But, a lesson that she learned very early in life was the one she forgot in that moment—good intentions paved the road to hell. Between her fatigue and the warmth of his body, she, too, fell asleep and her intention to leave drifted off even as she did.

Oh, sweet Jesus, but his head pounded!

Athdar tried to open his eyes, but the light hurt too much for him to do so. Covering them with the hand he could move, he adjusted to the brightness before trying again. Inhaling against the pain, he noticed that he and the chamber smelled like old whisky. He needed to wash and change out of these garments. Tugging his arm free of the weight on it, the sound of feminine murmurs surprised him even more.

Had he got drunk at the news of Robbie's death and ended up in one of the whores' cottages? Christ, what a mess that would be! He turned to see who shared his bed and blinked several times against what he saw.

Isobel lay up against his side, her leg wrapped around his and her face tucked on his shoulder.

His head dropped back and he closed his eyes, but that did not stop the images of thousands of ways to die from passing through his mind.

He would never…

He could never…

From the looks and feel of it, he certainly had shared Isobel's bed. From the looks of it, he yet shared her bed.

He sat up, ignoring the terrible burning in the pit of his stomach and the hammering in his head, and looked around the room, not daring to look at Isobel yet. The room was a mess, clothing all over, and they were tangled around each other on top of the bed. And the strong smell of whisky was all around him.

Still, things were not completely out of his control as long as he had not actually done anything to the lass. All of this looked bad, looked very, very bad, but it could be explained.

He'd been drunk as anyone in the hall could tell.

He'd lost control and sought her out.

All because you cannot control yourself. All because you did not think of the consequences of your actions.

Rurik's words came back to him just as Isobel stirred at his side and as the door to the chamber opened. Before he could warn off whoever entered, the scream rang out and the sound of the tray crashing to the floor woke Isobel, who also screamed.

Things went badly from there on.

Once Isobel was awake, he moved off the bed and rushed, or staggered as it felt, to the door to close it. He had no idea that Glenna's voice could hit that shrill tone, but it pierced his skull and made his ears want to bleed with its intensity. With the door finally secured, he turned to face Isobel. His stomach churned at the sight before him. No matter where he looked, all he could see was her blood.

A deep scarlet stain marred the pristine white gown she wore. A bloody sign of the worst kind of abuse he could have done to her. He could not meet her gaze to see the recrimination and horror there, so he fell to his knees before her to beg her forgiveness.

'Isobel.'

He could say nothing more. And even if he thought of the words to speak, the crashing of the door that knocked him flat to the floor would have prevented it. Athdar pushed himself to his feet and tried to block Isobel from the scrutiny of others, but it was not possible with the number of people who crowded into the chamber.

Expressions of shock turned to horror as they beheld the results of his night of drunken debauchery. He read disappointment and anger in their gazes as they—Padruig, Nessa, Broc, even Jean had made it up the steps to check on Isobel—gazed at him. But for Isobel there was only sympathy and caring.

'Nessa, please see to her,' he said quietly. 'She may have a need for Laria,' he admitted as he ordered everyone else out then.

He might have transgressed the bounds of proper behaviour greatly, but he was still laird and they answered to him. No one refused his command though they all waited outside the chamber until he left, as well.

'Athdar,' Isobel called out to him. 'Athdar, wait!'

How could she even speak his name without cursing him for what he'd done? He turned back to see her standing at the doorway, the red sign of his terrible sin visible to all. He would make this right somehow. He had to make it right…for her. She deserved none of this. He just did not wish to conduct their privy affairs in the corridor.

'Isobel, there will be time to straighten this all out once you have been seen to,' he said quietly. 'Let Nessa see to you, eat something if you can, and we will talk soon.'

She opened her mouth as though to argue with him, but stopped when Nessa placed a hand on her shoulder. Her mouth trembled as she nodded, accepting his explanation.

He ran his hand through his hair, pushing it out of his face and walked away, not meeting anyone's eyes. He needed to clean himself up so he could face the consequences of his actions. Once he rid himself of the stink of old whisky and cleaned up, he needed to consult with Padruig and others and to arrange for Robbie's funeral, as well. He barely got outside in the yard before his stomach clenched and he vomited. It took some time before his stomach calmed enough to complete his ablutions.

Then his sense of sorrow and failure nearly overwhelmed him as he thought of what he must face this day. Of the people he must answer to and be responsible for. He accepted one thing as he made his way outside— whatever had happened between them or as a result of his lack of control, it would be as Isobel wanted.

Whatever she wanted.

Chapter Thirteen

She could not have imagined that a day which had been as bad as the one yesterday was could have been followed by another one that was even worse. But, from the moment she opened her eyes—nay, even moments before that—it had spun wildly out of control as her life would now do.

How could she have fallen asleep with him? And in such a condition?

In the darkened chamber, lit with but one small candle, she'd never seen the injury to his hand when he reached for the broken jug on the floor. She'd never noticed the bloody stain on her gown where he grabbed it in the dark. Mayhap if she'd risen as she'd planned, she could have changed and no one would have seen it and made the hasty and wrong conclusion that everyone who'd rushed into the bedchamber had.

Including Athdar.

He'd lost his senses in the desolation of losing a friend, one of his oldest friends from the little he'd said, and then sought solace in too much whisky. That had driven him to the confusion that led him to her door— or rather Mairi's door—to find some comfort there, so deep in his misery and in his cups that he mistook Isobel for her. Her mistake added to his suffering, for now, now, she knew exactly what he thought he'd done.

Taken her virtue by force.

Her head swam with the implications and complications of this situation. She needed to speak to him before he made any decisions based on…based on her deceit. What if he sent word to her parents and to Connor about this? Then there would be no way of correcting her mistake and there could be war if her father sought satisfaction for what he thought Athdar had done.

'Nessa, please call Athdar here,' she asked, as the servants rolled the large tub into her chambers. 'I must speak to him before he does anything.'

'We must see to you, lass. Athdar…the laird can see to himself until you are…made comfortable.' The woman's fury was clear in every word and gesture. Nessa also believed the worst.

'Jean…' Isobel turned to the other woman in the room. 'I must speak to him first,' she begged.

'Here now, lady,' Jean whispered as she put her arm around Isobel's shoulders and guided her to the other side of the room. 'The laird said he would talk with you after you have had a bath and dressed.'

Jean glanced over her head and Isobel knew she was exchanging wordless gestures with Nessa. Once the room had been cleaned up and all the servants gone, Jean took her hands and sat her on the edge of the now-pristine bed.

'Should we call Laria for ye? Do you have any…injuries…that need tending to?'

When she looked from one woman to the other, they both blushed deeply at the questions. Isobel understood what they were asking and shook her head, trying to speak the truth to them.

'Athdar did not hurt me,' she said. 'I am not injured.' They shook their heads and tsked in reply. 'He did nothing...'

She realised that she was convincing no one of anything. Their minds were set on believing the worst, so she gave up the battle for the moment and sank into the tub's steaming water. Though he'd not hurt her, or truly even touched her, he had slept on her and his weight and the twisted manner in which she ended up—half beneath him, half next to him—had left her sore and achy. Isobel let the water, and the herbs they'd put in it, soothe her.

They did not rush her at all and only helped her wash her hair when she convinced them the water was cooling. Nessa stoked the fire so that it burst into flames, heating the chamber just before Isobel stood and climbed from the tub. Jean wrapped her quickly in two lengths of linen drying cloths.

She'd had enough.

'I need some time alone,' she said. 'I would like to dress myself.'

She just needed an opportunity to sort through her thoughts and come up with a plan before things went completely awry. She needed to know what to say to Athdar and how to explain the grievous error that had happened between them before he took responsibility for something he did not do.

'I will get ye something plain to eat, lady. And some of that betony tea that ye like so much,' Jean said, accepting her request.

Though Nessa looked as though she would argue, she nodded as she gathered up the soiled garments and followed Jean out. She could not fault them for their concern. It touched her heart to have them worrying over her, much as her mother fretted about her and her siblings, no matter their ages.

Once the door closed and the latch dropped, she sat on a stool before the fire and combed the tangles out of her hair. Letting it dry, she fought the growing urge to cry. Not so much for herself, but for Athdar and all the pain he yet carried within himself. And now this fresh guilt.

Her stubborn, selfish plan to come here and convince him that they were suited for marriage could now destroy her chances of that. Worse, if this misunderstanding continued too long, even more problems would happen because of it. She needed to see Athdar and clear this up. He did not deserve the trouble she was causing on top of everything else he felt responsible for.

So, she gathered her hair and braided it. Searching through the trunk in the corner, she found clean undergarments and stockings and put them on. A borrowed gown, for she'd not been able to keep all of her garments when she remained behind, that laced up the side and a tartan shawl and she was ready to leave the chamber and carry out her task to set things aright. Lifting the latch, she pulled the door open and found Jean waiting with a tray.

Letting out an exasperated breath at another delay, she stepped back inside and let the woman place the tray next to the bed. Realising that the woman's short stature belied a warrior's resolve, Isobel sat and ate. Hungrier than she realised, she consumed every morsel of the plain but filling meal. The betony tea she'd come to enjoy while working with Laria calmed her as she sipped the steaming decoction. Jean looked on as she ate and drank, pleased only when she finished every bit of it.

'Is Athdar in the hall?' she asked, rising and walking to the door.

'Is it wise to seek him out, lady? Why not rest here and wait for his call?'

Knowing the older woman meant only to be helpful and knowing she would never get past her peaceably, Isobel nodded. Taking the shawl and draping it over the chair, she went to the bed and got on it. Jean smiled and carried the tray from the room. Isobel listened at the hushed whispers outside her door and then closed her eyes to feign sleep when Nessa peeked inside to check on her.

A few more minutes of lying quietly and then Isobel climbed from the bed and pulled on her boots. From the quietness below, she suspected that Athdar was outside, in the yard or village. She would find him and they would talk about this.

She did not take a chance going through the hall and running into Nessa or Jean, so she put the shawl up over her hair, leaned her head down and made her way out of the keep's main door. Walking along the building, she found herself drawn to the boisterous—bloodthirsty, even— sounds from the enclosed yard where the men trained in arms and fighting. If there was something going on there, Athdar would be there—involved or watching at the least. As she rounded the corner of the keep, she found that she was not the only one following the sounds or the only one now watching the spectacle within the fence.

Athdar stood, surrounded by a half dozen men, taking them on. Some carried weapons, others did not. From his bloodied face and heavy breathing, it was clear he was not winning this battle or even holding his own. As she watched, she noticed he was not truly even fighting to his abilities. She'd seen him fight before—at Lairig Dubh, here—and this was not a fight. This was atonement.

Isobel pushed her way through the crowd to get to the fence. This must be stopped. He must be stopped. The people moved aside as they realised who she was and she rushed on. Spying Broc ahead, she ran to him and tugged his sleeve.

'You must stop this…now!' she said, loudly to be heard over the cheering. When Broc simply shrugged at her, she realised they, as well as Athdar, believed he was worthy of such punishment.

Men, she had found, were daft. They had this certain sense of judgement and justice that confounded her. They were…men! If no one here would stop this, she must. Gathering her skirts, she climbed up and over the fence, landing inside the yard.

Keeping hold of her skirts and stepping over God-knew-what in the dirt of the fighting field, she walked towards Athdar. Careful to stay out of the way of weapons, she approached him directly so she was in his line of sight at all times. One by one, each of his opponents saw her and stood down. Now only Padruig and Athdar continued fighting and the crowd grew quiet. Her voice could be heard now.

'Athdar, you must cease this now.'

She knew he saw her and heard her. Padruig did, for he stepped back for a brief second before turning back to face Athdar, sword raised and ready to strike again. She walked slowly, in measured steps, between the two men and approached Athdar.

'Athdar, I beg you to stop this now,' she said. Reaching over, she peeled his fingers from their steely grip around the hilt of his sword and took it from him. She dropped it to the ground and stood directly in front of him. Isobel lifted her hand to his face and touched his cheek. 'Cease this.'

'But, Isobel, I have dishonoured you…' he began.

'Nay, you have not. Only my actions can do that.'

He glanced over her head and around the yard where others remained, hanging on every word they could hear and action they could see. Still befuddled by his actions the night before and the grief of Robbie's death, he knew only that he must take responsibility for the actions, even if she decried it. In this, there was only one honourable way out.

But would she accept it? After his abominable treatment of her? He lowered his voice to her.

'Regardless of your assessment, your honour has been insulted. We know it. My kith and kin know it. As will yours.' She grew ashen then, as if accepting the price of whatever happened between them. 'There is only one way out of this so that you do not suffer the consequences.'

'Am I to battle your men for my honour then?' Her weak attempt to jest was whispered, telling him that this had shaken her, as well. He tried to ease her fears.

'Padruig might give you an even fight, but you could take the others down, of that I have no doubt,' he whispered back to her. Her lips trembled in a slight smile, but he sensed she understood. He stepped back from her, took her hand and held it up so all could see.

'Last night, I claimed Lady Isobel as wife in our custom of handfasting. And she accepted me as husband.' Shock echoed across the yard and he saw it in most faces there. Whether they accepted his words as truth or not, now, by publicly stating it before them, it was fact. 'No matter my clumsy and drunken manners towards her and no matter the misunderstanding of it this morn, the Lady Isobel is my wife.'

He watched as the same determined expression her father sometimes wore entered her eyes. But would she say the words that bound them for a year and a day? He did not deserve such consideration after what he'd done and could only hope she would accept this offer and let him make all things up to her. They could work out how this would end later, but first honour, his and hers, demanded this.

'And Laird MacCallum…Athdar is my husband.'

Her voice rang out clearly and did not shake as he was certain his had. She had allowed him to seek an honourable way to manage this disaster before his people. Though complete annihilation was yet a possibility once his overlord and her father discovered this un-sanctioned match, this gave him a respite to see things righted.

At first silence reigned, then someone in the crowd began clapping. Broc called out her name, 'Isobel! Lady MacCallum!'

The rest began chanting it in her honour, accepting his words and their vow—understanding that honour's demands had been answered.

'Isobel! Lady MacCallum!' they shouted. Then, *'A MacChauluim!'*

The sound was deafening as it echoed around the yard and off the stone buildings. Athdar waited for it to fade before kissing her hand and releasing her. They needed to speak, but first he needed to see to a few things.

'Wait for me in my clerk's chamber? I will be there

shortly,' he said to her. 'There are things to settle between us that this declaration did not.'

This time his words were met with acceptance rather than the usual mutinous expression and he nodded to her. Padruig walked to him, holding out the sword he'd retrieved and they both watched as his new wife walked away.

'She may have just saved your miserable life, but I suspect Rurik will still want your bollocks,' Padruig said, spitting in the dirt at their feet. 'What will you do with her now?'

'I have no idea,' he admitted. He'd not planned on having another wife, or even allowing another woman close to him, so he could not even gather thoughts about what next. 'I guess we will come to some agreement on things between us and then wait for her family.'

Padruig laughed then, aloud and hearty, the sound of it filling the yard. Others stopped and looked at him before carrying on with their duties. Padruig slapped him on the back, hard enough to make him stumble. 'I want to see that.'

Athdar went to the stables and to the barrels that held fresh water and washed himself clean of the sweat and blood that covered him. He could not speak to Isobel until he removed all signs of his debauchery. Though some walked past him, no one approached or spoke to him. He took the time to try to sort through how his life had spiralled so out of his control in such a short time.

If he could only remember what had happened between them last night. He rubbed his face and scrubbed his head, hoping that some memories would loosen within him. By the time he was well scrubbed and clean, nothing—no images, no words—had come to him. His only other choice was to ask Isobel, but after seeing her condition this morn, he did not want her to remember or relive whatever he'd done.

He made his way to his chambers and changed his trews and shirt for clean garments and then went to find her in the room he used for keeping his land rolls and records. It was more of a private sanctuary for him than anything else. Broc and others had urged him to request a brother from the nearby abbey to serve him as clerk, but he'd resisted.

Athdar approached the door, ill at ease about the coming discussion between them. He lifted the latch and eased the door open to find Isobel studying his collection, albeit small, of books. They'd been a gift from his mother on the anniversary of his birth for several years after he'd mastered the ability to read. Jocelyn had added to them, occasionally sending him something she thought might interest him. There was a Bible, some histories about Greece and Rome and his mother's book of hours. A modest collection for someone with the lands he held, but not as extensive as Connor's lands, titles, wealth, power or library.

'I had not thought to share these with you,' he said softly, startling her from her examination of them. 'You are probably accustomed to many more than that.'

'Oh, I am permitted access to the laird's library, but my own library numbers only a few more.' She turned then and watched him close the door.

'Would you prefer it open?' Did she fear him now in the quiet privacy? In spite of her brave intervention in the yard, she must have known she was safe there.

'Nay,' she said, shaking her head. 'I think we have matters to discuss that should remain between us.' Isobel moved around the table he kept there and sat on one of the stools. And then she watched and waited for him to begin.

'I...'

He was used to giving orders to men. He was used to making arrangements for the villagers. It had been years since he last answered to any woman as 'husband' and he could not think where to begin. With no memory of what had happened between them, he did not know how to apologise to her.

'You did me no harm, Athdar,' she whispered. 'I am not injured.'

He wanted to believe her. He had never in his life taken a woman by force and he had seen carefully to both Mairi's and Seonag's first time when he lay with them as husband and wife. He knew how to have a care for their tender sensibilities. And in spite of her apparent willingness to explore passion with him that night a week or so ago, he had no idea of what he'd done if drunk and unaware.

'I am well,' she said again, staring at his face. 'You were very drunk and came to the room confused and staggering. After you broke the jug, you fell down on the bed and dragged me with you. I...' It was her turn to hesitate now and he did not wish her to be more disconcerted by having to speak of it.

'Isobel, I know it will be difficult to remove the memories of last night from your mind. I want you to know that I will not force you to share my bed.'

He thought to give her reassurance, but that mutinous lower lip appeared once more, confusing the hell out of him. Added to that, his body reacted to the very thought of her in his bed and rose as though that deed was imminent.

'The handfasting satisfies the needs of honour, but

we can work out an acceptable arrangement between the two of us. If you wish it?'

'I understand that you were not yourself, Athdar. I have seen grief change people. I have seen men in their cups. You were devastated last night over your friend's death. I do not expect that behaviour will be repeated, so I am not worried over what will happen between us from now on.'

He wanted to laugh at how wifely her words sounded—the ones about that behaviour and not happening again could have been uttered by any married woman to her husband after a night's excess. She was extraordinary in accepting what had happened. But then her expression became serious.

'Are you able to accept this handfasting even though you have sworn not to marry again? Will you hate me now for making you break your oath?'

He lost his breath at her question. Not because he would hate her. He would not. But he had refused any thoughts of marriage for so long for such strong reasons, he wondered if he would simply be able to accept it and let his reservations and fears go.

'I will not hate you, Isobel. I think it was clear to both of us long ago that the feelings we have for each other speak of something other than that.'

She blushed then and glanced away, he hoped remembering the passion between them that night outside his chamber. A passion that promised to burn and delight them if allowed to burst into fullness. If he had not destroyed it in last night's debauchery. She tucked some loosened strands of her hair behind her ear and met his gaze once more.

'More than that, I…' He stopped then, trying to put into words how he felt. Athdar was not accustomed to sharing such things with a woman, but this situation was far different from any previous betrothal or relationship and Isobel deserved to know. 'I admit that I wanted no wife, for many reasons, but now that you are she, I think we can accommodate ourselves to it. And my first order as your husband is to stop trouncing me in our games of chess.' She laughed and he let the sound of it seep into his soul.

He could not admit to the depth of his feelings for her. Not tell her how much he liked and admired her. Not tell her how much he appreciated the way she'd acted more as part of his clan than as a guest these past weeks. For now, she knew of his attraction to her and the growing passion between them.

That would be enough for now. He would let her find her way in this and follow her lead.

And, God and the fates willing, they would have an understanding before her father arrived at his gates.

Chapter Fourteen

Lairig Dubh

'He comes,' Connor said to his wife as he watched Rurik approach the keep from the yard. 'And he looks none too happy about this.'

'I did not expect him to be happy, Connor,' Jocelyn replied. 'I—'

'I think I know what you had in mind, love. I just think you meddled far more in this than you should have. He has the right as her father…' His words drifted off as the topic of their discussion threw open the door and strode inside.

'Connor, there is still no word,' Rurik bellowed. 'None.'

'And there will not be any until the pass clears, Rurik,' he answered. He read the worry and the anger in his commander's, and friend's, eyes.

'She will be cared for, Rurik,' Jocelyn said softly. 'She is safe until we can travel back to her.'

'Your idea of safe and mine differs, Jocelyn, when your brother is involved.'

Connor watched as Jocelyn took offence at the words

and tone of Rurik's words and stepped between them. For as long as he'd been married to Jocelyn, he had never seen Rurik take a stance against her in any matter, so Connor was not quite certain about this disagreement. Still, his words had been an insult to Jocelyn's brother, one even he could hear.

'Athdar knows your feelings about him, Rurik. As does Isobel.'

'As does everyone here in Lairig Dubh,' Jocelyn muttered under her breath. Crossing her arms over her chest, she mirrored Rurik's stance. The battle was on and he stood in the middle of his long-time friend and the commander of all MacLerie warriors and his wife. Not an enviable place to be. He let out a sigh.

'He is an ally and my brother-by-marriage, pledged in fealty to my service, Rurik. He answers to me.'

'She is my daughter. He answers to me.'

A stalemate for now, knowing that Rurik would never disobey a direct order. 'When the pass opens, we will send some men to retrieve her.' When Rurik rose to his full height, Connor recognised his discontent and desire to argue. 'Those are my orders for now, Rurik. You have your duties—see to them now and until I give you leave to do anything else.'

'But, Connor…' he began.

Damn it, where was Duncan, his peacemaker, when he needed him for things like this?

'You may not like him, but Isobel is safe. She is her father's daughter and will not be taken advantage of or abused. You know it and I know it,' he offered, trying to reduce the tension in the situation.

A stricken expression filled Rurik's eyes for a second at Connor's reference to Isobel as Rurik's daughter and, if he had not been staring at his friend in that exact moment, Connor would have missed it. Something ran deeper here than Connor knew about. Rurik was hiding something about Isobel. He thought Rurik might have realised the slip, for he nodded to both of them and left without another word.

Connor faced his wife and could tell with a glance that she'd seen it, as well, but there did not seem to be the surprise in her gaze that he must have in his own. She knew something. She knew whatever it was that Rurik kept secret about Isobel. And from the unseemly haste in which she bid him farewell and left, almost on Rurik's heels, Connor suddenly felt like the only one who did not know.

And as the MacLerie and Earl of Douran, he did not like that feeling.

MacCallum lands

If, at this moment, she was exactly where she wanted most to be, why did she feel so horribly guilty? So guilty, in fact, that she wished the MacCallums had a priest here so he could hear her confession. As she sat at table in the hall, next to her husband, accepting the salutations of his kith and kin, all she could think of was the deception she was committing.

Oh, she had tried to tell the truth. First with Nessa and Jean and then to Athdar himself. But they all seemed to want to be deceived by the half-truths they thought they saw.

Isobel understood why he had offered her a handfasting union. Even if they believed her, someone would not. There would always be stories and questions about the real truth and her reputation and honour would suffer. Honour, to be preserved, demanded satisfaction and, short of her father killing Athdar, marriage was considered the correct, long-standing and customary response.

So, here she sat. Lady MacCallum. Married to the man she wanted to marry. Married to a man who did not want this. She glanced around the hall at the subdued wedding supper and wondered if any other man had been so dead set against marriage and then forced into it against his will? Could any good come of this? In the yard, he had sought atonement for what he thought he'd done to her, allowing his men to batter the sin out of him.

What then could she do to expiate her sins?

Their talk this morning, after he attempted to die for dishonouring her, had gone well. She tried to admit he'd not done what he thought he had, but he was intent on believing it…or suspecting it, for he had no memory of what had happened. After being battered and bruised in the yard, there was no way to differentiate the cut on his hand from the broken jug from any of the many other slashes and tears in his flesh.

Athdar rose and went to speak with his friend's widow. As she watched him speaking quietly to Ailis now that her husband had been laid to rest, a thought of how she could atone struck her.

If she simply carried out her original plan now, to show him that his worries about marrying again had nothing to do with a curse of God or the fates, she might actually help him.

Curses, she'd discovered in her readings, were like a good story—a small kernel of truth surrounded by layers and layers of lies, told convincingly over and over again. Athdar might believe in some curse, but Isobel would look closer with an unbiased eye to find that truth.

There was no other person who could seek the truth about his actions—the strange and frightening lapses in his memory, the inappropriate rages and more that none spoke of but knew of for a certain. As his wife, she could offer him solace in his moments of need. She could watch over him and protect him in ways no one else could or would, whether they be kith or kin.

Only his wife would have standing and power to do it. So, though she thought to marry him and simply prove the silliness of a curse, mayhap now her wifely task would be to save him from the darkness and loss she'd witnessed within him?

If she became the wife she knew he needed, one who loved him and stood by his side and encouraged him to be the man and laird she knew he could be, one who was faithful and useful, mayhap he could find it in his heart to forgive her when he discovered the truth?

For, the first he bedded her, he would find her virginity intact and expose the lie.

From his words, he would not rush that event, so it gave her time to show him that she was perfect for him, and to discover why he believed himself responsible for Robbie's death. And who the others were he mentioned. And why he thought that the women he'd chosen to marry were part of some curse.

Athdar rose from the stool next to Ailis and returned to her, hesitantly placing his hand on hers. This could be the nice part of being handfasted—she did not have to act demur when he touched her. She could accept it and some time soon, when they were accustomed to each other, even instigate it herself.

'I would speak with you about something, Isobel,' he said, sitting in his chair and leaning in nearer to her for a private moment. She noticed he did not release her hand.

'What is it, Dar?' she asked. His eyes widened at her use of it. 'If you would prefer me to call you Athdar…?'

'Nay, I like the way it sounds coming from you. My question is rather would you prefer to remain in your own chamber or if you will move into mine?'

There was a gleam of hope in his gaze as he asked her. Once more, giving her the power to decide something this personal. But then, it was not a private matter, was it? The whole clan would know she kept separate chambers and would believe that his actions had not made things right. Worse, it would give lie to his claim and public declaration that they had handfasted last night before he shared her bed if she now refused to sleep in his.

'Which would you prefer?' she asked him back. Other than for duty and honour and to right what he thought he'd done wrong, he'd given no indication what he wanted of her. He looked away and then back at her before speaking.

'Many marriages have begun on less than what we have between us, Bel. You know I like and respect you. You know I want you. I would like this to be as though tonight is our first night. I cannot take back what happened, but I swear it will never be like that again between us.'

He lifted her hand to his mouth and touched his lips to the inside of her wrist, sending chills of fire down her body. There was danger here, for if she granted his request, it would take her, take them, down a path from which there was no return.

And yet, was that not what had brought her here? It was not as though she wished for a different ending—she had come here intent on convincing him that marriage between them was the right thing.

So, why was she hesitating?

'Aye, Dar. I will share your chamber.'

He called one of the servants over and sent her off to find Glenna as soon as Isobel gave her consent. By the time they sought their rest, it would be together in his chamber. The guilt about allowing him to believe the lie still assailed her and Isobel made a promise to herself—until she knew he committed freely to this marriage, she would not allow him to consummate it. That way, when the year had passed, they would have no reason to reaffirm it in a formal marriage.

When the meal was done, Athdar stood and held out his hand to her. Taking it, she walked with him to his chamber. It felt incredibly strange to be permitted to enter a bedchamber alone with him and a bubble of laughter escaped as she watched him close the door behind them.

'After trying for so long not to be alone together, that seemed too easy,' she said to explain her mirth. 'Sinful somehow.'

Then she looked around the chamber. It was not as large as she thought it would be and rather sparse in its furnishings. A bed. Two trunks. A small table and chairs in the corner. A hearth. The other chamber seemed larger than this one.

'I do not spend much time here, other than to sleep. Unlike Connor, I keep this private and use the clerk's room for estate business.'

'Why do you not have a clerk?' she asked, as he paced around the chamber as though uncertain of what to do next. 'Your lands and holdings are large enough to warrant one.'

'I have just not tended to such things in the past.

Sometimes 'tis just easier to handle matters myself,' he explained. 'So, we are avoiding the obvious, are we not?'

Did he expect her to undress before him? Did he sleep naked? She glanced at the bed. 'You do not wish to discuss inviting a holy brother into your household?'

Isobel had the great ability to change the subject or, rather, to return to a previous one to avoid the current one if she so wished. A holy brother was the last thing he wished to talk about with her. But, from the way her hands trembled, the way she shifted from one foot to the other and the way she glanced at everything in the room but him, he knew she was nervous.

'Ah. I forgot to give Broc instructions for the morn. Let me go back down to the hall before he retires.'

Puzzlement and a frown flitted over her lovely face.

'Why not get settled for sleep and I will return shortly?' he asked, walking to the door. He would give her time to undress and get in the bed.

She nodded as he left. He did go back to the hall, but not to speak to Broc. Retrieving the chessboard and pieces, he thought it could help ease the strain between them in his chambers. And give them a way to regain their footing with each other. He did not rush or dawdle for he did not want it reported among his kith and kin that he avoided his chamber on this night. When a few minutes had passed, and no sounds came from within, he lifted the latch and entered.

Isobel lay in his bed.

He swallowed and then again, taking in the sight of a woman he'd wanted, but never thought he could have. He had pushed her away and pushed away the thought of any woman in his bed and in his heart for so long, this did not feel real and true to him.

Yet, Isobel lay in his bed.

He did not know, could not tell from where he stood if she slept yet, so he placed the chess game on the table, having a care to be quiet, and then he walked slowly towards the bed. Halfway across the chamber, he could see that she watched him.

'Ah, you are awake,' he said.

'I did not know where to settle. Do you sleep on one side or the other?' she asked, touching each side of the bed.

'I sleep all over it, I fear,' he admitted. It had been so long since he'd shared a bed with a woman—for sleep— that he could not remember. 'And you?'

'I have shared a bed when cousins visit and they have said that I, like you, sleep all over it. So choose a side,' she said.

'I will take this side,' he said, pointing to the one closer to the door.

She slid over and made room for him without hesitation. A good sign, that. He went around the room and blew out the candles that the servants had lit. Leaving only the one on the small table next to the bed, he turned his back and loosened his belt. He lifted the plaid from his shoulders and placed it over a chair. Then he dragged his trews off, leaving only his shirt on.

He listened to her breathing behind him. Each garment he removed was met with a slight pause, then she began anew. Athdar could feel her scrutiny as he undressed, but worried if she was simply being wary or if her curiosity was still strong. He hoped so. Turning, he walked to the empty side of the bed and climbed up on it. The ropes beneath the mattress groaned from his added weight.

Athdar found his body wanted to sleep as soon as

he settled on the bed. Between the amount of whisky he'd consumed yesterday, the beating he'd taken this morn and everything else that had happened all day long, he was exhausted. Without a word to her, he sank into sleep's grasp.

He woke when he felt her touch.

Startled at first, forgetting she lay at his side, he found her on her side facing him, tracing her finger along his shoulder and arm. The touch was light, not quite a caress and sometimes so gentle he thought he might be dreaming it. Then she slid it up to his neck and began gliding it along the edge of his jaw and cheeks. He did not move for fear she would stop her exploration.

Then, she dropped her hand and closed her eyes. He stared at her for a few minutes, deciding she was asleep and then slipped his hand around hers.

The second morning of waking with her at his side was much different than the first one.

His head did not hurt quite as much as the first time.

He was not met with a screeching servant and destroyed chamber.

Nay, on their second morning together, he woke alone to an empty chamber.

Chapter Fifteen

He slept like the dead. Far from taking over the whole of the bed as he'd threatened, he had not moved once he climbed on the bed and positioned himself there.

Laying on top of the bedcovers was his attempt to ease things between them and she accepted it. But some time in the night, he had slept so deeply that she did not think him breathing. Rather than shake him awake, she touched him, reaching over and sliding her finger along the muscles of his shoulder and arm. He shuddered so she knew he was alive.

Unfortunately, she wanted to touch more of him—so she did. Gently she slid just the tip of her finger along his neck and around the masculine curves, angles and planes of his face. She did what she had not been permitted to do before—touch him. He had drawn in a deep breath and she feared disturbing his much-needed rest.

Isobel lay quiet and unmoving then until his breath changed back into a slow, deep, easy pace. Deciding that she was much too awake to sleep, she slid from the bed, picked up his plaid and left the chamber. Her feet took her to her destination before her mind even knew it and she stood before the loom in the hall. She waited for her eyes to adjust to the dark and then sat before it, picking up the shuttle.

Her hands had moved more by practice than sight, adding several rows of new weaving before the sun's light began to brighten the day. Realising she should not be seen here, Isobel climbed the stairs and went to her old chamber, seeking out her clothing and other belongings so she could dress. The scant choice of gowns and not many personal items there reminded her of her need for more—at least until she could send for her things.

The thought made her homesick for a moment. What must her mother think of her escapade? How would she react when news of this newest wrinkle in things arrived in Lairig Dubh? She tried not to think about her father's reaction, but they would have to deal with that and the laird's as well. She thought Jocelyn might be able to temper Connor's opinion of this unsanctioned marriage, but her father?

Somehow, though her father could bluster and intimidate most everyone, her heart told her that he would be hurt by her actions more than angered by them. His anger he would no doubt aim at Athdar. After seeing her father take on Rob Mathieson when he came to claim her cousin Lilidh's hand, she knew the damage he would rain down on Athdar.

Well, what would be, would be, and she doubted that anyone short of Connor, and possibly not even he, could stop her father from seeking his own satisfaction for Athdar taking her in marriage without his consent.

Mayhap 'tis better to beg forgiveness than to ask permission?

Lady Jocelyn's words repeated in her thoughts. She

had little doubt that either action would have displeased her father in the matter of her marriage. So, they would face his wrath when next they met him.

In the meantime, she wanted to take the first steps to help Athdar and to begin their future. So, while weaving she'd sorted out her plan and decided to speak to Athdar for permission to make some changes here at the keep in anticipation of winter.

She was rolling her stockings up when the door flew open. Tossing down her gown, she turned to find Athdar standing in the doorway with a strange look in his eyes.

'What is the matter?' she asked, going to him.

'I woke up and you were gone.'

'Did you think I'd come to my senses finally?' she asked, jesting, but speaking what she suspected was what he'd thought.

'Aye.'

She smiled at him and shook her head. 'I could not sleep so I went to the loom to avoid waking you.'

'When?' he asked, dragging his hands through his hair and rubbing his face.

'An hour or so ago, I think.' She shrugged.

'More than that, I think,' he replied.

'It matters not,' she said. ''Tis something I do when I cannot sleep. Do you mind?' She stopped then, coming to a realisation that she'd not thought of before. 'I supposed that now I must get your permission for my actions?' He squinted at her. 'As my husband, I suppose you can tell me what to do.'

He laughed then, a true and hearty laugh, and Isobel liked the look and sound of it. His face lost most of the haunted look and she could see the younger man who lived within him. His deep voice echoed in the laughter and she smiled.

'Spoken by a woman who has never been married,' he said.

'As I am,' she answered. 'Mayhap I should seek out Nessa and Jean for counsel on such matters?'

He wiped his face then and shook his head. 'Aye, as your husband I am entitled to tell you what to do or not do, but as a man who has done this before, I have learned it's best not to try that.' He stepped back as she walked out the door. 'What plans do you have for this day?'

'I thought of that while at the loom,' she said. 'There are a few things…' She paused, not certain how he would respond to her desire to not only move things around in his home, but to bring in an outsider to see to some tasks he now did.

'Are there some changes you wish made here in the keep? Or in the village?' he asked. When she frowned, he shrugged. 'Every woman I have ever known wants something moved or changed. So, have at it.'

'You do not mind?' she asked. 'Should I tell you or rather ask you beforehand?'

'Nay. Though we did not accomplish it the more traditional way, you are lady here now. It is your home. Do as you wish.'

Mayhap his past experiences being married had led him to this manner of thinking about his wife's place? Her own mother exerted quite a bit of control over their household, though if you asked her father he would deny it. As would Connor about the amount of autonomy that Jocelyn had over Lairig Dubh. But, thinking about it, she realised that her mother and the lady always found a way to make their husbands believe that changes had been their ideas. It seemed to make changes more palatable.

'My thanks, Athdar. I will not change anything significantly without your permission, of course.' She faced him. 'I am going to the kitchens to speak to Jean and Ceard. Will you be down to break your fast soon?'

'Have a care if you think to suggest changes to anything in Ceard's kitchens,' he suggested. 'He does not take well to changes in the way he runs his kitchens.'

She nodded and went on her way, pleased that he would give his support. Many greeted her as she walked through the hall and in the kitchen. Ceard even paused and called her 'Lady MacCallum' twice in their conversation. She noticed that Jean glared at him several times during their talk and suspected that the cook's wife had more control of the cook's kitchens than his laird realised.

A short time later, she sat at Athdar's side as they broke their fast with steaming bowls of porridge, served up with brown bread and butter. Filled and refreshed, she bid Athdar farewell as he headed out to the village to work with the men there, repairing and readying several of the cottages and outbuildings where harvested crops were stored.

She spent her day much as the past days, part of the time with Laria and part working the loom. It would take her some time to learn all of her duties and to begin oversight of many tasks left to others in the years since there was a lady in place here. One thing she did see to, something she thought sorely missing, was the care of Athdar's chambers. It took some time to do, but she hoped he would be pleased by it.

Soon, the men returned to the keep as the sun set and supper was ready to be served.

But all she could think about was the night that would follow.

* * *

Athdar thought that he might have accomplished something good in a very bad way. And all day long, as he worked along with his carpenters and masons to make repairs to some cottages damaged in recent storms and to enlarge two storage barns on the edge of the village near the fields, he thought about Isobel going about her own duties.

Mairi had been more than competent and a wonderful helpmate to him as he became laird on his father's passing. Two years older than he, she had brought a certain quiet grace to the hall and they got along well as they learned to love each other. Everything seemed brighter then, coloured by their love no doubt, and many things were done the way she did them even now.

Seonag was, by the time he remarried, a younger lass, but her skills did not lie in running his household so much as managing the estate records. She had a keen mind for numbers and it was then that Athdar had stopped using a cleric to do that. She also taught him how to, so he continued after her death.

After that, various women among his older cousins and such took over some of the duties while Broc and even Padruig handled others. He would always hear Seonag admonishing him about keeping the numbers well, so he held on to that for more sentimental reasons than anything else.

And now? Isobel had a kind heart and he did not doubt that the changes she wanted involved helping some of those she deemed in need. Her visits to the village and to the weavers who worked in their own cottages were at the centre of it, he thought. She also had an extensive education and a sharp mind, so she could be an advantage to him in many, many ways…though right now, his body could think of one.

He'd been so wrapped up in his thoughts about Isobel, he never realised that all the other men had stopped working and now stared at him. Athdar shook off his reverie and looked at them.

'What is it? What?' He put down the mallet he used and wiped his hands on his trews, trying to remember what they were speaking about just a moment ago.

Broc nudged the man standing next to him. 'Did I not tell you? In spite of all his arguments all these years, he has taken to marriage like a pig in shit!' Athdar realised he must have looked like a moonstruck lad standing there, unmoving with his tool poised to strike…and not.

'The lady will put an end to his drinking,' another man said.

'Already did, from the looks of him.' Connal smacked his back and laughed. For a man recently entrapped by Isobel's charm, Athdar suspected Connal understood her appeal.

And though he did not feel as though she controlled him as a wife to a husband yet, Athdar knew to a certainty that she could…very easily…very quickly.

So, being trapped for honour's sake and in reparation for what he'd done to her was not a bad thing? Not if she could forgive him? Mayhap by this marriage not being his choice, things would work out? If he did not pursue it, she might be safe from the curse that seemed to strike every woman he chose.

'Enough!' he said, waving them off. 'There's work to be done here.' He tried to say it in a serious tone, to warn them off this teasing and taunting, but it came out on a laugh. 'I have a new wife to get back to, so let's finish this.'

Athdar knew that it was not like that between them, but he hoped that it could be. If he did not seek out a wife, if it happened without intention, then things might work out for them. This handfasting might be the answer to the curse he felt had followed him for his whole life.

The day passed slowly for him. Every time he glanced up at the sun to estimate how much more daylight they had, it seemed to be standing still in the sky. Each task completed was followed by another and another and yet another. He dared not complain or ask about the unending work or he would face more taunting.

Finally, the sun began to slide down the slope of the western sky and they gathered up their tools and supplies. There was more to be done on the morrow, so plans were made about where to meet and who would do what before they returned to their cottages or the keep. If Athdar's steps were a bit rushed or if he reached the keep ahead of the others, no one said a word. Though many, many knowing glances were thrown in his direction!

He did not see her when he entered the keep, so he sought out his chambers to change from the filthy clothing he'd worn for working into something less so. He opened the door to find the room within transformed into something…comfortable.

Athdar walked in and discovered more surprises awaiting him.

A bucket of water, still steaming, a basin, a bowl of soap and a washing cloth sat on one of his trunks.

A clean pair of trews and a shirt lay on the bed waiting for him.

A pitcher of ale and some bread.

A fire, well set and well tended, warmed the room.

All of this was different from what usually awaited him—nothing. An empty, cold chamber, his garments in the trunk, water for washing outside in the barrel next to the stables.

Isobel had clearly embraced her role as lady and wife as it came to seeing to his comfort and Athdar found he liked this.

He had washed and dressed quickly, wanting to find and thank her. Admonishing himself for nearly running down the stairs and through the hall, he slowed himself to a walk and looked for her. The hall began filling with those who took their meals with him here, so he went towards the table at the front. Reaching it, he spied Isobel walking in from the kitchens. He did not sit, but met her halfway and took her hand.

'My thanks for…' He glanced towards the upper chambers and kissed her hand.

'Everything was to your liking, then?' she asked, with a becoming blush rising into her cream-coloured cheeks. He noticed that she did not take her hand from his.

'Aye. I felt well tended.' He laughed then and kissed her hand again before releasing it. 'My thanks, Isobel.'

She began to speak, but not the way the self-assured Isobel usually did. This time, she stammered a bit, looking embarrassed by his compliments. Then, distracted by something behind him, she took his hand and led him to the table.

'Supper is ready,' she said in a loud voice.

Though he did not know what she'd planned, it was apparent that the women in the hall did. They pushed

and tugged and directed everyone to sit as Isobel did…
as he did. Then, the doors to the kitchen opened and
servants brought out platters of food.

As they ate, he noticed her signalling to servants and
watched their prompt actions in reply. It had not taken
her long at all to make a few changes. None of the servants, or even Ceard or Jean when they came out of
the kitchens, seemed bothered by the changes. His cup
was filled and his plate full, so he was pleased. From
the expression of satisfaction in her eyes and from the
matching ones on those serving the meal, Athdar understood she'd involved them in this change and they
did it for her.

'So,' he whispered as he leaned in towards her, 'how
did you accomplish such a magical thing? Ceard is not
known to be co-operative about changing the way he
runs things.'

'I pointed out that these few, small changes would
mean his chores would be completed earlier each night.
He seemed pleased by that idea.'

She'd found the man's weakness and used it against
him. It was a lesson he would need to be wary of when
dealing with her, he thought.

'Fear not, though,' she whispered. 'There will also
be a pot of stew or porridge waiting for anyone carrying out their duties past suppertime.'

So, she'd not missed the one thing that was Jean's
concern while getting Ceard to comply with her wishes.
Masterfully done.

They finished the meal and she motioned for him to
stand, a signal set by her for the other servants to clear
the table. He found he liked having everything there
until finished.

'I noticed the board set and ready in my chamber. Does this mean you are ready for a challenge?' he asked, taking her hand and marvelling that she let him do so. A good sign—she was becoming comfortable with his touch.

'Aye. A challenge for certain,' she said, nodding and smiling at some of those following her directions without her uttering a word to them. 'No quarter asked.'

'And none given, lady,' he replied.

It was a custom in Connor's home to say that and declare it an honest, no-holds-barred match. Whether the players be men or women, they were expected to play to the best of their abilities, no matter their opponent. He'd never noticed she'd never promised that in their earlier matches, leading him to the realisation that she'd let him win more than he thought she had.

As they climbed the steps leading to the bedchamber, he also knew he stood no chance of winning any game against her if they played in the privacy of a bedchamber. His mind would be on many, many things and none of them would involve which piece to play. More likely than not, he would be thinking about how to get her out of her gown or into his arms.

As he was at this moment.

So, if he wanted to put her at ease with him and even the balance of power in the game, he would need to come up with a plan that would bother her as much as her nearness in the face of his good intentions not to rush her bothered and stymied him. By the time he lifted the latch of his door and opened it for her, he'd come up with something simple and nefarious at the same time.

Chapter Sixteen

She could not catch her breath.

Oh, not from exertions, but from the way he spoke and looked at her. Isobel had feared overstepping in some of the changes she'd made but from his expression as he noticed them, she thought him very pleased.

As she worked this day, going from place to place in the keep, speaking to servants and others who called it home, she realised it was not truly a home—only a place to eat and sleep. Saddened by that and the lack of care that Athdar lived in, she decided a few things needed to be seen to quickly.

His chamber was the first.

She'd noticed the lack of care for him and his clothing when they had first arrived. Oh, she did not fault any of the household servants, for she learned that he had warned them off going in his chambers, giving them leave to do so only once a sennight or so. And though she could claim rightful reasons for her lack of an adequate number of garments now, he had no such claim. From speaking to the woman, Coira was her name, who saw to the laundry, Athdar would bring his clothing to her when he needed it cleaned. Isobel discovered one whole trunk contained worn-out or damaged garments that he never wore.

Coira had shown her to the storage closet where additional lengths of fabric and extra garments were and she availed herself of several for both her and Athdar. If she remained, if this handfasting stood the tests that would face them, she would see to it that his garments were completely replaced.

It was what a wife would do.

Now, he walked close behind her and she could hear his uneven breathing. It reminded her of the night they had kissed in the corridor and her body reacted, remembering the heat and the pleasure she had found with his mouth touching hers. If he kissed her now like he had then, she would not object. Nay, she would even encourage him in spite of the fear of him discovering the truth about her.

She stepped inside and was pleased to see that the water and basin had been emptied and cleaned and the chessboard lay ready on the table. He closed the door behind her and as she stepped away, he took hold of her and pulled her back against him, kissing the back of her head and wrapping an arm around her waist. She fell back against him, enjoying the way he moved her hair aside and kissed the back of her neck. Her body ached with every touch of his mouth on her skin. A throbbing beat deep within her and she wanted…more.

He released her and she tried to regain her balance. Her heart raced in her chest as she walked to the table. Sitting on the far side, she waited for him to sit. He poured her a cup of ale and brought it to her. If she did not gather her wits, this would be a very quick and embarrassing game for her. She drank deeply and tried not to look at him.

Once he sat down, they divided up the pieces and began.

It took an immeasurable amount of concentration to play this game when all she could think about was his mouth. She even found herself staring at his lips as he made his moves. The chamber felt very hot and she wondered if the servants had put too much wood on the fire.

'Before we continue, I would like to place a wager on the outcome,' he said. His voice had a husky edge to it as he spoke. 'The winner receives a boon.'

'A boon?' Her voice sounded squeaky and unnaturally high to her ears. 'What boon?' She needed to know what this wager meant.

'Whatever the winner asks of the loser, she or he must do.'

Her breasts tingled and her mouth burned at his words and she fought the urge to touch either one of them. He meant to do this to her—she could read it in his eyes. But from the way his mouth opened slightly and his breathing changed, it affected him as much. So, her chances of winning and claiming this boon were almost an even match.

Better than even since she had more skill than he did.

But every time he reached for a piece to move, he licked his lips, forcing her attentions there. To his mouth. To remembering how it felt against hers.

So, it was no surprise to her that the game ended with her as the loser. She pushed the pieces aside and faced him, ready to learn the price of his victory. Isobel met his gaze and waited.

'Kiss me.'

She frowned—that could not be his prize, surely not?

'I claim your kiss as my boon.'

'A kiss? Just a kiss?' she asked, not sure how that was a prize worth playing for.

'Whatever and however many you decide, Bel,' he said softly. 'I just want you to kiss me.'

Her body pushed her to move before she could think more about this. A kiss? A single kiss? On his mouth? Or more than that? She stood and walked over to him. He opened his legs so she could step closer to him. He smiled, welcoming her to him. Isobel looked down into his eyes, still trying to work out how to do this, when his next words proved her undoing.

'I beg you, Bel. Kiss me.'

Her mouth was on his without another thought about how or how many. She touched their lips together as he had before. Then she slanted her mouth and took his as she wanted to. Over and over again. Dipping her tongue inside until he touched hers back. Tasting him. Nipping at his mouth.

Leaving his mouth and trying to catch her breath, she traced the tip of her tongue around his jaw and down on to his neck, as he had done. He leaned his head back, giving her an easier path. She kissed where she had touched, tasting the saltiness of his skin, until she reached the place where the curly hair of his chest tickled her face.

Her knees wobbled and she leaned against him, still not done. She felt him rise and harden against her leg, but instead of being fearful, it made her feel powerful. She had done that to him. She had.

Isobel kissed the other side of his neck and then back up to join their mouths. This time, his tongue moved into her mouth and she hoped…she prayed…that he would take control and make her just feel. Instead, his hands never moved from where he'd placed them on his legs. Finally, aching with a need she'd not felt before, she asked him for exactly what she wanted.

'Touch me, Dar,' she whispered. 'Touch me, please.'

She kissed him again, waiting for the feel of his strong hands on her, but they did not move. Isobel leaned back and looked at him.

'Ah, for that, Bel, you must be the victor and claim it as your prize.'

She almost screamed at him. But it took her only a moment to realise he was serious. He still felt guilty, an unnecessary and untrue burden, for what he thought had happened between them. This was another way he atoned—making her the one in charge. She wanted to hit him and kiss him at the same time for this mad scheme of his.

So, she settled for another kiss before stepping back, determined to be the winner of their next game.

He watched as the steely determination he'd seen in her gaze entered it once more. He was getting deeper and deeper in trouble here. What he'd thought of as a way to let her become accustomed to the pleasures that could be between a man and woman would soon become his own downfall. His body ached for release. It had readied itself as soon as she stepped near to him and her plea to touch her simply made his rising flesh like the standing stones in the far field. If he touched her, he would have her beneath him in but a second and he would fill her to her womb in the next.

Nay, regardless of her ardour, she was an innocent and needed to be brought gently into this. A repeat of her first time would destroy any chance between them, so he clenched his fists and let her have at him.

He was strong enough to control this as long as not in whisky's grasp. He would be strong enough.

But, hell, after she placed her mouth on his, he knew he was going to die a painful, agonising, unsatisfied death over this. What a fool he was to make such a challenge!

He watched as she took her seat and placed her pieces on the board. Her face was flushed red, her mouth looked well kissed and plump and inviting. Her breathing was rough, but her body showed every sign of arousal. Ha! Now, the challenge was an even one.

Her play was haphazard at best. He took piece after piece, in spite of her every attempt to win. The only thing that kept him going was her clear desire to have him touch her. He nearly laughed aloud as he finally realised she wanted him to touch her intimately.

So, when he won this game—and it was evident he would—what could he choose as his prize?

He needed to handle her growing passion and desire carefully now after mishandling her body so badly. Step by step. Not too quickly, even if she thought that was what she wanted. He needed to have a care, a great care, for her innocence since he'd taken her virginity with so little.

Athdar knocked over the red king, claiming the game and the victory. For a moment she looked disappointed, but then her eyes lit up and she licked her lips in expectation of his request. Having decided what his boon would be, he stood, walked around the chamber putting out most of the candles and the lantern and banking the fire in the hearth. Then he faced her.

'My boon is…'

He tugged off his boots, loosened his belt and removed it. Then he climbed on the bed and laid down. He tucked his hands behind his head and met her gaze.

'Kiss me again, Bel. Here on the bed,' he said, in a voice that cracked from the desire he felt pouring through his veins.

It was a challenge he never should have made, for he could see her accepting it and plotting his demise, or at least the demise of his self-control. Isobel loosened her own laces and let her gown drop to the floor. She stepped out of it and used her toes to tug her soft leather shoes from her feet. The last thing she did, the one that made him begin to pray, was to take the tie off her braid and shake it free. As the lovely, hip-length blond curls flowed around her, his body shook.

She moved slowly towards the bed, gathering up the bottom edge of her chemise so she could climb up. Kneeling next to him, she moved her gaze over his body as though he was Ceard's latest sweet dessert.

This had been a mistake, possibly the biggest miscalculation he'd ever made in his life. And, from the hungry gleam in her blue-green eyes, she was going to make him pay for doing this.

'More kisses, then?' she asked softly. 'Do you have any rules this time?'

Damn his control! His answer slipped out before he could think about it. 'Just your mouth on me…mine!'

She noticed the slip and smiled, a wicked curving of her lips before she licked them and leaned down to him.

Oh, she began at his mouth, but clever and bold lass that she was, she did not stop there. She tasted his mouth, sliding her tongue to his, plunging it in deeper when his tongue moved away, until she had to stop to take a breath. When she glanced down at his body and shook her head, he should have surrendered and called this off.

'Take this off,' she said, grabbing the hem of his shirt and tugging it up. He leaned up and let her take it off him. When he lay back down, he slid his hands up and took hold of the headboard. He was going to need it.

Her mouth touched him everywhere. Her tongue tasted his skin and her lips kissed a path from his mouth to his stomach, stopping only at the waistband of his trews. His body arched against her mouth over and over again and her gentle laugh taught him not to tease her this way again. Her hair swirled around her, its feather-like touch on his skin intensifying every touch of her mouth.

She paused along the way to touch and outline the various scars he'd gained in fights and battles through his life. And licked and kissed them each in turn. When his hardness twitched against the fabric of his trews, she watched it before looking back at him. He held his breath when he thought she was considering whether or not to give that part of him such attention. Lucky for him this night, she proved how innocent she was and ignored that randy part of him that craved her touch.

Climbing back on to her knees, she came back to his mouth and kissed him, open-mouthed, hot, wanting. Dar knew what she wanted, so he released the headboard and wrapped his arms around her and kissed her back. Rolling so that he covered her, he plundered her mouth the way he'd wanted to, pressing his hardness against the softness of her belly. She tangled her fingers in his hair, held his face to hers and opened to give him as much as he could take. Their tongues danced with each other and nothing was not done then: licking, feeling, tasting, biting...

Hunger. Lust. Need.

He tasted them all in her mouth and gave them back. Then, when he knew he was nearly too far gone, he fell back away from her, panting heavily on the bed. As did she.

A few minutes passed before he felt as though he could breathe and speak again. As the passion cooled, the room felt chilled, so he got up and helped her under the covers, before putting his shirt back on and removing his trews.

He knew he would not sleep this night, not with the erection he had and the heat still pumping through his body. Once she had settled, he lay there, trying not to think about her lush body and her willing mouth. He turned on one side and then on the other.

'I cannot sleep,' she said, her words echoing through the chamber.

'Nor I,' he admitted.

'I will be back,' she said, as she slipped quickly from the bed and left the chamber.

So now he knew he was not the only one left unsatisfied.

He knew also where she would go and that she was safe, so he remained there abed, trying to cool his blood. Some minutes passed and then longer and still she did not return. Part of him felt extraordinarily prideful in a masculine way for having been able to arouse her like that. But the randy part chastised him for not seeking satisfaction. There would be time enough for that between them.

The room grew colder, the bed chilled and he no longer wished to be there alone, so he went to find her.

The cold stone floor felt good somehow on her stockinged feet. She needed the coolness on her skin. She would have peeled off the length of plaid wrapped over her chemise and rolled on the floor if she thought it would help her. Sitting before the loom, she tried over and over to find the rhythm needed.

And could not.

Knowing that no one was watching her now in the dark, she dropped the plaid and let the chill air of the hall permeate the thin linen of the chemise. Her nipples ached. Even the material of the undergarment teased them too much. Finally, minutes passed and her body relaxed.

Passing the shuttle over and under the threads, over and again, she watched the pattern shape under her hands.

This tension within her was the price of her lie.

If he did not think he'd abused her, he would have continued to the conclusion of the act. But convinced he'd hurt her, he would not.

And she knew not how to make him believe the truth before he discovered it for himself.

Mayhap that needed to happen? But would he ever trust her when he discovered the truth and knew that their handfasting was not necessary? Too distracted to think this all through, she turned her thoughts to something that bothered her.

When Athdar was drunk and grieving, he mentioned childhood friends that included Robbie. Yet no one knew the names when she'd mentioned them today. Childhood friends that no one knew? It made no sense, but she decided to speak to Athdar about it.

She'd no sooner thought about him then she could feel him standing behind her.

'It is cold down here, Bel,' he said, draping the woollen plaid over her shoulders.

'The cold felt good,' she said, as she put the shuttle between the threads and wove another row. She liked that he shortened her name to Bel. The first time he'd said it almost on a moan. It was something no one else ever did, save for her father.

'Are you staying here again? Did I drive you from the chamber?'

For all his strength and bravery and self-assurance, a hint of doubt lay under his words. Fear, even. As though he would force her away.

'I am not leaving, Dar,' she said. Turning to face him, she told him what she'd thought most about. 'I am staying, regardless of what my father has to say. If you will keep me, that is?'

'In spite of how things began?' He moved closer to her then, bringing his heat and his strength.

'I worry more that you did not want marriage and now have one. You have been convinced you are a danger somehow. Will that always stand between us or can you reconcile yourself to this?'

Mayhap because she'd watched him for so long it was possible for her to see the pattern in his actions. Before she knew she wanted to help him, she saw it.

'We are joined now, Bel. There is no going back.'

He did not know they had not consummated the public claiming that was part of handfasting. If he did, he might feel differently. That was her worry.

He took her in his arms then, wrapping himself around her and just held her. They stood like that for a short time, until someone asleep near the front of the hall coughed, reminding them that there was no privacy here.

'Come,' he said, taking her hand and leading her back to their chamber.

'There was something I wanted to ask you about, but forgot,' she said as they reached their room and he closed the door. 'You said something strange when you…when you were drunk. I asked Nessa and Jean, but they have never heard about the people you mentioned.'

He lifted the bedcovers and she climbed under them. He remained on top as he had last night.

'I cannot believe that neither Nessa nor Jean knew people who I knew. They are the same age I am.' He shook his head and shrugged. 'Whose names did I speak of?'

If he could not remember what happened or did not between them, it should be no surprise he did not remember speaking of childhood friends.

'You mentioned Robbie, of course. That is how it began,' she explained. 'Then Duff, Kennan and Jamie.'

Though his body reacted, he shook his head, denying he remembered. 'I do not remember.'

'I understand that. But who are they? Who were they?'

He shook his head again. 'I do not know those names. I had no such friends.'

'I must have been mistaken,' she said. In the face of his denial, it was foolish to insist he knew boys or men he claimed not to know.

She lay quietly for a while, waiting for sleep to take her. Athdar was quiet, too, then. Isobel had just fallen asleep when the screaming began.

Chapter Seventeen

Isobel stood in the corner of their chamber, staring in terror at him. Athdar had no idea of when she left their bed or what had happened. He tried to get out of bed to go to her, but his arms and legs would not move. Looking down, he realised he was completely tangled in the bedcovers.

And covered in sweat.

The door crashed open at that moment. Two guards came running in, followed by Broc. Weapons at the ready, it was clear they expected the worse here.

'Halt!' he yelled, finally freeing himself from the bed and going to Isobel. Her face was as grey as the ash in the hearth and she was shaking. He stumbled across the chamber and slowed before he reached her.

'Isobel? Are you well, lass?' he asked.

She blinked several times as though finally seeing him and then shook her head. Broc approached after waving the guards out.

'We could hear you below,' he said. His expression was dark with concern. 'What happened?'

'Me? What do you mean?' Athdar asked without taking his eyes off her. From the way it looked, she was the one who must have been yelling.

'It sounded as though you were under attack. You were shouting. Loud enough to wake most everyone in the keep.'

Athdar looked at Isobel and she nodded, still shaking.

'I am awake now,' he said, lowering his voice. 'You can go now.'

Broc looked at Isobel and waited for her nod before bowing to both of them and leaving.

'Here. Come. Sit.' He held out his hand to her and she took it with one of her trembling hands. She walked to one of the chairs and sat down. 'Can you tell me what happened?'

'You do not remember?' she asked, narrowing her gaze as she searched his face. 'None of it?'

He glanced over at the bed, at the bedcovers twisted and pulled loose, and back at her. He poured a cup of ale from the pitcher and drank it down. Then he filled it again and pressed it into her hands and waited for her to drink of it.

'None of it, truly. Tell me, please?'

'You had just fallen asleep when you began thrashing. I moved aside and tried to wake you. You opened your eyes and looked at me, but Athdar, you did not see me.' She shivered, then shook her head. 'You looked right through me.'

He did not remember any of this. Pushing the hair out of his face, he stared at the bed, willing himself to remember.

'Then it seemed like you were running and falling and screaming all the while. No words. Sounds. Like... like the screams of a wounded animal.'

'I…' He could think of no explanation, nothing, to say to her. But the worst thought did come then. 'Did I hurt you, Isobel?'

'Oh, nay, Athdar. You would never do that,' she said as she put the cup down and came to his side where he sat. She stroked his hair and put her hand on his shoulder now. 'It was difficult to watch and not be able to help you in some way.'

He was at a loss for words, for an explanation, of any of this. One thing was clear—he had terrified Isobel. How could he not remember?

'Here now, go back to bed,' he said. He stood and guided her to the bed. 'I want to go talk to Broc.'

'Why not wait until morn?' she asked. 'Let it go for now.'

He was going to ignore her suggestion, but the exhaustion struck him then. Waiting until morning would not hurt anything. Mayhap by then he would remember something about it?

She moved over and he climbed on the bed next to her. Though he suspected she would not sleep, she did and did it quickly. The touching thing was that she slipped her hand into his before doing so.

The hours had passed slowly then. He watched as the first rays of the sun began to bring light back to the chamber. When the sound of the servants going about their duties trickled in, Athdar slid from the bed, leaving her there asleep and sought out Broc…and some answers, he hoped.

He received some strange glances all through the morning, some bold and direct, others more surreptitiously given, as he carried out his duties. After having kept Isobel up most of the night, he gave orders to let her sleep this morn. He was sure there would be hell to pay, but she needed some rest. Instead of remaining in the hall to break his fast, he took some bread and cheese and a skin of ale and walked to the village to survey the work being done.

While in the village, he sought out one of his father's kin, an old cousin who had lived there all his life. Athdar had a strange feeling that what had happened last night, had happened before. Something about it seemed familiar and yet he could not draw it to his mind. Old Iain lived with his granddaughter and still had the biting sense of humour Athdar always remembered of him.

'Iain, you lived in the keep when I was a child, did you not?' he asked, once they were alone. Iain's granddaughter seemed to know he wanted a private talk with her father, so she'd taken her bairn and gone to visit a friend.

'Aye. I was in charge of the stables then.' Iain laughed loudly then at some memory only he knew. 'Taught ye to ride yer first horse, I did. Ye were a canny lad when it came to horses. Aye, ye were.' The old man reached inside his tunic and pulled out a flask. After taking a swig, he offered it to Athdar. He took a mouthful and handed it back.

'Do you remember any stories about…well, about me having night terrors?' He was embarrassed to ask, but could think of no other way to bring up the subject.

'Yer sister was a terror,' he said. 'Drove yer maither nigh to madness, but lasses can be like that, ye ken?' He laughed again. 'My own Jessie there—' he nodded in the direction where his granddaughter had gone '—she gave me a fair run as weel.'

'Do you remember stories about me?' Athdar asked

once more, hoping he could guide the man's wandering mind back to the topic. 'When I was a boy?'

Iain closed his eyes and for a moment Athdar thought him sleeping. Then he opened them and stared right at him.

'After that summer, ye did. Sometimes in the night. Sometimes in the day. Ye would lose yer way and wake someplace else wi'oot remembering how ye got there. Yer da would say the nights were the worst time. They sent ye to yer uncle's until it passed.'

'Which summer, Iain?' he asked. The old man ignored him or forgot to answer, Athdar did not know which. 'How many years did I have then, Iain?'

'The sad summer,' he finally said. 'Sad days, those.' Iain seemed to drift off into his thoughts then.

Shocked, but at the same time not, he knew now that last night was not the first time something like that had happened. But in all these years, he did not remember it. 'Since then, Iain? Do you know of any other times since then?'

'Did ye ken I taught ye to ride yer first horse? Aye, I did indeed. A big, black one. Yer maither, God rest her soul, feared ye would be killed, but yer da was proud of ye.'

Iain looked off in the distance and began telling his granddaughter, who had not yet returned, of Athdar's skills on a horse. The man's lucid moments gone, Athdar thanked him and left. Jessie waited a short distance from the cottage and passed him as he walked back to the main part of the village.

Troubled and puzzled by the man's words, he wondered if some illness he'd suffered as a child had returned now. But what was it and why now? Surely Jocelyn would have spoken to him about such a thing?

She was older by a couple of years and would have re-membered. It made no sense that she would keep such a thing from him.

The only thing he could do was to see if it subsided or worsened over the coming days. With little more in-formation than what he knew before, Athdar returned to the village and worked alongside the men to complete the repairs they'd begun the day before. They had been lucky and the clear skies held for them. As the month of November moved on, there would be fewer and fewer of these days in which to do this kind of work.

They pushed on, later than they usually would have, claiming every moment they could before ending for the day. Satisfied with what they'd accomplished, Athdar, Broc and the others headed back for the keep.

And once more water and clean clothing awaited him and the meal was served when he arrived at the table. But this night there was no sign of Isobel. He asked and was told she had eaten already. No one seemed alarmed by her absence, so he ate along with the others and waited until everyone was finished before letting his curiosity overwhelm him. Leaving the table first, he pulled Nessa aside and discovered that Isobel rested in her old chamber, feeling a bit ill.

He climbed the stairs two at a time and went to her room. Knocking and saying her name softly, he lifted the latch and opened the door. But for a huddled pile in the middle of the bed, he could see nothing but the top of her head peeking out from under the massive pile of bedcovers. Laria sat by the bed and watched him as he entered.

'Does she sleep?' he whispered.

'Nay, she does not' came a muffled reply from the bed, instead of one from Laria. He tried not to laugh over the absolute misery in her voice. She pushed the covers down and began to sit up when Laria ordered her not to move. Even he knew not to disobey the healer's words when given in that tone.

'My thanks for tending to my wife,' he said, glimpsing for a moment the strange expression on the woman's face before it became a tolerant smile. 'I will sit here until she sleeps.'

He expected her to argue—she always did—but instead she rose and held out a small bottle to him.

'Three drops in her ale and she will sleep.'

With that, she turned and left the chamber without another word spoken. As soon as she had, Isobel pushed the covers back and sat up just as she had tried before. She did not look ill, but if she was abed…

'Here now,' he said. 'You should be lying down.' When she gave no sign of listening to him, he warned her, 'Must I get Laria back in here to make you obey?'

'I pray you, no, please.' Isobel sat now, pushing herself back against the headboard of the bed. 'I need to sit up for a bit.' He held out the cup of ale to her. She shook her head and waved it off.

'So what ails you?' he asked. Her bright blush told him not to pursue it, but he did. 'Are you ill? A fever?'

'It will pass, Athdar. By morning I will be fine,' she said, with a peevish tone in her voice. That irritable inflection told him exactly what malady had her abed and it was one most women did not wish to discuss with men. He should have known that.

'Your courses, then?' he asked. She nodded and would not meet his gaze. This was possibly the first time a man other than her father, and he would never have done so, asked her about such a personal matter. No wonder she was peevish. 'So, if you are not contagious, why did you come back here?' Neither Mairi nor Seonag had ever moved out of their chamber for such a thing.

She sighed loudly then and shrugged. For once, the bright, intelligent, fluent-in-several-languages Isobel seemed lost for words. Then she whispered her reply.

'I did not wish to disturb you in your bed,' she said.

'After last night, you mean?' At first he did not think she would answer, but then she nodded.

'I was thinking about you and last night and wondered if I was the cause of the disturbance. After all, you did not want a wife and you were forced into marrying me. I thought mayhap the condition was brought about by that?'

Although he had not thought Old Iain's information very helpful, he decided to share it with her to make her understand that she was not the reason for his sleep disturbances.

'Isobel, I have discovered that I experienced such a condition as a child. Though no one seems to remember how or when it occurred, I was told by an old friend of my father's that it happened for a while in my childhood and then disappeared. Thinking about it, I wonder if Robbie's passing and the grief over that brought it back?'

'What do you think?' she asked.

'I believe it might be so. I cannot know until or unless it happens again, but I suspect that whether you sleep next to me or not will not make a difference in it.' He walked around the chamber, putting out the candles and then motioned for her to slide under the bedcovers. 'But, if it is up to me, I would rather have you in bed with me than to sleep alone...again.'

'But I am...' She could not say more.

'Disobedient? Wilful?' he asked, climbing in with her, this time under the covers. 'Beautiful? Lovely? Warm?' he continued describing her as he pulled her down next to him, turned her on her side and moved up against her. Even with his garments in place, he knew she would feel his hardness, but it mattered not. 'Rest now. I will be here if you need me.'

He felt her body relax into his, curling against him, as her breathing became deeper and slower. With her there, he felt safe somehow and he let sleep overtake him.

Upon waking on the fourth morning of their marriage, Athdar found his wife next to him, no screaming, no chaos, and decided he liked it more than he thought he would.

She felt much better this morn, better in fact than she expected to, but not so well that she did not take advantage of a few extra minutes of dozing comfortably in the warmth of Athdar's embrace. Isobel felt the moment when his body awakened and then when his mind did. It would be difficult not to notice such a thing when lying like this. When she was certain he no longer slept, she spoke.

'You slept?' she asked softly.

'Aye,' he whispered in her ear. 'And you? How do you fare this morn?'

She turned on her back then and looked at him. The terrible, haunted expression was gone and, though he'd slept for some hours, he still looked exhausted. With too many tasks left undone, she knew he would never remain abed.

'Were the repairs finished?' she asked, sliding to the side of the bed and regretting it immediately as the cold air in the chamber surrounded her instead of Athdar's warmth. She went to the trunk that remained in this room and took another borrowed gown from it. She really must see to her own wardrobe soon. 'And the barns?'

'Connal is an excellent carpenter. He directed the building of the framework so the others could add work on the walls. The cottages will stand another winter's assault and we now have more space for the additional crops harvested.'

He got out of bed and stretched to his full height. They'd awoken in the same position as they'd slept, so he was, no doubt, stiff from being in one position. She rolled her neck a few times, working out the spasms there. A soft knock on the door was followed by Glenna's voice.

'Lady?' she asked. 'I've laid out water to wash in the laird's chamber. Do you have need of anything else?'

Isobel opened the door a crack. 'Nay, Glenna. My thanks for remembering. I will see you in the hall.'

'You already have retrained my servants?' She met his gaze and did not see anger or irritation in his eyes. 'That did not take long.'

'I have found that, with few exceptions, your people would have seen to your care if you had let them.'

He winced.

'And that they have been well trained, but not allowed to perform their duties.'

Another wince as the truth struck home. He held his hands up in a gesture of surrender.

'I am gladdened then that my lady wife has freed them from the oppression of their laird and allowed them to work,' he said. His mouth curved into a smile, not the terribly wicked one that made her want to touch her mouth to his and taste it. Nay, this one was genuine and it warmed her heart.

She decided she liked marriage if it meant moments like this between them.

'I am going to dress and will see you in the hall?' she asked.

At his nod, she left and went to his chamber to wash and dress. The first day of her courses were always the worst and she felt better now knowing that was past. Just as Athdar and the men had things to accomplish, so did she…and the women of the village and keep.

It was time to make her first significant change and she hoped he would support her in it.

Is he finally remembering?
Could he be?
'Tis too late now to save the others….
Or himself.

The last death was not pleasing.
The next one will protect the secret.

And the last one?
Him…
Or her?

Chapter Eighteen

He'd seen her in the village as she approached each of the women involved, but she avoided speaking to him while she was planning this change. She'd discovered that the four weavers, all widows with children, each worked separately in their own cottages. During the winters, they could be isolated for weeks at a time due to the storms.

That did not sit well with her.

So, after speaking to Nessa and Jean, her plan was to move them to live in the keep, at least during the winter, and to build a weaving corner in the hall where they could work together. Their children would be kept close, the older ones given chores, and it would benefit everyone. After Athdar's comments about Connal's skill, she approached him to build some screens that could be used to separate the area off from the rest of the hall, making it like a separate room. If this all worked, she would ask Athdar about building a place for them within the walls.

Her dowry, once settled on him, could pay for that and more.

Like another tower where they could have their own

chambers, leaving the rooms on the second storey to others and other uses.

Maybe even to build a keep big enough to be named.

But, the dowry was dependent on her father's approval and she did not want to think about that just yet. For now, she wanted to concentrate on what she could change and that was the weaving.

Connal promised to send his assistant to measure for the screens and Isobel planned to use some of the tapestries she'd found that could not be completely saved or repaired. Cutting them down, she could use the pieces on wooden frames for screens.

Her plans now in place, all she had to do was convince Athdar to permit the changes. As she waited for him to arrive for supper, she decided to use his sister's approach—beg forgiveness rather than ask permission. It would take several more days before it could be accomplished, so she kept it to herself and engaged the servants and others involved to keep her surprise.

Athdar sat next to her at table and studied her face.

She was up to something. Just as he knew when Jocelyn had some plot underway, so did he know with his wife now. He could demand the truth, even force the servants—who wore the very same expression—to reveal it, but Athdar sensed that she, and they, were trying to please him.

How could he be mean-spirited and not allow them that?

Uneasy, he glanced around the hall to see if there was anything different there. Her loom had been moved aside. The tables used for supper moved forwards. Nothing else.

Isobel smiled at him then and he wanted to kiss her.

He leaned closer and when she did not move away, he touched his mouth to hers. For a moment, she opened to him and he deepened the kiss, sliding his hand up under her veil to hold her head to his. Then the growing silence around them forced him to stop. Once conversations had been resumed around the table, he whispered to her.

'Will it be painful, this change you are planning to make?'

She startled and then laughed at his words, not misunderstanding them at all. Then Isobel shook her head.

'Not painful at all…for me.'

He took her hand in his under the table and stroked it until she shivered. 'A hint, mayhap? A small one to put my mind at ease?'

'Nay, Athdar. Everyone is under pain of death if they speak of it before it is complete.'

'I will ask Glenna,' he said, acting as though he would stand. She clasped his hand and pulled him back down.

'She will not speak of it.'

'Laria, then?' He looked around for the healer, but she was nowhere to be seen.

'Laria knows nothing of it.' A smug little smile curved her lips. She still did not release his hand.

'I see I will have to challenge you to a game of chess, then, for the answer.'

Her body reacted to those words in a most appealing way. He watched as a shiver of anticipation shook her. Her skin, from the neckline of her gown up through her face, blushed and he was torn apart with the need for her.

'I think not,' she said. He felt her hand and the leg

on which it rested entwined with his grow warm in reaction to her memories of the boons claimed.

'I think I will reserve those games for other pur-
poses,' he said. 'For other nights.' He lifted their hands
up and kissed hers. 'For this, I suspect waiting is my
only option.'

He heard her expel the breath she'd been holding
within and watched as she nodded.

'I think you may have ruined chess for me,' she admitted, her voice breathy and soft.

'Oh, nay, Isobel. I think that once the purpose of
our game has been met, we will be able to play again.'
She met his gaze then and he saw no hint of fear there.
Nothing but curiosity and desire lay in her blue-green
eyes and he had only to wait on her word. 'You will tell
me when I can challenge you?'

'Aye, Athdar,' she whispered back. He was about to
kiss her again when Padruig called out to him.

'Let the lady eat, Athdar. Give her some peace!' his
friend called down the table to him.

The hall filled with the laughter of friends and family
and Athdar leaned back and allowed her to finish her
meal. They had accepted her as their lady, even helping her in whatever scheme this was she had planned.

He had not told her about the morning in the yard
when she'd stopped him from fighting. Though he battled six, including his closest friend, dozens had challenged him as her champion over his treatment of her.
Dozens had taken her side, believing he had wronged
her in the most grievous of manners.

So, this banding together to help her in her plans did
not surprise him at all. Not at all.

'Is there much more to do in the village?' she asked,
as she put her spoon and napkin on the table. Being the

last one eating, she signalled for the table to be cleared away. 'The old ones say storms are on the way soon.'

'Nay. With the barns done and harvest in, only the butchering and preserving.'

She shuddered then, a look of disgust distorting her lovely face. 'I am fortunate that Broc wishes to oversee that duty.'

She glanced around the hall then, looking for someone.

'Who do you seek?'

'Ailis. I asked her to sup with us.'

'Ailis?'

His eyes went dark and then empty. There was no recognition of the name she'd said at all in them. Watching him, she was reminded of the same kind of blank expression during their chess game here in the hall. He'd been telling her about the strife between him and her father and he had drifted away in his thoughts for a moment when his eyes took on this very empty stare.

'Athdar,' she said quietly so as to not draw the attention of the others at table. She put her hand on his leg and squeezed it. 'Athdar.'

It took a short bit of time before he came back to himself. He blinked several times and then frowned at her. 'Who were you looking for?' He glanced around the hall then, clearly not remembering what she'd said.

'Ailis, Robbie's wife,' she said, watching him closely this time.

'I do not see her,' he said.

'I wonder if she has family to help her through the winter?' she asked, still observing him closely. 'I did hear her mention a son, but no others?'

'Ailis is a MacDougal, from Lorne,' he finally said. 'She may decide to return to her family there.'

Did he even realise the break in his words? That, for more than a moment, he was gone? Lost somewhere in his thoughts or memories? So lost, he did not even know it happened?

Looking around, she was certain that no one else noticed it but her. He shook himself as though waking and stood, holding out his hand to her.

They went to his chamber and he took notice of all the small changes she'd made there. She lay in his bed that night, wrapped in his arms, but slept little.

Something was wrong here. Something was wrong with Athdar and no one else seemed to notice it.

Isobel knew with a soul-deep certainty that she had to get to the bottom of it. But if he did not know that something was awry, who could she ask for help?

Laria. Laria had lived here for decades. Surely, if there was a problem, she would know. When the sun rose the next morning, Isobel decided she would ask the healer.

And Broc. He was the same age as Athdar. He'd grown up in the keep with his father, the last steward. It was possible he would know.

With her purpose set—help Athdar whether he knew he needed it or not—she closed her eyes and sleep came.

Rains arrived instead of the dawn, making all but work inside the keep difficult, if not impossible. Unable to see to moving the looms, Isobel remained inside, claiming some fabric from Coira's trunks and cutting out two new gowns for herself. Her skills were practiced enough to make plain, working gowns, but to make something more ornate, she would need help.

For Athdar, she planned three more shirts and pairs of trews, for he wore his clothing out quickly. The weavers and seamstresses would have plenty of work to do over the winter to get everyone who depended on the laird for the living dressed as they should be.

When she went to speak to Laria, the woman was not in her workroom. Broc, too, was not in the keep, helping with something in the village. Her decision to speak to them would have to wait.

For the next two days, everyone worked at their own tasks, but Isobel did manage to have several men disassemble the four looms in the various cottages and bring the pieces to one of Broc's storage rooms so they were ready to be put back together. Then, taking advantage of his absence on the third day when he and Padruig rode to a nearby village, everything was done, the screens assembled and everyone waited for his return.

Since her courses had finished and there was plenty of time before Athdar was expected back, Isobel had a bath sent up to their chamber. After the hard work of the last few days, the steaming water felt wonderful, soothing away her aches and pains. She thought she might have fallen asleep, only to be awakened by the sound of the door opening and closing behind her. Expecting Glenna to come and help her wash her hair, the deep voice that spoke surprised her.

'Lass, what did you do to my hall?'

She startled and began to stand before remembering that she was naked in a tub. Isobel sank down in the water as low as she could and waved him out. 'Athdar, I am bathing,' she screeched.

'I can see that, Isobel,' he said as he walked around to the front of the tub, making no attempt at all to avert his gaze from all that she exposed in her position. 'Even better, I can see you.'

He reached into the water and touched her leg, sending shivers and chills along it in spite of the steaming heat in the water. Then he encircled her ankle with his fingers and began to lift her leg from the water. She grabbed the sides of the tub to keep her head from going under the water. She realised that the easiest way to keep herself balanced was to let him do it, so she did.

Until he picked up the washing cloth that lay next to the tub, she had no idea of his true purpose. Then he dipped it into the bowl of soft soap and began to spread the lather on her leg. He crouched down, attending to the task with more seriousness than she knew he felt, never moving his gaze from her leg.

He was playing a game with her—she knew it. He was going to continue until she stopped him. How did she play this?

Isobel was going to stop him, but the pure pleasure of his touch, sliding the cloth along her skin, enticed her. Did she act the maiden with him, demur, and object? Or did she allow him what he so clearly wanted? And what her body demanded of her, too?

'Athdar?' she said, shifting so he could lift her leg higher. Then his fingers reached her thigh, kneading the muscles gently with the soapy cloth, and she lost the power to think.

'Isobel?' he replied though he asked no question.

'May I have a boon even if we do not play chess?' She stopped talking then, stopped breathing, she thought, as well, as one of his fingers grazed the place between her legs. Her breath hitched and that place ached as she waited for him to move his fingers again.

'A boon, wife?' He took his hand away then and she almost screamed and dragged it back to where she wanted it most. 'Have you done something that should be rewarded?' He left her leg up on the side of the tub and reached for the other. When she lifted it herself, opening her legs and most every bit of her to his gaze, he laughed. 'Oh, aye, you have.'

She wanted to let her head fall back and simply enjoy the riotous sensations he was causing, but she could not. First, before this could go anything further, was the matter of...

'I want you to bed me,' she said, forcing herself to speak when she wanted to moan as his hand moved on her other leg now.

'Lass, I do not think you have to ask me for that boon,' he said, his voice now a husky whisper.

'That is not the boon,' she said, gasping as the cloth moved higher and higher. Her body answered by arching almost into his hand. 'I need to tell you something first. Before it is too late.'

'Oh, Isobel, it was too late when I walked in this chamber.'

He stopped then and stared at her as he stood and walked behind her once more. The heated breath on her neck was the only warning before his hands began moving down her shoulders towards her...

'Athdar! My boon!' she gasped as she caught hold of his hands and stopped them. 'You must know the truth. I will not deceive you about this any longer.'

He did stop then, lifting his hands and walking back to where he could see her face. His expression grew guarded and he looked ready to face some grave disappointment.

'Tell me your truth, Isobel.'

Sitting there, naked in the water before him, and telling him this secret that stood between them was terribly uncomfortable for her. She brought her legs back into the water and thought on how to make him understand.

'I am still a virgin, Athdar.' The truth, plain and clear.

He frowned and shook his head. 'Why do you defend my actions? I saw the blood on your gown.'

'You cut your hand on the jug and then grabbed my gown. You did not take my virtue by force that night. This handfasting was not necessary and can be annulled. There has been no consummation between us.' She just spit it out in simple statements.

'I did not?' he asked.

'Nay, you did not. Not yet.'

'Thank you,' he whispered heavenwards. 'You are certain?'

She laughed then. After being married to two other women who most certainly came to his bed innocent, she thought he would understand that a woman knew such things. 'Aye. Certain.' She moved, sloshing water over the side—quickly cooling water. 'That brings us to the true problem.'

He walked a few paces away and then turned to her. 'And what is that?'

'Whether or not to wait our year and a day or to annul this now?'

Silence so deafening it hurt her ears filled the room and the space between them. Here was his chance. If he accepted that she spoke the truth, if he spoke now, she knew her father and mother would see to an annulment as soon as she returned home. With all the connections Connor had to the Church, both in funding various churches and monasteries and in donations to their good works, an annulment would be no problem at all.

'You know,' he said in a low voice, 'I knew your intention before you ever arrived at my gates. I may have misjudged the strength of your efforts, but I knew you wanted me to consider marriage to you.'

'Was I that obvious?'

He laughed then and nodded. 'Terribly and completely obvious. But then I was trying to avoid that state and trying to avoid considering you as my wife.'

'And now?' she asked. Her voice trembled because she did not want this to end now. She did not want to return to her parents. She wanted to be here and to be his wife. She wanted him to love her as she did him.

He did not answer her directly. Athdar walked to the door, lifted the wooden bar from its place leaning on the wall and he dropped it down into the brackets on either side of the doorframe. Then he came to her side and held his hand out to her, waiting for her to take it. She met his gaze and recognised the frank desire in his dark eyes.

'Now? Well, I do not want a year and a day to decide. I do not want an annulment. I have decided that I'm keeping you. And after this night, my fair Isobel, there will be no doubt that you are mine.'

Chapter Nineteen

Athdar wanted to fall down on his knees in thanks when she told him her truth.

She said she was a virgin. He had not taken her by force.

Could he believe it, though? She had no reason to lie about something like this. The first time she'd said that nothing had happened between them, he had thought she was just trying to protect him. But now? By giving him a way out, she could avoid coming to his bed. He looked into her eyes and could read the truth there.

She accepted his hand and he helped her to stand in the tub. The water sluiced over the lovely curves and down her limbs as it fell back into the tub. He would have understood if she tried to hide herself from him, but not Isobel. She let him look his fill of her and so he did. He watched the way the pale rose-coloured nipples of her breasts tightened into enticing points that he would taste before long. She let him see the pale, golden curls at the junction of her legs and the long, shapely thighs he'd just touched. Her hair, damp but not wet, swung around her body like a rich, thick curtain and his hands itched to touch it.

Her chest rose and fell rapidly as he bent down and lifted her in his arms. Carrying her over to the bed, he placed her there in the middle and stepped back. She shuddered, but he did not think she was cold. He covered her with one of the large drying cloths and then reached for his own belt.

Isobel's eyes widened as she realised his intention. If he had seen her, it was her chance to see him. She'd touched so much of him with her mouth during the tortuous night of kissing, but now she would see all of him. Peeling off his shirt and trews, he walked back to the tub and washed the dust and sweat of the day's travel off him. Then, with a deep breath, he faced her.

She'd seen naked men before. Bathing at the river. She'd seen her brothers many times, even now that they were young men. But not even having kissed his chest the shameless way she had could have prepared her for Athdar. Aroused and rampant. For her. Isobel swallowed several times and waited as he moved towards her slowly.

Would it be a bad thing to reach out and touch him?

'Nay, lass, not a bad thing.'

She covered her mouth, laughing. She'd not meant to say it aloud but she had. It exposed her desire to him, but instead of making her feel shameful, it made her feel strong. So, she did—she reached out and touched his flesh.

It moved beneath her hand—even as she wrapped her fingers around it she could feel his hot blood pumping through it. Sitting up and kneeling, she drew him closer. He did not resist her at all. His eyes were black with desire now and he panted in short, shallow breaths.

'Does it hurt?' she asked. She gentled her touch then, tracing her fingers around the width of it.

His eyes closed, his head fell back and he moaned.

Her body answered the sound by sending heat and moisture to the place between her legs. It ached there and she wanted him to…to…to do something to make it…more.

She wanted more. 'Athdar,' she whispered. 'I want…'

Those were the last words she remembered speaking for some time.

He took her by the shoulders and brought her face up to his. Then his possession, his claiming of her, began in earnest. She leaned in to him and opened her mouth to his. The kisses began as gentle touches, lips on lips, but soon he took and took and took her mouth, thrusting his tongue inside and suckling on hers. When her hands drifted to his chest and she slid over the rough curls there, he took hold of her head and plundered her mouth until she lost her breath.

He pulled back, but he was not done.

'Lie back,' he said gruffly. He guided her back and then gathered her hair around her head. Then he tormented her as she had done him, showing her how strong his self-control had been.

His mouth moved like a storm over her—touching, tasting, kissing, licking the length of her body. He laved each of her breasts, cupping them and rubbing his thumb across the sensitive tips until her body bucked and arched up off the bed. Then he blew on them before suckling each one. Just when she thought he was done, he touched them again, rubbing the edges of his teeth across them until she moaned.

He laughed then, a wicked one filled with dark, hot promises of pleasure yet to come. She tried to pull him back to kiss her mouth, but he slipped from her grasp, sliding down her body and lying between her legs. She could resist nothing he did, her body pliable under his hands. But when he lowered his mouth, *there*, she grabbed his hair and made him stop.

'Oh, no, lass. I will show you my favourite kind of kiss,' he whispered, moving her legs apart. 'Lift your knees like you did in the tub.' He sounded so pleased, she did it—lifting her knees and opening that most private part of her to him.

Before she could think of such a thing, he was there, tracing the sensitive folds of skin and parting them with his tongue. At first she held his hair, ready to stop his intimate invasion, but then she released her hold and dropped her head back…and just let the sensations overwhelm her.

His mouth. His tongue. His lips. His teeth. Her body blossomed beneath his mouth and he did not pause. Everything within her tightened and ached and tightened more, her blood screaming through her body as she moved towards something. He knew what he did to her; he laughed and dipped in to plunge his tongue deep inside her.

She wanted to beg him for something. Beg to stop. Beg for more, but her hips raised off the bed to meet his tongue's thrusts. Then, just when she though there could be nothing sweeter than the touch of his mouth there, he slid his fingers inside her and she screamed out the pleasure.

More. Worse. Better. More. She chanted in her thoughts as he pushed her harder and faster. He was relentless in forcing her on, bringing her to some edge where her body could take no more and then pushing her harder and further, ever further.

'Athdar,' she moaned out. She wriggled against him

then, pushing her body against his mouth, demanding something of him.

'More. I beg you.'

He slid one finger forwards and touched some small place deep within the folds that made her fly. When his mouth replaced his finger and began licking and suckling it, everything within her began to unravel. She was falling apart in his hands.

Her entire body trembled then, shaking and shivering as the tension he'd built exploded free. From her skin to the very centre of her. From her head to her toes. Everything within her tingled and throbbed, for endless moments…or minutes…or hours. She lost herself then and thought she might fall asleep until she felt him nuzzle the roughness of his day's growth of beard against her there.

His fingers were yet within her and all it took to re-awaken her body was one slow, leisurely stroke of them as he slid them out from between her legs and up to her breasts. Every touch pulled some connection between there and the place he'd just…attended and the aching inside her continued anew.

'Athdar,' she whispered as his mouth came down on one sensitive nipple again. His erect flesh touched her belly as he dipped to taste the other one and she reached to take him in her hands.

He hissed at it and pulled away. 'Nay, lass. Not yet.'

She wanted to argue, but he climbed over her and took her mouth in a hot, breath-losing kiss. He groaned against her lips as she touched his back, moving her hands over the muscles of his chest and then around to his buttocks. Holding them in her hands, she squeezed them as he moved between her legs.

'Easy now, Bel,' he whispered against her mouth. 'Open to me.'

Now. He would take her now. Now.

Her body shook as he placed the head of his flesh where his mouth had just been and pushed against her. He slid deeper and deeper inside of her, the moisture of her release easing the way. Then, suddenly everything felt too much. Too tight. Too much. Too big. Too…

He thrust once and she felt him fill her completely.

Her body tightened around him then and he hissed again as he waited for her to adjust to him. All she could feel was his flesh stretching hers. Then, he moved, just a bit, and her body eased. He withdrew inch by inch until only the slightest part of him remained within her. She felt empty and wanted to protest.

He kissed her then, just as he thrust again, quickly and deeply. And then he did it again…and again. Thrust and drew back, thrust and drew back, until her body poured out for him once more and she felt him swell in her. Then one more time he buried his flesh in hers and she felt the spill of his hot seed.

He whispered her name over and over, in time with the pulses of his flesh, until it stopped. Then he buried his face against her shoulder and panted as she did.

She would be the death of him if it was like this every time they joined.

Though he was glad he could give her pleasure during her initiation into the intimacies between a man and a woman, he never expected she would be so open to it. Her body still held his inside and he did not want to leave her. But, more now would be too much for her innocent's body, so he eased out of her and moved to her side. Sliding his hand over her belly, he could feel the ripples of her orgasm yet moving through her body.

Several minutes passed and he was sure they both dozed off to sleep in the lethargic satisfaction that came from a good bout of lovemaking.

He'd meant what he told her—he was keeping her. Her father be damned. Connor be damned. She was his now and what had begun in misunderstanding was now consummated in honesty.

She was his.

She stirred a bit, opening her eyes slowly as though testing to see if she was asleep or awake. He lay quiet, giving her a chance to adjust to the new intimacy between them. When she kept her eyes open, looking at everything in the room but him, he spoke to her.

'Was it as you thought it would be?' he asked.

He remembered his first time—a mad rush to completion before he could be discovered behind the stables with the lusty and willing laundry maid. But, for women, well, he'd always thought their first time was something that needed to be special.

'My thoughts are so scattered, I cannot think,' she whispered. Then she turned slowly towards him, but he noticed the wince that crossed her face as she moved.

The chamber grew cool then, enough that he noticed the gooseflesh rise on her skin. Then his stomach grumbled, reminding him of his missed supper and late arrival home. She reached out to touch him and hesitated. He guided her hand to his stomach and held it there. The next time the noise happened, she smiled.

'I am yours, as well, now, Lady MacCallum,' he said, trying to put her at ease.

Her eyes flashed at his words and he thought he'd made a very large mistake. Aye, she would be the death of him if her appetite for the pleasures of the marital bed were close to her curiosity and boldness.

'You did not eat, then?' she asked, sitting up and pulling the drying cloth around her shoulders. Another wince reminded him of his husbandly concern for her.

'I entered my hall to find it in complete disarray, my wife nowhere to be found and more people than were here this morn now living here. Needless to say, I came looking for you to straighten this out.' He tried to remain serious, but could not. 'What the bloody hell did you do to my hall, lass?'

He got out of bed, heard the soft knocking at the door and went to see to it. Isobel squeaked, pulled the cloth over her head and dived down on the bed to hide herself. Surely she should know that there were no secrets when living in a keep? No surprise to him, a bucket of steaming water sat outside their door, placed there by the servants who understood what the sound of the door's bar dropping meant.

'It would be easier to do this in the tub, Bel,' he said. 'If you can find your way out from under that cloth?'

As soon as the door was secured, she peeked out from her hidey hole and then climbed from the bed. She looked at him and his manhood and then down at her legs. Her blood marked his cock and also her thigh, a sign of her virginity now taken. While he helped her wash and dress, she could not stop blushing from his private ministrations now.

'I am accustomed to finding my own meal in the kitchen,' he said. 'You do not have to accompany me there now.'

'I would like to explain what in the bloody hell I did to your hall,' she said without breaking into a smile.

He laughed then, kissing her quickly and nodding.

'Come, then. You can explain this mad new scheme of yours and why I now have four large looms and a small one where only one stood when I left this morn.'

They both tugged on shoes and walked hand in hand down to the hall and the kitchen. Since most of the keep's inhabitants already sought their rest, they moved quietly so not to disturb those who slept. The kitchen was empty and dark, so Athdar lit a lantern from the hearth and set it on the table in the corner. Isobel retrieved two bowls from the cupboard and spoons and ladled out some of the leftover stew from the cauldron.

'You missed dinner?' he asked, as she served it to him.

'Nay,' she said, shaking her head. 'I ate at supper, but find myself famished now!'

Isobel brought a jug and cups to the table and then sat with him. In many ways, he enjoyed this intimate dining with her alone more than the many formal meals he'd eaten before. He waited for her to eat and once she slowed, he spoke.

'So, tell me of this weaving plan of yours?'

'In Lairig Dubh, you have seen the weavers' building?' He nodded. 'I know that we do not need as many as they do, but I thought that it might be easier to have them in one place. For the winter especially.'

'So the one place is here in my keep?' Her eyes sparkled in the candlelight as she spoke and he found himself transfixed on the way the light was able to pick out all the shades of gold in her hair. By the time he remembered that he was listening to her plan, he'd missed a good part of it.

'And the older children will be given chores. What think you?'

Athdar wanted to laugh—he'd been trapped by his

infatuation with his own wife. She seemed pleased by what she'd accomplished. He was willing to allow her this.

'Can you show me?' he asked, only to give himself more time to figure out if he had any objections or not.

They finished the food, put the bowls, cups and spoons in one of the buckets to be washed and Isobel led him to her new weavers' corner. Tall screens made out of tapestry and wood separated the area from the rest of the hall. The five large looms faced a centre point, allowing room around them to walk and work. The small loom sat in the corner, waiting to be used. Trunks sat along the wall. 'Threads?'

'Aye. And supplies, extra weights and anything we need.'

'We?' He knew she planned on working with them and that was part of the reason she set it up so. And the thought of having her here, on long winter nights, working on her loom, pleased him.

She studied him before saying anything.

'You are jesting?'

'Aye.'

'And you are not angry that I did this without your knowledge?'

He pulled her into his arms and kissed her. He'd been wanting to ever since they're left their chambers. Athdar did not think he would ever tire of her or of wanting her. Now that that beast had been loosed, it would be impossible to cage it again.

'It pleases me that you want to make things better here.'

'I promise to move them back if this does not work out to your liking,' she said against his mouth.

'Very well.' He leaned down and touched their

mouths together, liking very much the way she melted into him as soon as he kissed her.

They sought the privacy of their chamber and if anyone noticed the change between them the next morning, the way his gaze softened when he looked at her or the easy way they touched whenever they met during the day, no one thought it awry. For the first time in a very long time, Athdar MacCallum was happy and content.

It took several days to move everyone into the keep and the decision that pleased Isobel the most was that Ailis agreed to stay and work as a weaver with the other widows. Isobel thought this might help the woman in her time of grief and it might help to have others around her who had gone through the same thing. Only one of the women was older—most had lost their husbands within the last several years. The best thing for Ailis was the opportunity to have her son raised in the keep.

With her days busy and her nights lost to the pleasure and passion she discovered in Athdar's arms, November days passed quickly. Men constantly waited by the pass to send word of its opening to travel, but it never came. Now that she and Athdar were joined, the thought of being here, undisturbed and with him, felt like a boon rather than a hardship. By the time her parents could travel back here, well, it would be too late to do anything but wish them happy.

Isobel forgot about speaking to Laria or Broc about Athdar's childhood to seek some answer to what plagued him, but decided instead to find the old man, the old laird's cousin, who lived in the village and see if she could learn anything more from him. On the next clear day, she made her way to the cottage where he lived.

When knocking brought no reply, she lifted the latch and pushed the door open slowly. 'Iain?' she said quietly. Stepping inside, she looked around at the small cottage. Two rooms, this main one and one behind a closed door. With no sign of anyone at home, she opened the door and called out again, 'Iain?'

A powerful odour struck her as she eased the door open wider, one she recognised. It was the smell of death. Peering into the shadows, she saw him, sitting in a chair next to a now-cold hearth. Her heart pounded so hard she thought it would burst in her chest. The best course of action would be to call Broc or one of the men to come, so she turned prepared to do so.

As she left the cottage, a young woman approached, carrying a wee bairn on her hip. This must be Iain's granddaughter. Oh God, did she not know, then?

'Lady,' the girl said, nodding to her. 'Did you want to speak to my grandda then?' She shifted the babe and reached for the door latch. 'Did the laird have more questions for him?'

'Nay, I came to speak with him. Pardon, but I do not know your name,' Isobel said, positioning herself in front of the door. The girl needed to be warned before she entered.

'Jessie, lady,' she said. Smiling, she kissed the bairn's head. 'And this is Iain, named for my grandda.'

'And your husband? Is he nearby?'

'Oh, nay, lady,' she said, shaking her head. 'He works in the fields, but for now he is stationed at the pass, waiting for signs that it is clearing.'

'Jessie,' she said softly. 'I went in to speak to Iain already.' She could not think of how to ease the blow, so she touched the girl's shoulder and told her. 'Your grandda has passed.'

'He…is he inside?' Jessie asked.

'Aye. Here, let me hold the bairn for you,' Isobel said. She reached out for the little boy and waited for Jessie to go inside. A few minutes later, the young woman came back out, dabbing her eyes.

'I stayed with my aunt these last two nights. He seemed fine when I left.' She took her son back and cuddled him closely. 'He has lived a long and full life,' she added with a sigh.

'Should we open the shutters? Let some fresh air in before you try to have him moved?' Isobel asked.

'Would you mind if I went for my uncle, lady? Could you wait here? It's just down the path a short way.'

'Go.' Isobel watched as Jessie went to fetch her uncle.

She opened the door wider and then went to open the front shutters. As she did that, the light pouring in struck the green glass object on the table near the small room. Walking over to it, she picked it up, realised what it was and pulling the stopper out and sniffing it only confirmed it for her.

This was the bottle of sleeping elixir that Laria had left in her bedchamber the first night of her courses.

Isobel had searched for it the next day. Athdar remembered putting it on the table next to the bed and then no one had seen it. She'd questioned all those with access to her chambers and all had denied knowing about it.

Now here it was.

And Iain was dead.

Three drops to sleep the night, Laria had directed. *No more or you may not wake.*

Isobel held it up in the sunlight and peered through the thick glass.

Half the bottle was gone…and Iain was dead.

Chapter Twenty

They laid old Iain to rest near his long-dead wife and everyone came back to the keep to eat and drink to his memory. Isobel kept a close watch on Athdar, fearing a repeat of his desperate behaviour that happened after Robbie's death. Iain had lived a long life and, though not recently ill, certainly suffered the various indispositions of the aged. No one, not even his beloved granddaughter, thought anything was amiss in his passing. No one.

Except her.

Another toast, the last one, was made in his honour and the villagers went back to their cottages and their chores and duties. Jessie's husband Micheil had been summoned home for the burial and would travel back to the pass once more.

'Does that dark expression foretell of trouble?' Athdar crept up behind her and slid his hands around her, pulling her to lean against him. When she shook her head and nodded at Jessie and the bairn, he said, 'He was a good man who lived a long life.'

'That is what everyone said.'

'Did you speak to Micheil?' he asked. 'He said the weather has been clear in the pass for these past two days. A good sign then.'

'Only if you are ready to face my parents.'

She had not thought about much else than the matter that bothered her now—her suspicions that someone had intentionally killed off an old man.

'Tell me what has you so preoccupied, love.' He kissed her neck and held her tight. 'Something has kept you up these last two nights.'

Unable to sleep, she'd sought comfort first with Athdar and then, after he slept, she sought the loom and its ability to soothe her. Usually, once she found the rhythm and pace to her work, her mind could sort out problems. She practiced entire chess games in her thoughts that way, trying and perfecting moves before she ever used them on opponents. Something about the way the threads moved on the loom and the way the shuttle separated and then combined the warp and weft made her see other patterns around her.

But it had not helped her this time. Too much was unknown to her and she did not who to ask. And now with her suspicions, it could be dangerous to do so. She had almost convinced herself she was seeing connections where there were none when Ailis walked through with her son.

Athdar froze behind her, becoming like a statue, motionless, not even breathing, as the boy passed them by. He drew in a ragged breath and she stepped from his embrace to aid him if he needed it. His face was as white as her chemise and his eyes stared at the boy and every step he took. Ailis had not noticed, but the boy did, staring back until his mother tugged on his hand and they made their way back to the looms.

'Athdar,' she whispered to him. Once again the frightening empty gaze now met hers. She reached up and touched his face, trying to get him to look at her. 'Athdar, please look at me.'

She tapped against his cheek, but he did not respond. The hollow stare, bordering on desolation, terrified her.

Just as she was going to call Nessa or Jean over, he blinked over and over again and then continued speaking to her as though he had not stopped reacting for several, long, tortuous moments.

'So what is it?' he asked, putting his hand over hers. 'Do you miss your family, then?' He smiled then as though nothing had happened. 'I will speak to your father and work this out.'

Someone called his name and he kissed her and went off, leaving her stunned and unable to figure out what had happened and what had caused it.

Some of the children ran by and Isobel realised Ailis's son had caused this reaction. Since she did not remember meeting Robbie before he died, she walked over to Muireall.

'How many years does young Morvin have?' she asked as the boy came into sight again. Glancing over, she saw Athdar leaving the hall so she did not worry that he would see Morvin again.

'The little lad is nigh on seven now, lady.'

'He seems a pleasant boy,' she said. 'I did not meet his father—does he favour him at all, do you think?'

Muireall squinted, watching Morvin scamper by on his way to Ailis. 'Oh, he has the verra look of his da, especially at that age.' She smiled. 'He has his height, as well.'

She noticed Laria enter the hall and wanted to speak to her about the sleeping elixir. Muireall saw her watching and nodded at the healer. 'They were all about the boy's age.'

'They?' Isobel faced Muireall. 'What boy?'

'That terrible summer. They…' Muireall stared at the window above them for a moment and then shook her head. ''Tis no wonder she is as bitter as she is.'

'Lady,' Laria called out to her. Isobel wanted to ask Muireall about what she'd said, but Laria approached, her speed belying her age at that moment.

Isobel wanted to stay and learn more from Muireall, but Laria took her by the arm and led her away. Just as well, for she wanted to ask about how much of the elixir she'd made and if, by chance, she'd taken some to old Iain. The old man could have followed her instructions incorrectly and her suspicions would be completely unfounded.

The other women began returning to the looms and their work as she walked away with Laria to the healer's workroom. They'd almost reached it when Laria remembered someone in need of her care and she excused herself from Isobel.

Not willing to waste the opportunity, she sought out Jean to see if the woman knew anything about this new information that Muireall had shared. But Jean and Ceard were both in the midst of preparing for the evening meal, so Isobel left disheartened.

There would be time and chance again, so Isobel went about her duties, with ever a watchful eye on Athdar whenever he was in the hall.

She had done it again.

Isobel had convinced him to make another change in his household. As he sat in the abbot's chamber, speaking with not one but two holy brothers, Athdar did not know whether to curse her and praise God for sending her to him.

Nay, that was not true. She was a gift to him, one that he treasured deeply in spite of the short time they'd actually been together. Although only weeks had passed since she had arrived with his sister to visit, he felt as though they'd been together for years. They'd fallen into a routine for their days…and their nights, though thinking about those nights was not something he should be doing now or here. So he concentrated on the task before him—choosing one of the brothers to come and be his clerk.

The idea came up one night as they lay together, talking about plans and dreams. Although older than her by years, her enthusiasm invigorated him. Of all the hopes she mentioned, the one she kept coming back to was that she wanted him to name the keep. Her dowry would help to make it grand enough to bear a name, she'd said. It was the first time they'd spoken of what she would bring to their marriage.

He laughed aloud then, remembering the expression on her face when he asked what she thought her father would do first upon arriving here. Athdar said if she were his daughter, he would kill the man who'd taken her without permission. She predicted her father would be ready to discuss the matter civilly. Rurik Erengislsson never met a fight he didn't like and, even at his age, rarely found himself the loser in challenges. His fists and sword skills spoke first for him and for the MacLerie for whom he stood. If you were left with enough pieces intact to live after facing Rurik, then they talked to you afterwards.

Athdar realised he wanted to get back to her now, so he glanced at the two, picked the one who looked the most studious and invited him to come to…his estate. Mayhap they did need a name for it?

* * *

Finally, hours later he was home and went looking for his wife to share the news of her success. Although he expected to find her with Laria or in the kitchens, she was not there. He checked their chamber and there was no sign of her. Leaving their room, he looked down over the weavers' corner, as she liked to call it, and could not see her. He did see Ailis so he called out to her. Both she and her son looked up at him at the sound of her name.

The boy.

The boy was down there.

Down there.

The boys.

The next thing Athdar knew he was holding the crying boy in his arms and Ailis was trying to take her son from him. Looking around, everyone in the hall stood staring at him. He let go of the boy and let his mother take him.

What had happened?

Why was he holding Ailis's son?

When had he left his bedchamber and walked here?

Worse, as he glanced around reading both surprise and confusion on the faces of his people, he had no idea of what had happened in those moments, few or many, before just now.

'Go back to your duties,' he called out. 'My apologies for frightening your son, Ailis.'

What else could he say? He had acted like a madman and so many had seen it. Then he remembered the last time it had happened—in his chambers when he came back to himself and Isobel stared at him in terror. Rubbing his forehead, he tried to remember that incident and could not.

Nor this one. Sweat poured down his back and he

rubbed at his face. Was he losing his mind? Was madness taking control over him?

Isobel walked in just then and met his gaze. She would hear about it—they, her people now, would tell her and she would wonder about the sanity of the man she married. Just as he was doing.

Something was wrong here. Something was wrong with him.

He needed to think about this before facing Isobel and her inevitable questions. He nodded to her and left the keep. Athdar walked to the stables and got his horse, not yet tended from his recent arrival, and headed out of the gates. Though he heard Padruig call to him, he ignored him and rode off into the forest. Without intention or destination in mind, somehow he ended up at the mill.

He had stood watching the water flow through the mill for hours without being able to sort through things. There were blank areas in his memory, places where nothing but blackness existed. Sunset came and went before he made his way back to the keep.

With no answers.

As though sensing his inability to address the myriad of questions she would ask, Isobel said nothing about it. She carried on a stream of conversation through supper with everyone at the table, making his brooding silence almost unnoticeable. He left the table as soon as it was seemly to do so and she let him go to their chambers alone. He was sitting at the table, staring at the chess pieces, trying to sort things through in his mind when she walked in.

Athdar's frustration over this began to boil within him. With his parents gone and his sister not there, there was no one he could ask to help him sort out the tumultuous confusion. With no words to say to her, flooded with embarrassment over these lapses in memory and strange behaviours happening more and more, he just opened his arms to her and she stepped into him.

The only thing, the only person he could count on was Isobel. She centred everything she did on him and his needs. Though she'd not said the words, he knew she loved him. This night, he needed to hear them. He needed…her.

He said not a word to her, but she understood the turmoil within him.

Witnesses had described the scene in the hall that happened just before she'd arrived—Athdar screaming from the balcony at Ailis's son, calling him by his father's name and running down the stairs at breakneck speed and falling to his knees in front of the boy. Then Athdar stared for several minutes before grabbing the boy in a fierce hug until the boy's screams seemed to rouse him from the stupor he'd fallen into.

She suspected he had no memory of this time, like the others, and that he had done this in front of his people was probably tearing him apart.

She wanted—nay, needed—to help him, but now she could see that he needed something basic from her. Something that would reconnect him with her. Something to show her love to him and let him know that she was there for him. The bleak expression in his eyes invited her to act.

Isobel stepped from his embrace, removed her clothing and then pulled him to stand before her. Circling him, she undressed him slowly, peeling away each of his garments until he stood naked before her. His arousal did not surprise her now—he became so at her slightest touch or glance, making her feel powerful in their relationship.

He needed comfort first, so she guided him to sit on the bed and she climbed up behind him. She removed the ties around the ends of the small braids he wore at his temples and then ran her fingers through the length of his hair, massaging his head and then his neck. Then she moved his hair aside and kissed down his spine.

Somehow she knew he needed more than just her touch this night. In the face of his doubts and questions, he needed to know that she was there for him. And she needed to tell him the truth that had lived in her heart for so long.

She moved around him and knelt across his leg, trying to ignore the aroused flesh that made her own body ache in anticipation. She took his face in her hands and kissed his mouth. Over and over, as he usually did to her, she kissed his face, his lips, his chin, his cheeks and then she opened and possessed his mouth. As she slid her tongue in his mouth, she felt his hands encircle her waist. When he finally gave her his tongue, he guided her forwards and up until she could take him inside her body.

Sliding down his length, taking him in inch by inch, she kept her mouth on his. Her breasts tingled as the curly hair on his chest teased her nipples. She lifted her mouth from his and exhaled a sigh of pleasure. Their bodies joined as one, now she wanted his heart.

'I love you, Athdar,' she whispered against his mouth.

He stopped then, tugging her hair and gently pulling her face back. He searched her face as though seeking the truth.

'I love you,' she repeated.

He turned her face, staring into her eyes. He knew she'd given herself to him, but now she gifted him with her heart when he most needed it.

'Ah, lass,' he whispered. 'Say it again.'

'I love you,' she repeated. Then she pulled herself against his chest and began to ride him. 'I love you,' she chanted in a whisper against his face. 'I love you, Athdar MacCallum. Always.'

He took control then, turning their bodies as one until she lay beneath him. She reached up and touched his face with a breathtakingly tender caress. His body urged him to move, to take her, to claim her and mark her, but his own heart wanted to savour this special moment between them. He moved in her in a slow pace, so slow that it made his control scream, but he wanted her to feel the love he could not give voice to…not yet.

Every time he filled her, she gasped. The sigh she made as he withdrew was music to his heart. He wanted this to go on for ever and never have to face the rest of it—the questions, the doubt.

'Athdar,' she moaned. 'I can take no more of this. Hurry!'

He laughed then—her soft voice had turned demanding and her hips thrust up to meet his. He loved hearing her demand more of him. He wanted to give her everything.

He loved her.

Athdar took her, then he thrust faster and deeper, feeling the walls of her channel tighten around his flesh. His release was close, oh so close, and he felt the spasms beginning deep within her body that foretold of hers. Then, just before he thrust for what he knew would the last time before they reached satisfaction, he lifted his head and met her gaze.

'Never leave me, Bel,' he whispered. 'Never.'

She smiled then.

'Never.'

Then, canting her hips, she wrapped her legs around him, drawing him into her fully. Her body exploded and melted around his as she screamed out her release. His seed burst forth as he filled her, plunging his flesh deeper and deeper still as her muscles convulsed around his cock.

He could not breathe then. He could only feel…her body and his flesh as one…her heart pounding in her chest…her love accepting and claiming him.

If only he could remain here for ever.

But he could not. He needed to find out what was happening to him and why.

Turning to his side, he pulled Isobel close, not sure of even what to say. They lay in the heavy silence for a short time before she faced him.

'Tell me how I can help you, Athdar. Tell me what to do.'

Her soft plea hurt because he could not answer her.

'Give me time, Bel. Just give me time.'

She said nothing then, just nodded and rolled to her side once more. Athdar moved in close and held her, unwilling to break the bond between them.

After watching her plan her changes and handle problems, he would love to have her help. But until he knew the problem himself, he could not even ask the questions.

His breathing grew deep and regular and Isobel hoped that their joining had helped him. Speaking the words of love to him had been terrifying and, though he'd not said them back to her, she doubted not that he loved her. It was in his gaze every time he looked at her. It was in his words every time he spoke of her or praised her before his—their—people. It was in every touch and every caress. If he could not say the words, she did not worry over it.

She listened to him breathe and marvelled over how far they had come together. Sliding her hand over his hip, she just left it there so she could keep some connection to him as they slept. A few minutes passed as she drifted in and out of sleep and then she noticed something was not right.

Reaching for him, she felt only emptiness next to her. The bed was cool to her touch, which told her he'd left some time ago. Both of them seemed to use the night to sort out their thoughts and just as she sought out the loom, she had known him to walk when he was bothered. So, she waited a little while for his return.

When she estimated it had been more than an hour, and how much before that she knew not, she left the bed and dressed quickly. With his plaid wrapped around her, she began her search for him.

Chapter Twenty-One

She crept through the hall, finding no sign of him.

Had he left the keep?

Isobel went through the kitchens, again without seeing him, to the back door where a guard always stood… and thankfully did now.

'The laird?' she asked, trying to keep her voice calm.

'He headed for the stables, lady,' the man said. 'Should I go tell him you wish to speak to him?'

'Nay,' she said, walking past him. 'I will seek him out there.'

It took a few minutes to find her way there. With little moonlight to brighten the yard, it was difficult, but soon she approached the fenced yard behind the main building. Again, no one was there so she followed around to the door…the open door. Tugging it wider, she stepped inside and looked around. Though there appeared to be about eight stalls, only three were being used. A torch placed high on the wall showed Athdar standing in front of one of them.

She walked to him, stopping not far from him. The horses neighed softly, hoping she brought a treat, but she had none. Athdar did not seem to hear her or them.

He just stood shifting something in his hands back and forth. As she got closer she could see it was a length of rope that was looping around one hand. When he reached the end, he dropped it and began again.

'Athdar?' she said. Remaining where she was, she said his name once more.

'Rope. I need the rope.'

He did not precisely say it to her, more at her, and then he looked around the open room and along the floor as though searching for rope. Seeing none, she did not know whether to go and get some or not. He spoke again.

'Dear God, where is the rope?' There was such pain in his voice that it hurt her to hear it. It made her move.

'Here, Athdar. Here it is,' she said, picking up the length he'd dropped once more and holding it out to him.

As he turned to look at the floor, she saw that empty gaze and knew his mind, his thoughts, were not here.

'Where is it? Where is the rope?' he asked again, falling to his knees and searching through the hay for something that was right before his eyes.

'It is there, Athdar,' she said.

'No matter telling him, lady.' She jumped at the sound of another voice. Turning, she discovered Broc standing behind her.

'What is he doing?' Athdar continued feeling through the hay and did not react to their voices.

'He walks while asleep,' Broc said. 'There are stories he did this as a child, but then it disappeared before he married…Mairi.'

'It is back, then,' she said. She had heard about people who did this—they could have conversations, even eat and drink, and all the time were sound asleep. But she'd never seen it before Athdar began it.

'I think 'tis what happened in your chamber that night,' Broc explained.

She started to say that it did not explain the several times when he had not been sleeping, but decided it was something best kept private for now.

'Has it happened at other times?' he asked, moving closer as they watch Athdar repeat the task over and over.

'In the hall. This day.' Everyone there had seen it and many had told the tale of it, so it was not a secret. The other times, she would keep to herself.

Athdar got to his feet then and walked past them as though they were not there, the rope left forgotten on the floor.

'I should go,' she said, not willing to let him out of her sight. 'Broc, I would speak to you on the morrow about this.'

Isobel also wanted to know why Broc was watching him this night, but there would be time to ask that after she made certain Athdar was safe.

Isobel followed Athdar back through the yard and inside the keep before she realised he wore no shoes. And he seemed not to notice as he walked over the cold stone floor and steps. He went directly to his chamber and lay down on his bed. She sat on the chair and watched him sleep until she fell asleep herself.

Only when he had roused her in the morning and asked why she slept on the chair did she decide it was time for some plain talk between them.

Isobel sat in the chair, slumped over and sleeping with her head leaning on the table. Athdar slid from the bed and went to her, only then noticing the mud on his feet. Confused, for not only were his feet filthy but also he was dressed, as well, he touched her shoulder and she startled.

'Isobel, why are you sleeping there?'

She rubbed her eyes and he noticed the circles when her hands dropped away. She gathered the plaid around her shoulders and shivered before answering him at all.

'I wanted to know if you left again,' she whispered as she stood. 'So, you do not have any memory of the stables?'

At first he thought she must have had some nightmare until she glanced down at his feet—his bare and filthy feet which were not in that condition when he settled to sleep wrapped around her. A sick feeling in his gut told him he would not like what she would tell him, so he turned the chair and sat down.

'After you fell asleep, you left our bed and the keep. I found you in the stables,' she explained. She sighed and shrugged, clearly exhausted. 'You were searching for a rope. And then more rope. You were frantic.'

Then he noticed the tears and—damn it!—Isobel never cried. He tried to take her in his arms and she pushed him away.

'Tell me about Robbie and the other boys,' she said, dashing her hand across her face to wipe away the tears. 'What happened?'

'Robbie? Robbie died. You know that,' he spat out. 'What boys do you mean?' Did she mean Robbie's son?

'Jamie, Kennan, Duff and Robbie?' she asked. 'Those were the names you cried out in your drunken sleep that night.'

He shook his head and tried to think about the names she'd said. He did not remember saying them then and could not bring them to mind now. Although he knew Robbie more recently, he could not place him as a child. He shrugged. 'I cannot remember any by those names.'

'Try to remember, Athdar,' she urged. 'You had about seven years. They were your friends. Something happened to them.'

Her words were like blows to him—his mind reeled and a dizzying blackness began to rise within him. He tried to think of himself as seven again, a child, a boy the same age as Robbie's son. Something stirred in the blackness of his memories then. Horrible. Nauseating. A wall he could not, he dared not, approach.

His stomach clenched and he bent over from the pain of it.

'Athdar, let me help you,' she said. But the pain and the blackness welled up in waves, threatening to claim him.

He thought about something else, not boys, not him, not friends, and it all subsided. He took in deep breaths, trying to regain control and he felt better until she mentioned them again.

'You are not helping me, Isobel,' he yelled at her. He had to make it stop. The blackness. The swirling. 'Leave it be!' She jumped back away from him. Clearly he had to be forceful about this or, like his sister, she would meddle and make it worse...again. 'Leave it be and leave me be! Now!'

At first she seemed cowed by his order, but then her lip, her God-be-damned lower lip, edged up, showing her defiance.

'I cannot help you if you do not try, Dar,' she said. Her voice echoed in his mind and the blackness that waited there.

'I do not want your help. You overstep yourself

in this. I did not ask for your help. Leave. It. Be,' he shouted.

Did she cry then? Nay, not her. She gathered the plaid around her shoulders and left the chamber without another word. And, thanks be to God, without asking more questions.

Athdar looked around for something to drink then— both to ease the pain in his stomach and to make him forget all the names she kept saying. It was important that he forget and never remember them.

Finding nothing, he went to the kitchen to get some from the barrel kept there. From the looks he received along the way, he knew others had heard the exchange. Well, good and fine, that now they remembered that he was their laird and the one who gave orders here.

Isobel was stunned. She watched as Athdar battled something within himself, his expression changing moment by moment, once she spoke the names. She could see him arm himself with anger to push her away. She'd seen others do that when the cost of accepting or admitting something would be too much and now saw him doing the same thing. Usually it was caused by pride, but this time? She had no idea of what could cause such a reaction in him.

Husbandly orders or not, she had learned how to accomplish things without a husband's knowledge and in the face of a husband's resistance from the best women at doing such things—her mother and his sister. She would need more information if she wanted to help him. Thinking about who would know such things, Muireall's name came to mind.

After washing in her old chambers, Isobel decided to seek out Muireall before she came to the keep for the day's work. The older woman had not yet moved all of her belongings out of her daughter's cottage, so Isobel waved off Jean's offer of food as she left to find some answers to her questions.

Thinking about all the things spoken about the Mac-Callums' past, she thought of Laria who had been here through all of it. Who had grown bitter as Muireall had said.

And she needed to speak to Broc about last night. Why was he in the stables when Athdar was there?

No matter who she had to seek out, she was going to find out what held Athdar in its grasp.

Muireall met her at the door and they walked back to the keep. Isobel did not wait long to begin her search.

By the time they reached the keep, Isobel knew about the terrible accident: a bridge collapsed, killing three boys and injuring one more. Only Athdar had survived unscathed.

And, the most surprising thing she learned was that the mother of two of the dead boys—Duff and Kennan—was Laria. Muireall's comment about Laria being bitter made more sense now, though she could not imagine how the woman could remain here and serve the man who was the only boy uninjured when her sons died. It made no sense that Laria and the boys' father remained here after such a loss.

The image of that green glass bottle flashed through her thoughts again. Laria's sleep elixir. Iain dead.

Was this all connected? Isobel knew she was missing something about this, something very important. She really wanted to talk to Athdar, which was out of the question.

Jamie and Robbie's parents had moved away right

after the accident—something the old laird arranged. So Athdar's statement about knowing Robbie only as an adult made sense—if he had somehow forgotten about Robbie being part of the accident.

But could someone do that? Put something so far and firmly behind him that he did not and could not recall it?

Her head hurt by the time they arrived back at the keep, both from the lack of sleep and from trying to figure this out. She realised one thing: she could not barge into the workroom and ask about Laria's dead sons. Even if there was a connection somehow between what caused Athdar's suffering and the woman, it would be a cruel thing to do to a woman who'd lost bairns.

Isobel remembered one of the MacLerie villagers— Margaret—whose husband and only child had been killed in a terrible accident, leaving her alone. Connor and Jocelyn had made all kinds of provisions for her since the deaths had occurred in their work in the harvest. Margaret had seemed well enough, bearing up under her grief until one day she simply cleaned and shuttered her cottage and walked off a cliff.

God rest her soul. Isobel crossed herself and offered up a momentary prayer for the poor woman. No one, not the woman's neighbours or closest friend, had had any idea of the terrible grief she had kept inside or the plans she'd made. Inconsolable people saw no way through and suffered terribly.

Walking through the kitchen, Isobel knew she must rest. She could speak to Laria later. So she told Nessa, who had now agreed to serve as a housekeeper for them, overseeing the needs of the families there, that she would be in her chamber. No one questioned it as she walked through the hall.

* * *

Athdar knew the moment he poured the whisky that it was the wrong thing to do. Last time—well, last time had turned out disastrously and led him down a path that saw his avoidance of marriage be thrown by the wayside. All things considered, he had got more in this bargain than Isobel had. He had got a woman and wife who only wanted to see to his needs and she had got a cantankerous old man who was too set in his ways to accept her help.

Not that he intended to tell her that. And from the glares being sent his way by the servants, he had no intention of letting her know she was right.

His head yet pounded from whatever had happened this morn. He remembered the feeling of it as it happened, but could not make it stop. When he even tried to think about last night, his head hurt.

She said he had walked to the stables and looked for rope. It was like the other night when he woke to find her huddled in the corner and Broc at the door with the guards. And then again yesterday when he'd come to, holding Ailis's screaming son.

Robbie's screaming son.

Had the boy reminded him of something he could not or should not remember? Athdar rose and climbed the stairs, deciding to return to the last spot he remembered. Outside Isobel's, looking for her. So, he walked to that place and looked over the wall, much as he did whenever she was below.

Three women worked at the looms. He laughed roughly as he saw two spinning wheels there now. More changes brought by Isobel. When he leaned over to watch them work, he experienced…nothing. No dizziness. No blackness threatening to swallow him whole.

Nothing.

He walked a few paces to another vantage point and looked down again. Stared at the looms and the women and the other servants as they carried out their duties. One or two peered up at him and looked away when he nodded. One more time he moved, trying another view before accepting that he could not make it happen. It just did.

The door to her chamber opened and Isobel stood there. He thought she would slam the door in his face, but she did not.

'Do you need something, my lord husband?'

He clenched his teeth against the hurt sarcasm in her voice. He had treated her abominably, no matter if he was right or wrong. He'd never heard Connor raise his voice to his wife as Athdar had. He would have to offer...

'Isobel, I—'

'I do not want to speak to you right now,' she said. 'I will see you at the noon meal.'

Then she slammed the door in his face. As he turned to walk away and looked over the wall, this time he saw some of the women below smirking. They'd heard and approved.

He had forgotten this part of marriage—the give and take of it. The bad with the good. And, in spite of being on the wrong end of it now, he liked it. They would have differences from time to time, but they would have to find their way through it all. Mairi had been strongminded and never hesitated to speak her mind and make him see her side to disagreements. Mayhap he had let his fear of some curse, imagined or real, cause this aversion to marriage, which he'd used to avoid it for so many years. Had it been a mistake?

It mattered not. They were married, by custom now and by formal ceremony as soon as her parents arrived and the arrangements could be worked out. He had claimed her, body and heart, as his and he would keep her. No matter what.

Chapter Twenty-Two

Lairig Dubh

'I will wait no longer, Connor.'

He had never seen Rurik like this before. Not when he had brought Margriet back and was present at Isobel's birth. Not when he faced war and death and destruction. Nothing had brought the man to his knees as this situation with his daughter had.

'The report is that the snow is melting and the pass should be open in two more days.' His commander loomed over him, standing across the table with his massive arms crossed over his chest. God help Athdar MacCallum for bringing down this man's wrath!

'I am going now. Duncan travelled that pass in the dead of winter when he needed to,' Rurik said. 'A few feet of snow will not stop me.'

'And, friend, we were all so much younger then,' he offered. 'This is not the same situation now as then. Isobel is in no danger.'

'Athdar is—' Rurik searched for the right words, but Connor cut him off. Without the women here, he could be frank with him.

'Athdar MacCallum has had an eye for Isobel for the past year. When he visits here, he watches her like a hawk does its prey. He wants her,' Connor said boldly. When the expression on Rurik's face spoke of death, Connor then eased his words. 'And he is honourable and he answers to me. He would not disgrace or dishonour your daughter, or any woman, for that matter.'

'He is not dependable and acts without thinking, Connor. You know that.'

'And he was no more than a boy when you had your confrontation,' he answered. 'And he paid the price. He went home, he learned, he married. Athdar took his place as laird and has been a good one for his lands and people.' He stood and walked around to his friend. Putting his hand on Rurik's shoulder, he said, 'And a marriage to your daughter, in spite of your personal feelings, would not be a bad thing, old friend.'

Rurik wanted to argue; Connor could see it bubbling up from inside the warrior. In the end, he nodded in acceptance.

'If they marry, you do not have to like him or even see him more than you do now.' Connor laughed and then grew serious for a moment. 'But, if you cause strife for him, it will also cause you problems with my wife. And that...' He did not need to finish it.

'Damn it, Connor! I cannot stand when you use Jocelyn against me.'

'Her brother is blood, Rurik. You, although friend for decades, will not win in that battle. So, step carefully when you get there.'

Rurik cursed again, something that crossed the lines between several different languages and was rude in all of them. 'Are you saying I cannot make him pay if he has hurt my daughter?'

Connor laughed then. Rurik's forebears were true Viking raiders—bloodthirsty, brutal and ruthless—and at times like this he could see how the blood had been passed down through the generations between them and him.

'I am simply saying that I support you completely, if you wait for two more days and try not to kill him.' Rurik's expression eased then. 'Mayhap Duncan should come with you? He could work things out in a more civilised way.'

'If he has hurt my daughter in any way, Athdar will need more than your peacemaker to get him out of my justice.'

Rurik grunted then and left. As Connor watched the most loyal man he had ever known leave, he was certain of two things.

First, Athdar was going to face a father's wrath when Rurik arrived on MacCallum lands.

And second, Rurik had a new son-by-marriage and did not know it yet.

God help them both!

Isobel felt better after she had slammed the door in his face and even better once she had slept for a couple of hours undisturbed. Knowing that Athdar was working somewhere and with others, she knew he was safe. Not that she did not want to hit him with something hard herself...

When she went downstairs, the hall was filled with people and it all felt good. The new brother arrived sooner than expected and Broc was showing him around. He would begin taking over clerking for the estate.

The spinning wheels were now in place and the winter would be a productive and safe one for everyone who worked on spinning thread and weaving cloth.

Broc walked back in without Brother…Angus and went into Athdar's private chamber. This would be a perfect time to speak to him and in a perfect place. Retrieving an item she'd hidden deep in one of the trunks of threads and weights, she tucked it inside the small purse she wore on her gown and then followed him inside. He put a package on the table.

'Lady Isobel,' he said with a nod. 'A packet came along with the good brother from the abbot for your husband.'

Isobel pushed the door closed. She turned and faced the man who was loyal to her husband, all the while feeling guilty as though asking him to betray his laird.

'I need your help, Broc.' She sat down at the table and found a piece of parchment to use. The quill and ink sat on the shelf next to her so she opened the bottle, dipped the quill and stared at him.

'I thought that Athdar has taken on a clerk now.'

'I pray you to be serious. I know he counts you as his friend and I need your help.'

The lively, womanising steward grew more serious than she'd ever seen and nodded. 'Tell me what you need.'

'Have you always lived here?' she asked first. She needed to know if he would have been here when this terrible accident happened.

'Aye, lady. From my birth.'

'First,' she said, lowering her voice so they were not overheard, 'do you have any memories about the accident?'

He frowned and shook his head. 'Accident?' He

glanced across the chamber as though thinking about it. 'Nay. When would this have been?'

'Around the time Athdar and Robbie were seven years of age.'

'Oh.' He shook his head again and though he denied it once more, she saw something flash in his eyes that told otherwise. 'He, they, are two years old than I. I would not have been old enough to remember events then.'

He was lying. She did not know why or what, but he did not speak the truth. Dare she continue to ask questions or should she stop now and hope he would not reveal her interest to Athdar? Athdar needed her in this, so she went on.

'How long had Athdar been married to Mairi when she died?'

'Is that not something you should speak to him about, lady?'

'Broc, I believe he is in danger. I need to know more about how many have died here and how.' He studied her intently for more than a minute, then, just when she believed he would refuse, he answered.

'They were married for more than a year. She died within days of giving birth to their son.' Sadness at his friend's loss weighed heavy in his voice.

'Had she problems during her carrying? Bleeding? Pains?' she asked. From what his sister had said, there had been no sign of trouble.

'Nay, she was healthy and happy until the day she died. She bled to death. Laria could do nothing to stop it.'

Isobel was about to write down the details until he mentioned Laria's name. 'Did she try?'

'Oh, aye, she did. Stayed with Mairi for days at the

end. Helping with the delivery. Tried to save both of them,' he said, his voice now a whisper and filled with remembered grief.

She scribbled some notes, in Norn, on the parchment. Something her grandmother had taught her long ago. A number of people here might read and write Gaelic, even English, Latin or French, but none would read or write the native language of her father and mother's people. It was useful to know at times…especially when she wanted to keep something private.

'And tell me of Seonag?'

'Seonag and Athdar were married almost four years when she passed. A fever. It was a year when several villagers perished from it.'

'Did anyone survive it?' she asked.

Broc stood and went to one of the shelves, searching through the record rolls until he found the one he wanted. He frowned and read further. 'I thought that others had died. It was only Seonag.'

'Athdar was with her?' He nodded. 'And did not catch it?' He shook his head, his eyes wide as he perceived the line of her suspicions. Before he could ask her anything, she posed her question to him. 'And Laria?'

'Treated her for days without success.' He narrowed his gaze and studied her own expression for a moment. 'You think that Laria caused their deaths?'

Did she reveal the rest of it to him? There was the matter of his earlier lie.

'Why did you lie before? You know of the accident, do you not?'

He let out a breath and looked away for a minute, as though deciding whether or not to trust her. His head nodded slowly before he met her gaze. For a moment, she saw the same desolation there that she'd witnessed in Athdar's gaze when he was lost to himself.

'Aye. But not about the accident as much as about what the laird did to make it all go away.' She was right then and had not made incorrect assumptions based on what Muireall had told her.

'I was younger than Athdar and his friend and they chased me away from following them that day. But I did,' he said, staring off again as though seeing it all again. 'I followed them far enough to know that they did not go anywhere near a bridge. They went in the direction of the old mill.'

'The old mill?' She'd been to the current one only and had no idea there had been another.

'Aye. The river changed directions after some storms about ten-and-five years ago. The old mill ran dry and so the laird had the new one built farther downstream where the currents were still strong. But there was no bridge up on that part of the river that could have failed and killed those boys.'

The sounds of scuffling footsteps outside the door gave them pause. It moved on, but Isobel wondered if someone had been listening. She still needed to know so many things.

'Tell me, from that time on, what happened to the families of the boys. Duff and Kennan and Jamie and Robbie?'

'Laria yet lives here. You know that. And Robbie so recently died.'

'Her husband?'

Broc shook his head. 'Passed about the time that the other families left the village.' Broc sat down once more and did not look comfortable as he thought about her questions. 'Robbie. Ailis said his heart just gave out. He was complaining of chest pains for some days before it happened.'

He leaned over and put his head in his hands. The colour had left his face and she knew he followed the path she was pointing out. Every death they spoke of could be caused by one or more of the decoctions, potions and medicaments that Laria produced or used. Broc then began to pull out certain rolls and check names and the years when other people died. By the time they finished, Isobel had a list of more than a dozen suspicious deaths, all of which involved Laria.

'I still cannot believe that she did this all. All these deaths? What made you suspicious of her?'

Isobel reached into the small purse and took out the green glass bottle and placed it on the table between them.

'That is one of the bottles Laria uses. I ordered them for her from the glassmaker in the next village. She used different colours for different potions.'

'How many of each does she have?' Isobel asked, although from working with Laria, she knew exactly how many of the costly items there were.

'Two of each.'

'I will tell you that if you searched her workroom and her supplies, you will find only one green one there. This one—' she picked it up '—I found in old Iain's cottage when I discovered him dead. He had been talking to Athdar about his sleep disturbances. I went to ask him some questions and he was dead. And this sleeping elixir was full when last I saw it.'

His shock was clear on his face and in the way his hands trembled. 'Have you added him to your list?'

Isobel nodded.

'What should we do now?'

She leaned back and it was her time to shrug. 'There is still more to this than I know and I worry about Athdar's reaction to any of it. He has been…having these spells. They are happening more frequently, more so now since Robbie's death.'

'They have happened before, too. With Mairi's passing and Seonag's, and a number of those on your list.' He shook his head then, glancing at the list though he could not read it. 'At each of those. Most times no one notices. Sometimes the bad dreams strike him. Other times, it's what you witnessed in the stables.'

'And you keep watch over him? Why?' she asked.

Broc stood and walked to the door before turning back for a moment and she witnessed the terrible sadness in his eyes.

'Because, though he could not save the others, he saved me that day. In not taking me along, I survived when all the others died.' He lifted the latch, but she shook her head to stop him. A terrible thought entered her mind then and he needed to be warned.

'Does anyone know what you just told me? That you were supposed to be with the boys? That you know which path they took?'

'Nay. I have never spoken of it to anyone until this moment, until you.'

'I would keep it that way, Broc. I think Laria is going to kill again and Athdar will be her target. Do not give her another one,' she warned.

'And you, lady. Have a care for your own safety while watching out for your husband's.'

He left first and she replaced the bottle in the purse—she would dispose of it when she could—and made certain all the rolls and records were placed back where they'd been. It was only when she reached for the latch that she noticed how badly her hands shook.

She still had to work out how to prove any of this to Athdar. He would not or could not let himself find the truth of the past and until he did he was in danger. As she went to the kitchens, she finally pinpointed the one thing that yet bothered her—why? Why all these people and not Athdar himself?

The time is almost here.
He's fallen in love with her.
It only matters if it causes him pain.
The anguish of losing someone he loves.

She thinks she knows the truth.
I struggle not to laugh at her efforts.
She loves him.

Which should die first and which should watch?

Chapter Twenty-Three

He slept alone and decided he did not like it. At least he thought he slept without her. He got up several times to see if she sat at her loom trying to sort him out, but always turned back at the last moment.

Athdar let Isobel sleep in her own chamber because he could not figure out how to take the first step back towards her. He did not understand what was happening to him and her questions just reminded him that he had no answers or explanations.

He thought that by doing some of the things she'd asked him to do, it would ease things between them. Such as bringing Brother Angus to work for him. And though she did not know it, her mention about the lack of regular masses being said had caused him to discuss building a chapel and having a priest in residence instead of calling one to see to funerals and baptisms… and weddings.

He'd spoken to Broc about having a builder and stonemason plan for a new, larger tower on the north corner of the keep—one like Jocelyn and Connor had with their large, private chambers at the top and their children's nursery beneath them.

He'd even come up with a name for it all—something simple, something his, theirs—*Caisteil Chaluim*—Callum's Castle.

All plans that he thought would please her.

He'd kept busy yesterday, working in the village once more.

The worst thing was not being able to tell her the whole of why her questions bothered him so much. He had not figured it out right away, not until the dark of night when he could not listen to her breathing next to him.

She thought him a good man. She thought him a good laird to his people. She thought him a caring and strong man.

All lies.

For deep within that churning darkness or madness that rose when he thought of the past, shame lived. He did not remember why or how it was part of him. He only knew that terrible shame was part of his past—and remembering it all would remember that, too.

He had failed Mairi. He had failed Seonag. And somewhere in his past, he had failed grievously and others, many, had paid some price for it. He understood that the dreams and the strange spells he suffered were part of it. He did not want to look too deeply or closely at his past, for he knew that by doing so he would fail Isobel.

And he knew he could not bear to do so.

He wanted to be the man, and the husband, she thought him to be, but he lacked the courage to do that.

When word came that day that the pass was open, Athdar knew his time was running out. Her parents would arrive and convince her of all the reasons why she should leave him behind and the only reason he could come up with for her to stay was love.

But, if secrets of his past came crashing out, would that be enough? He prayed it would be, but feared he would find out soon.

Laria was nowhere to be found. Isobel had contrived a number of reasons to seek her out, but she was never in her workroom or in the keep or in the village. Isobel decided to only have dealings with her with others around until she could either prove or disprove her suspicions. She would not purposely put herself in danger when she believed the woman to be using her talents for healing in the most diabolical way and causing death instead.

Standing in the workroom she'd helped to set up, Isobel studied the various plants and herbs, some dried, some ground, some steeped and so on. And, because of what Laria had taught her, she could explain how each one could be used to bring about death—how to kill someone.

How she wished she had her parents to discuss this with. Or Jocelyn. But most of all she wished she could approach Athdar.

Unfortunately, though they had pursued many philosophical and logical discussions during their many hours together and during their chess games, this conversation would be neither calm nor detached. There was, she understood now after speaking to Broc, something dark and horrifying that had wrapped around Athdar's memories of the accident, or event, that had cost three boys their lives.

Bringing up the subject, even if it was his idea, would lead to that emotional and physical reaction she'd seen already—either the benign spell or the vitriolic reaction. Like the wild boar that became more deadly when cornered, this fear deep within him would not be dispossessed easily and she worried that exposing it would harm him more than help him.

So, how could she handle this wisely?

Thinking back about his objections or reservations about marriage, she remembered how he thought himself cursed by God or fate. He'd told her that plainly, giving Mairi and Seonag and Tavia as examples of how she might come to an end if they married. Now, if her suspicions proved out, she knew that what he'd thought was a curse of fate, damning any woman who married him or was planning to do so, was almost certainly the work of a woman driven mad by inconceivable grief.

The one thing that lay behind all of her worrying and all of her efforts to relieve him of the burden of guilt under which he'd lived for years was that she loved him. She wanted to love him. But freeing himself from his past was something she could not do for him.

Once she laid out all of her information and thoughts about how Laria had managed to do this, it would be up to him.

And that was what had her hands shaking when he summoned her to his chambers. She loved him, but did he love her enough to try to break from the prison he might have created?

He'd only intended to tell her two things: that the road was open and he expected her parents within days and that Laria had been called to assist a birth in a neighbouring village. One of the village girls had brought the news, saying that Laria had left immediately and would return in a few days.

Now, he had a third, more pressing thing to ask her about, one that crowded out the others.

When showing Brother Angus his system of organising his records and rolls, a scrap of parchment covered with strange words fell out from between two of them. To his surprise, the good brother recognised the words—Norn, he said, because he'd been raised north of Caithness where the Norse inhabited much of the area.

It was a list of names beginning with the names she'd asked him about, continuing on to his wives, his betrothed, Robbie and old Iain and others. He could make no sense of it, but it made his stomach churn and his head hurt. Part of him wanted to put it back where he'd found it. Part of him wanted to burn it. But seeing it, he knew that she was pursuing something that could be dangerous for both of them.

Her soft knock distracted him, as the sight of her always did. He missed her. He wanted her.

Always.

'Come.'

She opened the door and entered. 'You wanted to see me?'

'I wanted to talk to you.' Her eyes brightened—a good sign, he thought—but how would she react to what he'd found? 'Sit. Please.' She fidgeted in the chair, so he walked over and sat at the table with her, the chessboard a reminder of so many things.

'I would like to talk to you, as well,' she said.

Why was he so nervous? Then she saw the parchment there in his hand and knew he'd found her list. But did he understand it and the significance it had?

'What is this, Isobel?' His words sounded thunderous between them.

'What do you think it is, Athdar?' His jaws clenched then and she waited. He could not have read it himself…

'Brother Angus is from Caithness,' he said and she understood.

'Then you know what it is,' she threw back at him.

'I would know why you probe and pry into my private life?'

'I am your wife, am I not? Do I not deserve to know what has, who has, come before me?' she asked. She reached over and took the list from his hand and met no resistance. 'And how and why they died?' Then she knelt down before him and took his hand. 'Athdar, something is wrong here. It has been wrong for a very long time and I think it has nothing to do with a curse. I think that Laria has been avenging herself on you.'

She let out her breath then and waited for his reaction. She could see him battling even now about whether or not she was the one losing her mind to madness. Isobel knew she must stay calm or it would not end well.

Then she realised that a calm and even approach would not break through the walls his past had built within him to protect whatever secrets lay there. Taking a deep breath, she said the words she believed would force him to face the truth he could not.

'Jamie. Duff and Kennan. Robbie.' She waited a moment and then repeated their names. 'Jamie. Duff and Kennan. Robbie.'

'I told you before and I will tell you again—I do not know those names.' He pushed away from her and stood, pacing across the chamber and putting an ever-growing distance between them, a distance she wondered if they would ever bridge again. 'Why are you doing this?'

'Jamie was the tanner's oldest son. Robbie—your

best friend. Duff and Kennan were Laria's own sons. And they died, along with Jamie, in some terrible accident that only you know about, Athdar. You need to remember. Or I fear she will continue to kill people until you do.' She knew she pushed him hard, but only by remembering what he would or could not remember would set him free of the terror that controlled him now.

The logic behind Laria's madness had come to her in the night. Not at her loom as such clarity usually came to her, but while staring at the ceiling in her chamber, imagining another game of chess being played. It was not about revenge as much as it was about inflicting as much pain as possible before ending it.

A web woven of waiting and watching and planning…and killing. Not all at one time. Not all guilty of the sin at the centre.

Isobel knew now that Athdar was the one at the centre of it all.

'Laria has no children. She is a widow and never had children,' Athdar protested.

Isobel was new here. Isobel was wrong. This was wrong. Children? Laria had had children? Nay, he'd never heard her speak of them in all the years that she'd served his clan. Or had he forgotten them as he had others?

'Duff and Kennan. Only an eleven-month separated them in age. They died the summer you and Robbie were seven.' She stood and walked to his side. When she touched his hand, he pulled away, running it through his hair as he turned from her.

Could her words be true? If so, who but a madman forgot his friends? Something dark trembled within him, pulling his reason aside as he forced himself to listen to her. Then, shaking his head, Athdar tried to push the doubt and the foreboding aside, but something in his past, something dark, would not ease his path.

'I said that Laria has no children. And Robbie has been my friend, since he married and moved here some years ago.'

Thoughts and questions swirled around in his mind, but he did not know which to think about or to say. Her words disturbed him deeply and he wondered if this turmoil could truly be something much more dangerous than forgetting.

Was this madness after all? Had he ignored the signs? The voices he heard. The times when he was lost to himself. The times when he did things with no recognition or memory of them. The rage and fear that seemed to live just beneath his skin, always threatening to explode.

Oh, God in Heaven, he was a madman.

And Bel had married him, tying her fate and her life to a man who lost all those he dared love. What if the truth was that he was somehow causing it all? That he had taken the lives of those named on her list? That his madness kept him from remembering dark deeds done? How could he protect her if she needed it from him?

He tightened his hands into fists and released them over and over as the confusion and fear tried to gain control of him once more. But who would protect his Isobel if he did not?

Isobel watched the terrible pain and fear inside of him try to protect itself. It had ruled his life, it had held him prisoner, for years and years, even without him knowing it.

His expression went blank, the emptiness taking control so he could not think past it. But he was struggling there, she could feel it, see it…and her heart broke.

If he could not take that first step and claim control over his soul, how could she do anything to help him? Pain burned in her chest as she understood that she could not remain here, could not continue to be his wife, if he was not willing to believe her. Their ending, she feared, was approaching and she could not stop it from happening now.

Worse, even though he'd read her list and knew her suspicions, he would not accept that someone else was to blame here. If he could not try to believe her, she could not help him as she thought she could.

How presumptuous she'd been. How certain she knew the best path for him and that she would be the one to show him along it. What a fool she was.

There would always be some trigger lurking and waiting to cause these spells. If there was happiness, guilt would lurk in his darkness. If sad, fear would. A never-ending pattern and he would never break free. Isobel gave up in that moment.

He could see the heartbreak in her eyes as she met his gaze then and waited for the words that he knew would damn him to the darkness that always waited there.

'Athdar,' she said, her voice calling him back from the edge that moved ever closer. 'I cannot do this. I cannot live with your past and this pain between us. I cannot live in fear of saying the wrong word or doing the wrong thing. I cannot live not being able to help you.'

'You said you were mine always, Isobel.' He needed her to stay. He needed her love. He needed...

She stepped away from him then, the pain of her small movement making it difficult to breathe now.

'I want to be with you always, Dar,' she whispered to him. 'But you will not let me help you and you will not take the steps to help yourself.'

Athdar had heard her words and wanted to believe them. He wanted to believe there was no curse. That everything had been caused by one person. Now though, he feared at his core that he might be more responsible than anyone.

And if it was him, if he was battling not only a terrible past, but also a horrible mad future, how did he protect Isobel?

There was only one way to make certain she was safe, from a curse, from a madman if his own madness was the cause of it, or from a madwoman if she was correct about Laria's involvement in his past. He stood tall and looked past her at the window of the chamber.

'I expect that there will be some visitors soon. I asked you here to tell you that the road is open to travel now.'

'My parents? My father is on his way?' she said. Confusion entered her eyes at his change in their topic.

'Aye. I expect your father to be the first one through. I think you should make plans to leave and meet him so that you can return to Lairig Dubh.'

Would it work? Could he drive her away from him, from here? More importantly, drive her to safety? He waited for her to speak, hearing only the sound of her breathing, shallow and low.

'And that is what you wish, Athdar?' she asked. She clasped her hands together, searching his face.

He knew the words that would bring this to a close, and even knowing they would keep her safe if he could not, his heart did not want him to say them. To use them against her.

'For years, I'd convinced myself that I did not wish to marry again. Then you came here uninvited and, well, now we are married.'

He saw her draw in a breath as though preparing

for what he would say. Turning away, he only knew he
could not say them while watching the pain in her face.

'It was a mistake to do this—to marry again was a
mistake. You are a mistake.'

Her gasp cut him in two. He forced himself not to
turn at the sound and waited for her to leave.

If he was descending into madness, it would be without her.

The sound of her footsteps moving across the
wooden floor echoed in the emptiness that would be
his life without her. He dared one slight turn of his head,
one last look at her that would have to last him for ever.

She paused before the table and reached over, taking one of the pieces before she ran from the chamber.
After the door slammed behind her, Athdar walked to
the chessboard and realised which piece it was.

She'd taken his black queen.

It mattered not for he would not play with those
pieces again. He would not look on that board, for he
could only see her when he did.

Now that he had managed to drive her away, with
his words and his lack of faith in her, he wondered if
the madness would rise up to claim him completely.

Chapter Twenty-Four

The morning came and she dressed in silence. Walking through the hall tortured her with its many and wondrous memories and she would keep them close to her heart for ever. Surely longer than the year-and-a-day of their marriage.

Though some of the women were already there to begin working, she could not speak to them or to anyone else. Only Padruig tried, but she had to wave him off. Nessa hugged her and wished her well. Jean fought back the tears she could not and turned her face away. Even Ceard crossed his arms over his broad chest and muttered about Athdar.

He needed them now. He needed his people because she would not be here to help him. A failing for sure, but she knew the limits of her abilities and her love. Staying would kill that faster than leaving would let it die. Broc had everything arranged and she found the horse saddled and ready outside the keep. Two guards, already mounted, waited on her to leave.

She had little to take with her since her clothing had returned with her mother. So, a small bag tied to her saddle was all she took…and the black queen. She could not leave her behind to be played by someone else.

Mayhap she was a more jealous woman than she thought?

With enough provisions to take them through the pass—two days' travel at most now that the snows had melted—she would meet up with escorts from Lairig Dubh. Broc had sent out messengers ahead to make preparations to take her the rest of the way…home.

Soon, Athdar's keep was but a shadow behind her and the road opened before them. With so much pain in her heart that she was almost numbed by it, she could not talk to the guards, choosing silence as they rode. Only questions about her comfort were asked and when they did stop to eat the food packed for them, she avoided them.

They'd eaten their midday meal and were about to mount when one of the guards began gagging and coughing. Then the second one did the same. Horrified, Isobel watched as, within a few short minutes, they lay unconscious and near death. They'd shared the same food and she waited for the symptoms to strike her down, praying that Athdar was safe.

But they had not shared the skin of ale.

Could there have been something in the ale? She had, instead, drunk from a skin that contained the betony tea she so liked. Jean said…oh, God, not that she'd made it, but that it had been waiting for her this morn.

The sun above became blurry and Isobel's legs felt weighted down. She knew Laria must be close, watching and waiting for her to fall, so she picked up her skirts and ran, moving slower and slower with each step. She fell then, tumbling into the field by the road, unable to move even though she knew that death, and Laria, tracked her.

Athdar!

Athdar, she thought as her body began to shut itself down.

Will he remember me or will I fade into the dark part of his memory like the others?

'Athdar?'

'Leave me be!' he yelled from inside. The whisky did not block out their voices or her memories.

She was gone. She had left him after swearing she would never leave.

'Damn it, Dar! Open this door before I break it down.' Broc's angry voice did not change Athdar's mind about opening it.

'Come on, man. Isobel is in danger.' But Padruig's quiet plea and mention of her name did.

He staggered across the clothes-strewn room and lifted the bar just moments before the two forced their way in. Knocked to the floor, he waited for them to climb off him.

'Where is Bel?' he asked, climbing to his feet and pushing his hair out of his face.

'This was just delivered from the village.' Broc handed him a small, folded packet.

Tearing it and cursing as he did, Athdar handed it back to Broc to open more carefully. Padruig paced, hand on sword, waiting for orders. When something fell to the floor from inside the packet, Padruig scooped it up.

He'd seen the writing before, when Laria wrote down instructions or a list of ingredients and supplies she needed. This was her writing now.

Come and learn the truth.
Come alone or she dies.
I am waiting.
Justice is waiting.

Padruig held out his hand and dropped the item that
he'd picked up into Athdar's palm after he read the note.

His black queen.

She did not think he saw her take it, but he had. He
just couldn't find the words to tell her not to, or to beg
her to stay.

Laria had Isobel and would kill her unless he found
them.

Only by facing the darkness inside his memory could
he get to her. His refusal to do that yesterday was what
put her on the road this day. He thought she would be
safer away from him, but that had simply put her into
Laria's grasp. Now, she was in danger and his heart and
soul knew he could not risk her.

He closed his fist over her favourite piece and read
the words again. Dear God, she had not told him where
to find them! Athdar knew he could not help her without facing all of it, even the dark, swirling madness
that lay inside him.

'I do not know where she is!' he yelled out. 'How
will I find them?' Broc grabbed for him as he fell to
his knees.

He had to think. He had to concentrate.

He had to remember the accident Isobel had spoken
of and where it had been.

He recalled the names she'd spoken over and over
to him, trying to open the dark pit within him to find
her. He said them aloud, caring not who heard them.

'Jamie. Duff and Kennan. Robbie.' *Nothing.*

'Jamie. Duff. Kennan. Robbie.' *Still...nothing.*

'Athdar,' Broc said. 'I know where they are. Where she is.'

'How do you know? Did Laria tell you something?' he asked, grabbing Broc by his shirt and pulling him close.

'I followed you. I followed you that day.'

'What day, Broc?' he asked as he flung his steward aside.

Black waves tumbled in his memories. Broc as a child, younger than him by a few years. Broc sneaking behind him, ever a few paces behind him. Unable to force what would come at its own pace, he walked away.

'Where, Broc? Tell me where?' he shouted. Athdar opened his trunk and got his dagger and his leather jack. Then he turned and waited for Broc to reveal the location.

'The mill. The old mill.'

Athdar wanted to argue with him that there was no such place, when the image of it floated into his thoughts. They'd run past the mill, laughing and avoiding the place where the currents were the strongest, and turned into the forest.

'I know where she is.' He began to run, out of the room, down the stairs, to the stable.

Padruig and Broc followed close behind him, catching up as he threw his saddle on a horse and tightened it into place. Leading the horse outside the building, he vaulted up on top of it. He wanted to leave, but he needed something. He needed to take something. Something...

'This,' Broc said, tossing a looped length of rope to him. 'You have to take the rope.'

He was completely at a loss to explain how Broc

knew such a thing, but it was exactly what he needed to take with him.

'We will speak later. After you bring the lady back,' Broc said, smacking the hindquarters of the horse and sending him into a trot.

Athdar was through the gates and heading for the mill, all the while trying to figure out the way to go. Then he heard the sounds of boyish laughter in his head and saw a shadowy group of boys racing ahead of him. Only madmen saw and heard people who did not exist. But he followed them, even while knowing they could not be real, through the forest. It took a while for him to reach the current mill. And then he knew in which direction the old one was.

The sun was beginning to fall lower in the western sky, making his stomach churn. He would never find his way to her in the dark, just as he could not find his way that night long ago. Blinded by sweat, he continued riding, urging the horse to continue its relentless pace. Whenever he thought himself lost, the five ghostly boys would appear before him, laughing and running as they had that day, never knowing the death that lay ahead. Finally, he saw the place where the path turned away from the river bed and into the forest and knew he was close.

The path disappeared, making it difficult and slower to get the horse through, so he dismounted and walked. After a step or two, he knew he needed the rope, so he pulled it free and carried it on his shoulder. He'd just turned back when he heard the crackle of dry brush behind him and was struck down, not by Laria, but by a giant of a man.

'Where is she, Athdar?' Rurik said, picking him

up and punching him again. 'What have you done with her?'

'Laria,' he choked out when he could get a breath in. He held his hand up to block the next punch. 'Laria has her. She is waiting for me.'

Rurik dropped him on the ground and crouched down near him.

'Why?' Isobel's father asked. 'What is she planning?'

Athdar wiped the blood from his mouth with the back of his hand. 'She wants to kill me. She is using Isobel as bait to draw me there.'

'What have you done now?' Rurik asked, as he grabbed the leather jack and hauled him to his feet.

Athdar thought of all kinds of things to say or not say, but only one thing, one person mattered right now.

'You can lay the blame on me later, Rurik. She will kill Bel by nightfall, if I don't get there.' He got his bearing, even as memories of being completely lost and running in circles through the dark forest flooded his thoughts.

'How did you find me?' he asked, as he began to trot towards the west, staring at the trees and looking for anything familiar.

'I tracked her, from the main road.' Rurik stayed with him, matching his pace even though his strides were longer. 'I found the guards escorting Isobel dead and followed the signs.'

They were close, very close, now, and Athdar stopped and stared through the thick trees for the place where—

The arrow took Rurik out with amazing precision.

'I told you to come alone.' Laria's voice echoed to him from some place further ahead.

'Rurik,' he whispered, crawling over to him where he

lay face down in the dirt. He did not move. The arrow had pierced him straight through his back.

Of all the ways he thought the proud warrior would meet his death when it came time, this was not it. Rurik should have met it with a sword in hand in battle and not shot in the back by a madwoman whose true target was Athdar. He was about to move on when Rurik grabbed his leg.

'Here, let me help you,' he said, grabbing the man's thick belt to pull him away.

'Nay,' Rurik gasped. 'Get Isobel. Protect my daughter.' Then Athdar felt his body go limp. He should take him back towards the mill. Broc would eventually send men and they would find Rurik and he might have a chance to survive. Any argument or thought of delaying to help Rurik was stopped when Laria spoke again.

'Remember, if you kill me, you will never get to her in time. Come along, boy,' she ordered.

He followed the sound of her voice as she continued to speak and watched for movement ahead of him. Then, just when he thought he would catch up to her, a wave of terror pierced him and he froze.

He had not recognised it at first, but now he did.

A wide chasm opened before him, the bottom not visible from where he stood. Then the sounds and sights of that day crashed inside his head.

'Come now!' he called out. 'It is not wide enough to stop us. Are you afraid to jump?'

They were, but he goaded them on.

'Get a running start and you will make it.' He saw the uncertainty on their faces and would not allow that to ruin their adventure.

'Cowards!' he shouted at them. 'Only cowards would disobey their chief.'

Athdar watched as they nudged each other, nodding and backing up to get a good running start to their jump. Smiling, he crossed his arms over his chest the way his father often did and waited for them to reach his side. One and then another soared into the air above the deep gash in the ground...

Their cries turned to screams as they plummeted down into the dark crevasse below them. Athdar watched in horror as the screams faded into a deathly silence. Only the sound of his breathing broke that still- ness as he crept over to the side and peered down.

The bottom lay about twenty feet below him and his friends lay strewn across the small floor of the gully.

He stood at the edge now and looked down, the bod- ies still fresh and bloodied as they had been over thirty years before. Jamie and Robbie, his cousins. Duff and Kennan, Laria's sons. Jamie dead already, his head twisted at an impossible angle. Kennan and Duff landed next to each, impaled on the old tree trunks that grew out of the bottom of the crevasse. Only Robbie yet lived.

Those bodies faded from his sight and were replaced with one more horrifying to him—Isobel lay uncon- scious at the bottom now.

'If she is hurt…' he began to scream out at her.

'She is the only one I regret,' Laria said almost qui- etly from across the ravine. 'She understood a moth- er's grief. She asked me to teach her. 'Tis sad you fell in love with her. Then I had to take her. You had to re- member the pain. You had to feel the pain I lived with every day because of you.'

How did you reason with a madwoman?

'Twas impossible to do, so instead he began to look for a way to her. Realising that she stood very close to the edge, watching Isobel at the bottom, Athdar began circling the edge. As he expected, she moved as he did, mirroring his steps from across the chasm and never letting him get closer to her. As he walked over the ground, he forced his steps deep into the marshy soil, trying to loosen it.

'I was a child, Laria. You know that,' he said, keeping an eye on Isobel to see if she roused. 'My only sin was being a stupid and proud child.' He remembered the words he spoke that caused his friends to plunge to their deaths now.

But he had been only a child. It had been a terrible, horrifying accident.

'You should have remembered them. You should have paid a price,' she shrilled, the madness and pain in her voice echoed through the dark woods.

She still had the bow with an arrow nocked and ready, so he had to be careful. When he thought the ground could take no more without pouring into the gulley, he began trotting. No matter that insanity fuelled her efforts, Laria was older than he and could not keep up the pace he set.

'I should have remembered them. I should have...'

Somewhere deep within him, Athdar had remembered them. It had caused his nightmares and sleepwalking and the pain that he had no explanation for. He might not have realised it, but he had held his friends in his soul while waiting for his mind to remember them.

'I remember them, Laria,' he called to her as he stopped there on the edge. 'I remember Duff and Kennan.'

Laria tried to stop then, wobbling and losing her balance as she leaned too far towards the pit. As she lurched back trying to compensate, she fell, sliding down the side, taking soil with her.

He watched as she pitched herself forwards in the last second and landing against one of the large rocks on the bottom. She died instantly, her neck broken from the impact. The only sound now echoing across the pit was that of his breathing.

Pushing his hair out of his face, he studied the loosened edge and tried to work out the best place to try to descend to Isobel. He listened for signs of her breathing and heard nothing, so he found the rope he'd brought and, after tying a knot in the end, tossed it around a sturdy tree and dropped the length down into the chasm. Fearing it would not be long enough, he smiled grimly when it reached the bottom. Thinking only about getting to Isobel, he took a deep breath and climbed down into the pit of his nightmares.

When he reached her, he touched her face and felt warmth where he feared the coldness of death. Without delay, he picked her up in his arms and managed to get a quiet moan out of her. Athdar allowed himself to hope he had found her in time then. He still had to get them both back up the side, but he would manage.

He had to.

It took him longer than he expected, but in a while he carried her away from the ravine and laid her on the ground. Tapping her cheek, he finally roused her from the drugged stupor Laria had put her in. Her eyes fluttered open and closed a few times before she focused on his face.

'Dar,' she whispered. 'You found me.'

'Aye. And I'm not letting you go. Ever, Isobel. You are mine.'

Chapter Twenty-Five

Bel smiled then, the corners of her mouth curving only a bit, but she fell back to sleep before he could say more.

A good thing considering the terrible news he would have to give her when she woke. Realising he could not carry her all the distance back to the mill where he could get help, he searched nearby until he found Laria's horse, lifted her in his arms and mounted.

Now that he knew she was alive and would be well, he took her to Lyall's cottage near the mill as fast as the horse would carry them. Leaving her in the man's care, he returned to where he'd hobbled his own horse next to Rurik's body. Knowing that Rurik's horse must be nearby as well, Athdar whistled as he'd heard Rurik do and the trained mount came to him. Once again, it took more time than he thought it would, but he could not leave Isobel's father in the dirt after he'd tried to save her.

It was hours into full dark by the time he led Rurik's horse carrying his body out of the forest near the near mill. By then Broc, Padruig and a full contingent of MacCallum warriors were there to help.

Isobel made her way out of the cottage then, a bit wobbly and escorted by the older man. From the look of her slow steps, she must be sore from her ordeal. First she met his gaze and took a step in his direction, but then she caught sight of her father's body draped over his horse. She gasped and began to run to him, only stopping when Athdar caught her up in his arms.

'I am sorry, love,' he whispered against her hair. 'Laria…shot him,' he said, trying to think of a way to soften the blow of her father's death.

'And damn near killed me,' Rurik muttered gruffly.

Isobel screamed and pointed as her father raised his head. They both ran to help the men move him. Apparently the half Scots, half Norse giant *was* hard to kill after all.

Using the cart from the mill, they took Rurik back to the keep where Ceard practiced his knife-wielding skills to remove the bolt. Knowing he was in the best of hands, Athdar took Isobel to their chambers where he planned to spend several days sorting through the reasons why they were staying together. And he allowed no amount of bellowing from his bride's father to disturb them during that time.

No MacCallum dared to approach their chambers and no amount of cajoling, suggesting or threatening changed that in the coming days. By the time Rurik fought his way out of that damned sickbed and made it there, it took him one glance to know he stood no chance of separating them ever again. He was quite certain he'd worn the same expression in his eyes when he'd rescued Isobel's mother all those years ago.

Worse, or better depending on how he examined the situation, Athdar's actions had saved the young woman who Rurik had claimed as the daughter of his heart when Rurik could not.

By the time Jocelyn and Margriet arrived, Rurik had begun to grow accustomed to the idea of their marriage, or rather, he'd begun to stop opposing it. Mayhap, considering that Athdar had also come back for him, even when believing him to be dead, having him as husband to his daughter was not the worst thing in the world.

Epilogue

Caisteil an Dòchais
Castle Dochash—Castle of Hope—
Spring, in the year of Our Lord 1376

It was not a year and a day but it was as long as Athdar was willing to wait before solemnizing their union. Though their new tower and chapel would not be ready for some time, they decided that the hall would do just fine for them.

And considering that she was well pregnant with his child, he preferred to have it done before she delivered. Surrounded by many more MacLeries than MacCallums, they spoke their vows and he could have sworn that even her father celebrated their marriage.

When Isobel recognised the pattern of what he thought had been his curse and exposed Laria's terrible plotting that had cost them a dozen or more lives over the last three decades, she had given him his soul and his mind back. Being able to finally talk about the truth of the accident and to understand his part in it now, looking back as adult, he was able to mourn the friends he'd lost fully.

The nightmares, the spells, all disappeared over the months since that night. Because of his love for her, he faced the black pit that night and rescued her. In truth, she had rescued him and he never let a day go by when he did not show her what she meant to him.

After the vows, after the celebration, after everything they had to do in front of their kith and kin, he carried her up to their chamber for the one thing he'd been longing to do with her…to play a game of chess with the winner claiming a prize of their choosing. He'd spent weeks with the recuperating Rurik, honing his game skills, and was determined to win.

Later after she'd explained what she wanted as her prize and Athdar did as she demanded, he held her in his arms and fell into a peaceful sleep, knowing that she was the true prize and she was his.

Even as he watched Athdar carry Isobel up the stairs, Connor knew that Jocelyn would claim victory. But, as the rumours around this keep told him, neither the winner nor the loser ever seemed to mind when love was the ultimate prize of the game.

'So, I wonder if we must allow them to claim victory,' Duncan said, clearly reading his thoughts. 'Did we set down any rules about meddling mothers?' he asked, always the peacemaker.

'Meddling was not permitted by the mother, but there was no rule about meddling aunts or other kin,' Jocelyn said.

'This is twice now you have overstepped,' he said to her as he lifted her hand to his mouth and kissed the inside of her wrist. She shivered, as he knew she would, in response. 'I think that gives us the win in this one.' He knew she would argue, but the result was the same—a well-made marriage for another child of theirs or their closest, most loyal friends and family.

'I think we can call this match an even one,' Duncan said. 'Which means that the women won the first, but these last two have been ties.'

'So we won?' Marian asked. She was thinking already of what prize she would claim from her husband—even Connor could see it on her face.

'I guess we must concede then?' He looked at each of the men who nodded or shrugged their assent without trying to show their anticipation for whatever boon their wives claimed of them this night.

The other couples began to stand, to go off to the chambers they'd been assigned during their stay when he just couldn't help himself.

'Of course, there is always Aidan.' Their eldest son was still not married, though it took little more than a look at the woman he'd taken as his leman to understand Aidan's delay in seeking it.

'Nay!' Jocelyn said. They'd barely survived their daughter's path to marriage, so she could not want to jump back in the fray so soon.

'Aye!' said Rurik. His friend just wanted to see another father fret over their daughter as he had over Isobel.

'I think we should see how things proceed when we get back to Lairig Dubh,' Duncan advised.

'So, for now, I supposed we will have to consider the women to be the victors,' Connor declared.

Within a few minutes, the table cleared and everyone went off to seek the pleasurable end now that this game they'd played was done…

Or was it?

* * * * *

Author Note

Post-traumatic stress disorder—PTSD—is a condition that we know about in today's modern world and it is diagnosed and treated by mental health professionals. But not too long ago, this condition was misunderstood and feared because of the sometimes frightening symptoms.

In the medieval world, this condition would not have been recognised and would have been one of a myriad simply called 'madness' by healers, physicians and the clergy. The methods of treating that were more horrifying than the condition itself.

Athdar MacCallum is a victim of a trauma in his childhood that led his mind to hide the truth because it was too terrible for him to process. His symptoms— nightmares/terrors, overwhelming guilt, sleepwalking, blackouts linked to triggers and more—were/are common in PTSD sufferers. But in 1375 Scotland, madness would have been the likely diagnosis for Athdar.

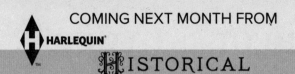

COMING NEXT MONTH FROM

HARLEQUIN®

HISTORICAL

Available November 19, 2013

THE TEXAS RANGER'S HEIRESS WIFE
by Kate Welsh
(Western)

Helena Conwell has built a successful ranch, but now raiders are hungry for her land. Only one man can protect her—Brendan Kane, the wild Texas Ranger she married at gunpoint.

NOT JUST A WALLFLOWER
A Season of Secrets • by Carole Mortimer
(Regency)

Ellie Rosewood is the talk of the *ton*. Her guardian, Justin, Duke of Royston, has one job—to find her a husband. But confirmed rake Justin wants Ellie all for himself!

RUNNING FROM SCANDAL
Bancrofts of Barton Park • by Amanda McCabe
(Regency)

David Marton lives a quiet life, until Emma Bancroft comes sweeping back into his world. She will never be the right woman for him, but sometimes temptation is too hard to resist....

FALLING FOR THE HIGHLAND ROGUE
The Gilvrys of Dunross
by Ann Lethbridge
(Regency)

Disgraced lady Charity West lives in the city's seedy underbelly. She's used and abused, yearning for freedom, and her distrust of men runs deep...until she meets Highland rogue Logan Gilvry.
